# GUSSIE & LUTHER

To Big Rob,
A great Friend and a
source of good
Feelings wherever he
goes!
                    Aaron Fox

## AARON FOX

ISBN-10: 1477641416
EAN-13: 9781477641415

"**O**ld Jew's dead—can't rob us no more. Hear what I'm sayin' old lady? Can't be' robin' us no more."

Gussie paid them no mind. The punks were high on some shit or another. They pounded on the store window, leered and mooned and danced obscene street dances. Sol would break their heads if he were here.

The store was dark except for the fragile February light weeping in through the filthy little front window. Something was starting to smell… Gussie hadn't touched a thing since Sol died. Probably the tomatoes had turned to mush.

This was the fourth day of s*hivah*, Gussie Steinberg style. Where was she going to find ten Jewish guys for a real *minyan* down here in the heart of *schvartze* town. All the old-timers are either dead or have moved away. And could "mister" Maxwell spare his father more than three days?

The punks had suddenly become silent. A tall black man in a cashmere coat appeared. His Caribbean features were at once striking and menacing. With a slight toss of his head he dispersed the hoodlums and pressed his face against the window, peering inside. Something told Gussie to look up. The face, pressed against the window, did not frighten her…she simply stared. Then their eyes met and memories poured into the lacunae of Gussie's mind. She struggled to get out of the rickety old chair and shuffled her *Enna Jetticks* slowly to the door. It was always a fight to get it open. It was badly warped. They said nothing, just stood there, looking at each other.

"Is that you?"

"It's me."

Then she buried her face in the warmth of his elegant coat and began to weep as she smelled his smells. Luther Hightree held her as he always had and kissed the top of her head. Then he gently steered her back into the store. "Where's Maxie? Why ain't he here sitting *shivah* for Sol?"

"You know about Sol? When did you find out?"

"I got the word." He found two chairs at the back of the store and they sat. "Where is Maxie? Why ain't he here?"

"Maxie Steinberg, my son, you mean? Or maybe *Maxwell Stone-hill* the fancy Harvard lawyer? Which one are you asking about?"

"So it's Maxwell now." A sardonic smile. " I hear you, Gussie. Nothing's changed." Luther had always agonized over his role in Gussie's fraught mother-son relationship with Maxie.

"Let him live and be happy. He flew in for the funeral and sat *shivah* for three days."

"Three whole days…ain't that nice. You shouldn't be alone, Mama," he said.

*Mama.* My god! How long since he was a little boy crying for a piece of baloney that he saw in the meat case?

His toe lifted a loose board in the floor. "Told Sol about that board a million times. Somebody's gonna' trip and get themselves a shyster and – "

"—Where did you go? You just disappeared. Sol went to wake you and you were gone. You broke his heart. Not a word from you all these years. Nothing." She struggled to emerge from her acedia.

Luther said nothing. The tenebrous store had depressed him. He glanced down at Gussie's swollen feet pushing her sensible *Enna Jetticks* into misshapen baked potatoes. "Them shoes hur-tin' your feet?" Gussie grinned.

"What's funny, Gus?" She could still make him feel like a little boy.

"Never mind my feet. When will I see you again?"

" I'm here, Gus. I'm here. Stay upstairs in the apartment and keep the doors locked 'til I get back to clean things up. The store will be okay." He put his hand in his pocket to reach for his money and he felt himself blushing. *Jesus Christ!* He knew she was glaring at him.

"Don't you dare," Gussie said.

It was a snake pit of writhing designer jeans and skimpy satin skirts gyrating to the beat of salsa music blasting through the super-hyped speakers. The flashing lights, purple, green, yellow and white, added to the insanity. Lindy Blanc was eye-to-eye with Luther as they did their moves—a tall, slinky, light-skinned, bad-news bundle of Negro, French, Spanish and God knows what else, originally from New Orleans, but now, from wherever the money was. Lindy's hair was shiny, straight and shoulder-length--the end product of money and hours spent in hair straightening salons. She loved to languidly brush it off her face, as though she had always had straight hair—that it was not a big deal. Her smart little dress cost Luther a bundle and he was on the qui vive for any guys whose eyes lingered too long on Lindy's callipygian ass.

The smells were getting to Luther—pot, perfume, sweat and vomit. A spaced-out chick ran her hand across Lindy's shoulder admiring her dress; "Lookin' good, girl friend," she shouted over the cacophony.

" My man knows how to dress a lady, ain't that right, baby?" Lindy shouted.

"Nothin' but Saks Fifth Avenue since she was seventeen," Luther preened. Suddenly he stopped dancing and pulled Lindy behind him as he bulled his way off the dance floor.

"What kinda' shit is this? Quit pulling on me."

"We got some talking to do."

"Talk, talk, talk. Man, I wanna' party." Lindy dug in and put her hands defiantly on her hips and glared. He thought he might slap her– he hated being dissed in public. His face convinced her that she had better mellow out. Somehow she managed to sound sweet once again though she was burning inside. "Where we going, honey?" He gestured toward the exit with a nod of his head and started his cool lope to the door, signifying that he was in control, with Lindy following, like a good girl.

Luther drove a midnight blue Lexus. The used car dealer had shown him a bedizened Cadillac and Luther gave him his "look."

"No," the intimidated car hustler quickly recovered, "this is not you. Let's find something appropriate for a man like you."

"A man like me? What kind of a man would that be?" Luther was making the smart-ass salesman tap dance. Luther had reduced the guy to gibberish.

"You just look like a Lexus man and I'm ready to give you a deal you can't refuse." They haggled for a few minutes and Luther got his price. "Let's go inside and write this up, Mister Hightree."

"That steering wheel cover is worn out. Give me a new on and we've got a deal," Luther probed.

"That wheel cover is genuine leather. They're very expensive you know," stammered the dealer.

"Then get me a very expensive genuine leather steering wheel cover ," Luther said, his face a marmoreal mask. Luther drove off the lot, his hands on a genuine leather, very expensive steering wheel cover.

Luther had a self-image that Sol had inculcated in him when he reached adolescence. "Don't talk and dress like a little jitterbug boogie," Sol had admonished him. "Look like a somebody and you'll be a somebody." Luther was bemused at Sol's attempt to talk street talk, but he nonetheless paid attention and did as Sol asked. His wing tip shoes and the muted shades of his sports coat reflected Sol's teaching. The street thugs couldn't read Luther. But they feared him. *What's that dude signifying?*

Lindy would have preferred a Caddy convertible but she rode quietly in the Lexus in high dudgeon as they drove into the heart of the black ghetto. "Why you dragging me down here when I'm dressed for a party," she caviled.

"Just be quiet, girl. I'm gonna' show you something."

" Don't show me shit. This your idea of a party night?"

"See those windows up there over the store? That's where I grew up. Used to live up there."

"What?"

"I said I used to live up there. And I worked in that store right down there for Sol and Gussie Steinberg."

"You lived with a Jew family growin' up? You pull me out of a party to tell me this shit?"

"You wanna' keep partying in fancy dresses?....then hush up, girl, and listen to what I'm saying to you. This little store is going to set us up for life if things go the way I got them figured."

"You high or something? What the hell you talkin' about, man?"

Unnoticed, a black and white police cruiser silently rolled to a stop next to Luther's Lexus. The blinding spotlight startled the couple as Peter Supelak, a fat, uniformed cop, hand on his holster approached the car. As Supelak peered at Luther, a spiteful smirk crept across his purple kielbasa and beer face. "Well, if it ain't my favorite punk, Luther the grocery boy – all duded-up now," the purple face said, spraying the air with stale garlic. "You through hustling and getting ready to go back into the grocery business, boy?"

"Don't you be callin' him, `boy', " Lindy spat.

"Okay, how's `nigger' suit you, you smart bitch."

Luther squeezed Lindy's arm to keep her quiet. "Just checking out the old neighborhood, officer."

"Yah, well just check your ass out of the neighborhood," Supelak said.

"We're goin'," Luther said. Then that special look transformed Luther's face. "You're officer Supelak, if I remember—ain't I right?"

"You got it, boy."

"Well, I guess you're still moochin' cold cuts from the Steinbergs then."

"Get the fuck out of here," the flummoxed cop barked as Lindy burst into a mocking, coloratura screech.

Sol Steinberg grew up running wild on the streets of the old Italian-Jewish immigrant neighborhood, a congeries of ethnic enclaves housed in the decaying , formerly elegant homes of the first families of the city. Sol was an orphan kid, dodging the social workers. No way was he going back into the Jewish Orphan Home. He barely remembered his parents who died in the influenza epidemic, post World War I. Joey Randazzo took Sol home with him one cold winter day; they were street-fighting buddies and Sol had nowhere else to go that day. Joey's father, Pete Randazzo, took a liking to Sol after he saw Joey and Sol kick the shit out of a pair of tough Irish kids who had called them greasy wops. Pete and his wife, Marie found room for Sol in the attic and he became a member of the Randazzo family, Pete, Marie, Joey and the twins, Laura and Louise. Pete changed Sol's name to Sal and transformed him magically into a Sicilian. Steinberg became Randazzo. And so it remained for several warm, wonderful, pasta-loaded years, with the plump and pretty Marie, directing things in the kitchen.

At Central High, Joey and Sol-Sal were an inseparable pair; swaggering, good-looking wise guys bursting into young manhood like the little black spikes of their inchoate, swarthy beards that made them look years older than the other kids in their class. They were both tall and sinewy-muscular with olive skin, big brown eyes and lustrous, black hair.

There was never any competition and sibling rivalry between Joey and Sol. They were "deuce," as Pete liked to refer to them.

When it came to girls, the boys had their pick of chicks with burgeoning breasts yearning to catch the eyes of the swaggering studs. Then one lunch period, in the crowded, boisterous lunchroom, there sat this luscious "Jew-broad" all by herself, munching on a sandwich. Joey spotted her first and made his Sicilian great lover face as he approached Gussie Berg. Sol picked up on the unfolding drama and followed Joey to this great-looking girl. "I'm Joey Randazzo and this here is my stepbrother Sal. You new here? Never seen you around before," Joey babbled.

"My family just moved here from Buffalo. I just transferred in. Hey! I'm already late for my geometry class. See you guys." And she picked up her books and rushed away, positive the guys were boring holes in her tight-fitting skirt. "She's tall for a Jew broad, ain't she Sol," Joey observed.

"And green eyes. Man, I never seen green eyes before," Sol added.

"Green eyes go with that sort of reddish hair she's got," Joey said. She was duly catalogued.

Sol made the first move a few days later when he took a deep breath and slid onto the bench in the schoolyard where Gussie was reading her lit book. Sol struggled to lower and steady his voice as he said, "Hey, shuffle-off-to-Buffalo, you doin' anything Friday? Would you like to see a movie?"

"Listen," Gussie said, "you're a nice guy I can tell, but I gotta' tell you up front—and I don't mean nothin' snotty or anything, but I don't date Italian guys. I'm Jewish, and I kinda' stick with Jewish guys. So don't take it the wrong way, 'cause I'm sure you'd be fun on a date, but you know what I'm sayin', right?" And she stared at Joey in amazement at he literally laughed in her face, "You got a screw loose, or what? What the hell is so funny? I talked to you like a human being and you laugh in my face? You can go straight to dago hell, mister wise guy," Gussie inveighed.

"What a mouth on a girl! You should try out for the movies." Gussie got up and started walking. "Hey! Wait a minute—I want to tell you something" Sol pleaded. Gussie kept walking without so much as a backward glance. "Can you wait a goddam minute? I got something important to tell you."

Finally she stopped and she just stood there, looking straight ahead. Sol caught up with her and spun her around. "Just stop, already with this shit."

"You got 'til three to take your hands off me before I scream for the cops."

"I'm Jewish! I'm Jewish. Just like you. My real name is Sol Steinberg. You hear what I'm saying? Steinberg! Steinberg! I'm a heeb, just like you. Now will you stop being such a— "

"Such a what?" Her voice was softer now. And she was smiling. "Why do you pretend to be a dago?"

"Because I am. Kind of."

"What do mean 'kind of?' You're fuckin' crazy."

" Such a mouth on a nice Jewish girl. Will you go with me to the movies?"

"Jew or dago date?"

"Jew. I'll explain it to you."

"Start talking, smart guy."

Gussie was touched as Sol told her about the Randazzos and how he came to be called Sal. She kept asking about his real parents—did he ever know them? Where are they buried? Did he have any brothers or sisters? They talked for hours until the crepuscular light and the eerie silence of the empty schoolyard warned them that it was time to for Gussie to get out of there. Sol asked if he could walk her home. And thus began the parlous journey through life for Gussie Berg and Sol Steinberg-Randazzo.

It soon became apparent to Joey Randazzo that Sol was drifting away. *Everyday with the Jew-broad at lunchtime! Everyday he walks her home. He hardly talks at dinnertime.* Joey was beginning to feel a sense of betrayal. Finally he confronted Sol. "So what's it gonna' be? You forgetting about your family for that broad? We don't do nothin' together no more. Even Mom is starting to ask what's goin' on with you. She ain't stupid…she sees that you're actin' different. You goin' steady with the Jew-broad or somethin'? "

"Hey, she's a cute broadie. What do you want from me? She's a nice kid to hang around with. You liked her too when you first saw her. Why don't you take her out? I wouldn't care…I ain't married to her, for crissakes." Joey put a headlock on Sol and affectionately grunted, "Lyin' sombitch."

Never once did Gussie invite Sol in to meet her parents. Gussie would glance nervously at the living room window to be sure her parents were not around before they embraced and kissed. The kisses had grown more passionate and Sol would pin Gussie against the house and grind his erection into her groin until she could force herself to moan for him to stop. As the days grew shorter and darkness descended in late afternoon, Sol and Gussie grew more aggressive until one late October day, the porch light suddenly came on to reveal the tableau of the two young lovers frozen in a mortified, adolescent embrace as Nathan Berg threw open the front door and magisterially said, "Bring him in the house already, before the neighbors call the police."

Sol thrust both hands in his pants pockets to balloon out his pants and disguise his erection.

"Ma, Pa, this is Sol Steinberg from school," Gussie choked out.

"I thought maybe it was Dillinger the way you were hiding," Nathan said.

"Stop, Nate. You're embarrassing the kids," Sonja Berg said, just a faint echo of her Prague accent in the plangent plea. Gussie's mother smiled and nodded her head nervously, struggling to find the proper words to dispel the tension that had suffused the room. "You live in the neighborhood, uh, uh, Sol? Sol is short for Solomon, yes?"

"I, uh, I'm not sure," Sol mumbled.

Sonja did not know how to respond, but Nate did: "Some fine gentleman you got here, Gussie. A guy that don't know his own name." Gussie's temper flared and she turned on her father and told him he was being rude. She defiantly helped Sol out of his jacket and asked Sonja if Sol could stay for dinner. *Stay for dinner!* Sol's eyes widened. He had never heard those words before. Sonja stammered that they only had "plain food" for dinner, that evening. That would be fine, Gussie replied. Sol stood there; a sudden urgency to pee overtook him at the prospect of dining with strangers. *Two forks* at each plate at the table.

The Berg's little home was different from anything Sol had ever seen. So pretty! Pictures on the wall and a glass cabinet filled with little figurines and ornamental plates. and a silver *menorah*. Lot of *tsatskes*. There was pale green wallpaper with a border around the top. Little table lamps cast soft shadows on the wine colored, mohair sofa with two matching chairs. Sol took it all in as he sat there in living room with Gussie and Nate while Sonja busied herself in the kitchen.

Nate was kinder as they dined. The rich wood of the dining room table and the padded chairs were far removed from the Randazzo's huge, round formica kitchen table.

Nate made sure that Sol had plenty of everything—the goulash with the soft chunks of meat floating in thick gravy loaded with carrots and potatoes. There was a long loaf of fresh rye bread from which Nate cut slices. Sol watched as the Bergs tore the bread into smaller pieces before buttering.

"So," Nate said as he folded his napkin, "what do think of Hungarian cooking? Really it's Czech but it's the same. We're from Prague––Czechoslovakia. You heard of it? Where are your people from?"

"He doesn't know, Daddy. He never knew his parents. They died in the flu epidemic after the war."

"Let him talk, for God's sake, Gussie. He hasn't said a word all through dinner."

"You cross-examine him and ask him things that he doesn't have answers for," Gussie protested.

"It's okay, Gussie. I can talk," Sol said, his voice taking on an edge of firmness.

"Sonny boy, you don't have to tell us anything. I'm not a policeman."

"No. It's okay," Sol said.

Nate rose and gestured to the living room where they would continue the conversation as Sonja and Gussie began clearing the table. Sol got the message—I'm on my own. Sol and Nate sat quietly for a few moments before Sol asked if he could use the bathroom. When Sol returned, Nate said, "My daughter's afraid I'm scaring you with questions so I'll be polite and shut up."

At the beginning, Sol temporized, making small talk, not knowing how to begin. Finally he blurted, "Look, Mister Berg, just ask me what you want to know. I've got a feeling that I kind of worry you. Like I don't know 'Is Sol short for Solomon' and stuff like that."

"Alright, I'll be honest with you," Nate said. "My Gussie, God bless her, is not like other kids. She does what she wants, how she wants, when she wants. You know what I'm saying? And all of a sudden she presents me with a guy that's a mystery man; a guy that doesn't know his family, his name, nothing! Am I worried? You're goddam right I am. You're probably a nice kid, Sol, but to tell you the truth,—you're not exactly what I had in mind for my only daughter."

Sol began to talk, slowly at first, as he gathered his thoughts and then his words built to an almost logorrheic outpouring of pure passion as he told his story: Sol, the wild, street urchin hiding from the social workers from the Jewish Orphan Home, sleeping in doorways and begging or stealing food; his friendship with Joey Randazzo and his life with the Randazzo family as *Sal Randazzo*. His commitment to Gussie to live as a Jew named Sol Steinberg.

"Some story," Nate said. And then, in the cadence of the typical Jewish father-in-law, he asked, "So, what are you planning to do when you graduate? This is 1932 and we're in a depression. So what are you going to do for a living? College is out of the question, am I right?.. What do you do for pocket money now?" Sol confessed that he earned a little money delivering pints of hooch to the customers of the small-time bootleggers in the neighborhood. "*Gott in Himmel,*" Nate moaned.

When the evening ended, Nate felt Sol's strong, firm handshake and despite his fervid wish that this street scamp would never see his daughter again, he felt a strange admiration for the tough orphan boy Gussie had brought home. No *goyim* would bully him the way the Slovak anti-Semites had humiliated Nathan and his family in Prague.

The Randazzo house looked as though it might slide off its foundation during the graduation party for the *deuce*, Joey and Sal/Sol. The raw tonnage of flesh jammed into party dresses of an army of aunts and cousins guided by the rough, callused hands of their cement worker spouses was beyond anything Sol had ever seen. It seemed as though everyone was cooking something in the kitchen. Pete Randazzo pulled out all of the stops; gallons of the best homemade dago red were uncorked and everyone was holding a water glass of the stuff. Ravioli, lasagna, aunt Angie's famous sausage, mounds of every imaginable variety of pasta were heaped on the plates. Tables had been set up in the back-yard and they were jammed with happy, excited relatives eating, drinking, hugging and talking as loud as they could in order to be heard.

Sol had tried repeatedly to find a low traffic location; he had begun to feel like a trespasser; after all, this was a Randazzo celebration. Repeatedly, he was hauled to the center of the action where he and Joey were the recipients of emotional toasts and vinous kiss-es. And then the dancing started; if the aunts couldn't find their husbands, they danced with each other….wild, old country Sicilian dances. Suddenly Sol was dancing—*come on handsome, loosen up… now you're moving that skinny ass of yours….spin me, spin me, atta' boy. You lookin' at my boobs? I'm old enough to be your mother! Where's your girl friend? You didn't bring no girl? Let's get a wine, I'm pooped.*

The day roared on and when Sol was sure no one would miss him, he sneaked out and ran to the corner drug store where he found an empty phone booth and dialed Gussie's number. His luck, Nate answered. Sol idiotically said he was calling to offer his congratulations. Nate thanked him. Silence. Finally, Nate handed the phone to Gussie. Sol babbled the congratulation thing again.

Gussie didn't get it. They had hugged and kissed at the graduation ceremony. Sol babbled on. The call was disintegrating into a classic solecism. Finally Gussie put an end to it and invited him to the house.

The Bergs had planned a modest family celebration. They invited Nate's sister Lillian and her husband Karl, Sonja's brother Sasha and his wife Miriam. Both couples had married children living out of town. Sol immediately felt as though he had been transported to another planet; these people were so refined and soft spoken. They all had that very pleasant Prague accent. They greeted Sol graciously as Gussie introduced him as "my very special friend from Central High." Sol was determined not to appear a street kid living as a Sicilian with an adopted family. His J.C. Penney blue suit fit him reasonably well, but the Randazzo party had him looking somewhat disheveled. No one asked about his family. Had they been prompted? Mostly, they wanted to know what the new graduates where planning to do with their lives. Gussie did a double take when Sol announced that he was thinking about the food business, maybe a grocery store. "Depression or not, people have to eat," he proclaimed magisterially as Gussie, red as the radishes, buried her face in her plate. Sol didn't have a clue.

The Bergs had ordered a delicatessen platter from the Cohen Brothers deli. It was way beyond their budget "I hope you brought an appetite," Sonja said, smiling sweetly. Sol could have choked the dear, sweet creature, but he did manage to eat the smoked sturgeon and a corned beef sandwich. And he felt like a normal human being for the first time in his life.

The North-Central States Food Terminal came alive at 3a.m. In the trading area of the Food Terminal there were hundreds of "fruit stores," as the places selling fresh produce were called in those days. There were also fish stores, chicken stores, butcher shops and grocery stores for the canned and dry goods. But the Food Terminal was where the fruit and vegetable store buyers fought for every penny as they haggled with farmers and wholesalers over the price of tomatoes, cherries, onions, cabbage and potatoes. They were a rough bunch, standing on the cold, wet cement floor under the glaring lights. Almost everyone had stopped at Kaufman's, the restaurant-bar at the end of the terminal. Stacks of hot cakes, ham and eggs, corned beef sandwiches, shots and beers or big mugs of coffee with "sinkers" were consumed there, prior to the opening of the market.

Pete Randazzo maintained a stand at the terminal where he wholesaled fruits and vegetables and ground out a moderate living. He was formidable— a big guy with a mop of graying-black hair and the traditional moustache. His hands were bruised and raw and his fingers resembled the parsnips that he sold. His tattered black sweater, rubber apron and boots were his uniform as he did battle on the floor of the terminal. His negotiating parlance was limited to a few phrases: *You wanna' rob me? —Come on, stick a knife in my heart—I don't sell garbage—I gotta' live too! You come up, I come down. Get the fuck out of here.*

After graduation Joey and Sol importuned Pete to "get them in" at the Terminal. Pete didn't think the boys could get up in the middle of the night and get to the terminal at 3a.m. and he did not wish to be embarrassed by their tardiness. Finally, with the proviso that the boys work in different sections of the terminal, Pete was miraculously able to "get them in." Their job was to unload the

14

trucks and box cars that brought crates of produce and canned goods from all over the country. It was heavy work, but the boys hung on. They knew they were lucky to be working at anything in 1932. *Roosevelt and his "happy days are here again," bullshit.* Joey often thought about Al Capone— bet he didn't bust his balls in the middle of the night.

Gussie's life after graduation was filled with disappointment and bitterness. Her father, Nate Berg, had wanted her to follow in his footsteps; he was an educated man... a chemist with a degree from the Prague Technical Institute. But it was not to be. The Czechs had a long tradition of tolerance for Jews, but with the break up of the Hapsburg Empire after World War I, Slovak nationalist elements had gained power and Jews were once again the scapegoats for the diminished glory of the Prague based government. Nate was forced out of his position at the Institute and eventually he and Sonja emigrated to America were he felt there would be opportunity. The Depression destroyed Nate's dream of finding a teaching position at a university. There was really nothing available in Nate's field. He was a lumpen intellectual reduced to working in a drug store as an assistant to the pharmacist. So there would be no college for Gussie, only a so-called secretarial school where she would master shorthand and typing, for which she had a consumptive hatred and bookkeeping, which she rather enjoyed.

She and Sol saw very little of each other that first year after graduation; Sol was asleep by eight every night except Saturday when they usually had a movie date. Joey had found a girl that he rather liked. Her name was Carla Byrnes and she was of Italian- Irish heritage. Often the young couples would double date on Saturday night. The Irish-Italian animus still existed in the old neighborhood and Carla was baited into making a choice should there by trouble with Irish toughs. To Joey, Sol was forever to be Sal, the Sicilian, in fights with the Irish.

The bitter cold of the winter of 1934 was starting to wear on Joey. He developed a cough which would not go away, and a succession of nasty colds made life on the wet terminal floor almost unbearable. He envied Sol. The little bastard actually seemed to love coming to work at the Terminal in the middle of the night, and Pete was constantly lavishing praise on Sol because the kid had gotten a reputation around the Terminal as a hard worker. And this annoyed Joey. He knew he was becoming jealous of Pete's affection for Sol. *The kid's a natural for the produce racket.* Joey knew it was true and that he could never measure up to Pete's expectations because he had no love for the produce business.

His romance with Carla was going nowhere. She was like one of those Irish nuns from Catholic elementary school— strict and prudish. There was no fooling around with her. He had once touched her breast and she pushed him away and started crying. She was a great looking girl and he liked showing her off, but that's as far as it went. He was looking for an appropriate time to end it all and find someone with some warmth. He envied Sol's close, loving relationship with Gussie. "You're banging the Jew-broad ain't you, Solly boy?" he would probe. But Sol was very circumspect and revealed nothing. This only added to the inchoate envy that he was developing toward Sol. The ambivalence he was experiencing troubled Joey; Sol had always been like a little brother ever since he brought him home off the street that cold winter night many years ago. And now, they were drifting apart and Joey felt himself adrift in the bleak, hopelessness of the Depression with a job he hated and a girlfriend that gave him nothing.

Several months later, Pete was shocked when Joey told him that he was quitting his job at the Terminal. "What are you going to do, sleep all day and listen to the radio?" Pete shouted in a fulminating rage.

"I'm joining the C's. At least I'll be out in the fresh air doing man's work instead of pulling slop out of a boxcar in the stinking Terminal in the middle of the night."

"What the fuck is the 'C's'?" Pete demanded.

"The CCC. Civilian Conservation somethin'. Corps. Corps. Civilian Conservation Corps. It's like the army, only it ain't. It's guys wearing khaki uniforms and planting trees and doing all kinds of outdoor work all over the country."

16

"Where'd you hear about that kind of a bullshit deal? You telling me you're quitting a paying job that I broke my ass getting for you to go play soldier planting trees? What the hell happened to your head, Joey?"

"Don't hate me, Pop...I'm very unhappy with my life the way things are. I got to make a change." He took his father's hand and rubbed it against his cheek feeling coruscating emotions that brought tears to his eyes. "You've still got Sol. He loves you like a father. Bring him into your business. He loves the Terminal. He'll be a big help at the stand. You're getting older, Pop."

"CCC," Pete muttered. "Fuckin' Roosevelt turning the country inside out."

It was a pathetic little cluster of silent, sad people standing on the loading platform of the shabby bus terminal in the pre-dawn, April drizzle… all the Randazzos and Sol and Gussie. They had come to see Joey off on his journey to the CCC camp outside of Vermillion, South Dakota. As the bus pulled away, Sol felt a terrible sense of loss. He struggled to catch a last blurry glimpse of Joey's face in the misty bus window. Would he ever see Joey again? Sure, he had Gussie who loved him so very much; but what would his world be like without the brother who had given him a life? He looked at Pete, weeping silently, his face turned away. He would be a real son to Pete. He would work his heart out at the stand. He would be what Pete wanted Joey to be. Oh God, Pete's feeling so much sorrow. Could I have done something that would have kept Joey here, Sol agonized.

At first, Pete was rather distant when Sol came to work with him at the stand. Though Pete had long ago renamed him "Sal" and made him an instant Sicilian, he never forgot that Sol was a Jew; not that Pete hated Jews or anything of that nature. Actually, he had lived among Jewish immigrants in the Central area and had done business with them at the Terminal for many years. Yet he asked himself over and over: *why did the little Jew kid work his ass off and get ahead at the Terminal while his son fucked off and did nothing with his life? Were Jews smarter? Harder workers? Shit, nobody worked harder at the Terminal than me, Pete Randazzo, a Sicilian.*

Soon, Pete began to feel a sense of comfort having the preternaturally quick and alert Sol at his side every morning. Soon they were eating breakfast together at Kaufman's before work began. Both men enjoyed corned beef sandwiches and Cokes on their empty stomachs.

One morning Pete sensed that Sol had something on his mind and he asked him if something was bothering him. Sol was diffident, wanting never to appear overly aggressive with Pete. Finally he spoke: "Lots of coloreds are moving into the neighborhood."

"I ain't blind. I see them moving in. Lots of money-hungry *gumbahs* starting to sell out to them. What are you going do? Some people got no respect for their neighbors. Me, I ain't running. I raised my family in Saint Cecilia's parish," Pete rumbled.

"That's not what I mean," Sol said, and he proceeded to offer his suggestion about starting to offer produce that colored people liked; things like collards, yams, turnips, rice and red beans. Pete was impressed. "How had Sol gotten this knowledge?" he asked. Sol remembered his days on the streets when he had wandered into a black section and noticed what the stores were selling.

The items that Sol had suggested proved to be good sellers and the Randazzo stand at the Terminal had stolen the march on the other purveyors. Soon Sol was sharing the responsibility for ordering with Pete and he was rewarded with a significant raise.

Sol could hardly wait to tell Gussie about the raise. He was now earning a salary, not just kid's money, but a real man's salary. He was twenty years old and he could perhaps afford a place of his own now; maybe a small apartment in one of the four-suite buildings in the neighborhood. He and Gussie could be alone without worrying about her parents. When Sol told Pete about his plans to get a place of his own, Pete's main concern was food…where was he going to eat? Who would cook decent meals for him?

Finally it was decided that Sol would come home, that meant the Randazzo home, for dinner so Marie could see that he was eating "right."

Gussie in the meantime, worked out an arrangement with her best girlfriend, Sylvia Margolies; both girls were in secretarial school and frequently needed to practice taking dictation in shorthand. It was convenient for the girls to alternate sleeping over at each other's homes several times a week; except that Gussie's "sleep-over" was at Sol's bare bones apartment on Sullivan street where she and Sol somehow managed their love-making on a surplus World War I army cot that was the crown jewel of Sol's bedroom décor.

It was not just the cot that made their lovemaking so awkward, it was Sol's utter lack of experience and it humiliated him to confess that he had never used a prophylactic before. Gussie had insisted that he use them. Gussie was the more experienced partner and she ignored Sol's request to reveal when and how she had lost her virginity. She taught Sol the rudiments of foreplay and explained that women want to climax also. Gussie was in control and it would stay that way for the remainder of their life together.

Marie Randazzo was worried; Pete's nocturnal coughing had increased in intensity to the point where it awoke him in the middle of the night after which he would roam around the darkened house, unable to get back to sleep. As a result he would leave for the Terminal an hour earlier than usual rather than sit around the darkened house.

Sol began to notice the dark circles under Pete's eyes and it worried him. He was now close enough to Pete that he felt comfortable urging Pete to see a doctor about the cough. Pete would simply laugh it off and rumple Sol's hair affectionately calling him a "regular little Jewish doctor." More and more, Pete assumed a passive role in the haggling with bargain hunting buyers. Sol stepped in the role of head man at the Randazzo stand and Pete would watch him *hundle* with the customers with something akin to paternal pride.

On a bitter cold December night Sol waited at Kaufman's for Pete to arrive for their usual breakfast. When he didn't appear by 3am, when the bell clanged signaling that the Terminal was open for business, Sol got worried. He gulped down his corned beef sandwich and headed for the stand where crates of produce awaited him. He wielded the claw hammer expertly tearing open the crates and boxes of fruit and vegetables which he arranged in the various bins. The Randazzo stand attracted most of the Negro buyers who were there for the collards, the pole beans, the okra, the chicory, the turnips —the complete panoply of foods for the colored store owners. The other wholesalers had started calling the Randazzo operation "boogie land."

"Their money's as good as anybody else's," Pete would bellow. But on this icy morning there was no Pete and Sol was getting frantic. There was a pay phone at Kaufman's and Sol thought about running down there to make a call to Pete's home even if he had to leave the stand unattended.   And suddenly, there was Laura, the Randazzo twin, weeping and hysterical running down the wet concrete platform. Sol grabbed her and wrapped his arms around her. Between racking sobs and hiccups  she blurted out: "Daddy's  at Mount Sinai—Mom found him on the floor in the kitchen.  He was blue, Sol. Blue! They don't know if they can save him! Oh God, Sol, is he going to die? Mom wants you to come. I've got  Daddy's truck…can you come now?"

A crowd had gathered and Sol reached out to a regular customer—a colored man named Marvin and asked him to watch the stand.  Marvin told Sol to go, that he would keep an eye on things. "Go man," Marvin said, "my store will keep. We'll watch your stuff."

Laura  lurched the truck the several blocks to Mount Sinai, not shifting gears, just grinding away in first gear.

Sol knew at once, as he ran toward the cluster of Randazzo relatives surrounding Marie, that things were critical.  "How is he? What happened?" he gasped.

"Heart attack—really bad, Solly. He wanted you here," Louise told him, her voice  high pitched and pinched. Marie did not speak.  She wept softly  in Sol's arms.  Finally a young resident came out of the operating room and asked for "Missus Randazzo." Marie  looked at him, her eyes begging him to say Pete was alive. "We've got him stabilized and breathing with oxygen.  He's going to make it, Missus. God was looking after him.  A few minutes longer and—well, it's a good thing you found him.

"God bless you, doctor, God bless you." She crossed herself repeatedly, violently, as though the violence would convince God of her extreme  gratitude. The others were murmuring prayers in Italian. Sol too was weeping,  drowning in the  emotion; transmogrified again into Sal the Sicilian; one of them.

The figure sloshing down the center of the Terminal platform in a pair of winter galoshes and an oversized, man's sweater looked vaguely familiar. *Holy shit! What the hell is she doing here?* Gussie's eyes were puffy, half-closed from lack of sleep. She had never gotten up at two in the morning in her entire life. She knew that Sol was killing himself trying to run the stand by himself. So she quit the secretarial school, which she hated, and came to help. Turned out she was a natural. "Our kale is fresh and beautiful this morning," she shouted to the buyers.

"What the hell are you doing?" Sol hissed. "Do you have any idea what you're yelling?"

"Never mind. You fill the orders, I'll pull in the customers. You don't know shit about selling."

"What a mouth on that girl." Sol instinctively knew who would be running the show at the Randazzo-Steinberg produce stand from that point on.

Pete knew that it would be months before he could return to work and then his work load would be radically reduced. So he made Sol an offer: Sol would be a partner, not an employee, and they would split profits 60/40, with Sol keeping the 60. And maybe after a few years, Sol would own the entire operation and Pete would call it a day and retire.

Sol and Gussie spent New Year's, 1935 with the Bergs; the usual sedate, quiet Berg-style evening. The kids were there because Gussie had an announcement that she was certain would upset Sonja and Nathan: she was going to move into her own apartment. After all, she was a twenty-year-old woman and it was time she went out on her own.

When Gussie made it clear she would not be living with Sol, a *shondah* for their friends and neighbors, the Bergs' sadness was somewhat softened.     But Nate could not reconcile himself to Gussie's withdrawal from secretarial school—*being a bookkeeper and a secretary to a big business owner was far more in keeping with her family's educational heritage than working at a "fruit stand" in the middle of the night*—but what could he do?  She loves this guy…this guy with no family,  no  background except with a bunch of *Italanors. Some father! Me,. a  professor from the Prague Technical Institute can only afford to provide his daughter with a job as a huckster selling  produce to schvartzes.  It pained Nathan;  he hated the Slovaks who had made him a poor, wandering Jew when he had been important, dignified, respected.*

Gussie's apartment on Quincy was a cut or two (or three) above Sol's digs on Sullivan Street.  And that of course would be where they would eat, sleep and make love. Gussie's place had curtains and a double bed with a decent bedspread.  Sol's window treatment was a stained, torn, brown window shade permanently hanging at half-mast from the roller; unable to be raised or lowered.

Gussie would handle the money when Sol and Pete met to divide the weekly take. The youngsters would be pulling in good money for the bleak Depression year of 1936 and Gussie was saving every penny of it. "We're going to have our very own business someday. Something with normal hours, not this craziness in the middle of the night," Gussie proclaimed. "Maybe even a store."

Pete was mending slowly but he was far from the  strong, tough guy he had been.  He beamed with appreciation when he and Sol divided the profits on Sunday mornings after church. Profits where going up. "That *madel*  of yours has made a real  business man out of you."  They would have a glass of Pete's homemade red  to celebrate.  Often a sadness would  cloud Pete's eyes and Sol knew he was thinking about Joey. It should be Joey  taking over the business.  Sol  knew what Pete was thinking and it blighted the joy that Sol  felt at his success.  It made it all the more imperative  that he and Gussie have their own business someday, though he would always have this achingly deep love for Pete and Marie.  Then, one Sunday morning when Pete had a glass or two more than he  was allowed, he blurted out something that had been lurking in everyone's mind: "When you gonna' marry that  pretty little *balabusta*

of yours?" Pete loved to use the many Yiddish expressions that he
had picked up over the years in the neighborhood. "You're making enough money to have a wife. And I wanna' make a wedding
for a son. You're my kid, Solly. I got no idea what's going on with
Joey. I'll make a real party here and we'll have a rabbi and her
folks and their family. A real big bash! What do you say, Sol? You
ready to be a grown man?"

Gussie was ready. She and Sol were as close as two people
could possibly be. She loved his little lost-boy vulnerability, his
clever scheming mind. She was proud of him. And he didn't feel
diminished when she sat on top during lovemaking; he was tough;
he was tender. But she was troubled at the thought of the wedding
being orchestrated by Pete Randazzo. She knew it would break
her father's heart. She told Sol that her family wanted a quiet little
ceremony in the rabbi's study at her father's *shul,*

Sol's sui generis, street boy's politesse caused him unbearable
anguish at the thought of refusing Pete's heartfelt offer to provide
a wedding celebration. Sol existed in a state of anomie never sure
which persona should prevail, Jew or Italian. For the duration of
his life he would remember the meeting with Pete when he had to
tell him there would be no wedding celebration at the Randazzo
home. And the young lovers decided not to rush into a wedding.
They would wait. How would things work out with Pete and the
possible purchase of the business? They could wait a little longer.

Joey came home in May of 1938. He was hardly recognizable; he was a grown man…bigger, heavier, stronger; broad-shouldered with heavily muscled forearms and a thick neck. His face was tanned but it was the face of a man who had done too much living. There were deep lines on his forehead and around his eyes; the eyes of a half-feral creature, surveying his surroundings, looking for weakness, fear.

He moved into his old room and offered perfunctory comments about the beauty of his twin sisters. He did not talk much at meals. Everyone had questions about his life in the Three C's which he brushed aside, saying it was hard work planting trees out there in the barren plains; that the men he worked with were mostly poor and uneducated. There was lots of drinking and fights would break out often. The food was good, and if you got sick you could see a decent doctor for free. He talked of places about which the family had only vague notions; Nebraska, Wyoming, Idaho. Laura changed the mood, asking if he had met any nice girls which brought a quick shadow across his eyes but no answer. He asked about Sol and Gussie and he showed no emotion when told that they were running the stand while Pete was recuperating and that they were planning to marry. Pete made no mention of his offer to host the wedding party.

Pete's long awaited private talk with Joey was a disappointment. Joey was vague about his future plans. He wasn't going back into the C's, that was for sure. Maybe the army, he was sure war was coming—all that Hitler and Mussolini stuff.

Joey was a stranger; Pete did not know what to say to him. Pete had wanted to resolve the issue of the family business; was Joey interested in the business? Did he have feelings about Sol eventually buying out the business? Joey said nothing but his eyes told Pete that he had struck a nerve.

Days past and Joey's presence hung like an incubus over the entire family. Who was this big silent man whose eyes seemed to look through people?

Finally the unthinkable occurred: Joey angrily told Pete that he was shocked that Pete had given Sol the option to buy the business. The business was a family business that should be passed from father to son. When Pete protested that Joey had shown no interest in the business, that he told him that he was unhappy getting up in the middle of the night and going down to the cold, damp Terminal to peddle produce to blacks; that he had to get away and had then enlisted in the CCC and disappeared from the family for years. "What do you want from me?" Pete cried.

Joey's eyes turned black—he wanted what was coming to him, he said—he wanted to take over the business and make something out of it for the entire family. "What do I do about Sol and now, Gussie?" Pete asked and was shocked by Joey's answer:

"You've always put that Jew-boy ahead of me…don't think I didn't know it. That's one of the reasons I ran away from here. Well now you gotta' be a real father and do what's right for your son. I want the business and I want that eager beaver little bastard out of here."

"You talk like an animal," Pete said. "What did they do to you, there in them C's?" Sol's been your brother since you where little kids. What kind of a guy did you turn into? I ain't kickin' Sol out, you hear me? He deserves what I'm giving him. And don't ever tell me I ain't a 'real father.' "

That seemed to end it.…Joey's cri de coeur. Joey made no more demands, though he stopped having conversations with Pete… only perfunctory greetings in the morning. No one seemed to know where he spent his days and his evenings.

Marie worried about Pete. Ever since he and Joey had their conversation Pete had been depressed and agitated. He wasn't sleeping well and he had no appetite. Finally he told Marie that it 'tore his heart out" to talk to Joey the way he did. His brain was on fire: Maybe he's right, maybe he's entitled to the business; maybe I should just tell Sol that I can't sell out to him. No! I can't hurt that kid. God, please tell me what to do.

It was Joey who finally gave Pete the answer to his dilemma: "There's going to be war and I ain't going in as a flunky. Guys that did well in the C's can take a test for OCS. If I can pass that test. I'll come out as a second looie and move up. Marie started crying. She pleaded with Joey not to go to the army. Though she loved Sol she pleaded with Pete to turn the business over to Joey so he wouldn't join the army.

Pete started having chest pains. Joey had put him in an emotional meat grinder. All he could do was pray. He went to mass early every morning to pray for an answer. Then suddenly, inexplicably, Joey changed; he tried to relieve Pete's anguish, telling him that his real love all along was the army; that the argument about the business was "pure bullshit;" that he was just feeling sorry for himself; that he never really wanted the "middle of the night routine." The army offered him a chance to be a "somebody." "Believe me Pop. Don't hassle yourself, I'm doing what makes me happy. I love you, Pop." And he kissed his father.

The kiss felt cold, unnatural on Pete's cheek. He was bewildered by Joey's sudden change; Pete didn't know who Joey Randazzo had become.

"Go spend some time with Sol and Gussie before you leave. Sol has always loved you like a brother," Pete pleaded.

Eventually, Joey went to the Terminal to see Sol and Gussie work the stand. Neither Sol nor Gussie knew anything of Joey's argument with Pete.

Joey's piercing eyes took in everything but he focused on Gussie; her buttocks as she bent over, her legs, the outline of her breasts under her T-shirt. Gussie could feel his eyes and it made her feel uneasy but strangely stimulated.

Sol had hardly ever became ill; but on this particular day he felt feverish and tired. Joey told him go home and get some sleep, that he would help Gussie finish the morning's business.

"I'm leaving tonight, kid, so this is so long for a while," Joey said as Sol got ready to leave. "Take care of things and keep and eye on my dad. God bless you." They hugged and Sol went home.

Gussie could feel it; she was not his brother's fiancée, she was a tempting piece of ass. And strangely, Gussie was not shocked or insulted. Nothing like this had ever happened to her before. She became wet. The new Joey was a frightening and exciting creature. He was a man—a big. strong, tanned, worldly man who had fucked many women, And now he wants to fuck me, she thought. And the bastard could give less of shit about what Sol thinks. For some perverse reason this stimulated Gussie.

The contrast between the two men was overpowering; suddenly Sol was a kid that she took care of; Joey was a man that knew he could take her whenever the desire hit him....the arrogant bastard! What would it be like to be with a creature like that? How would he smell? His hands are so big and rough. What would they feel like grabbing my ass? Squeezing my thighs? Would he be gentle? No, he would actually rape me. He would penetrate deep and hard. He's going to hurt me...I want him to hurt me. Oh God, what is happening to me! You a selfish thug, Joey...you son-of-a-bitch. How can you do this to a friend... your brother, for God's. sake! Oh, Joey, come on, fuck me. Fuck me, you lousy wop you.

By no assay of logic could Gussie understand what had driven her into Joey's powerful arms. She knew in her heart that such a thing could never happen again; what had happened here, behind the crates and bales of produce. Did she no longer love Sol? She would not allow herself to let that thought enter her mind. For he rest of her life this frightening episode would lurk in a hidden corner of her brain, reappearing with no warning for reasons she would never understand. It was something that had happened. Sol, I'm so sorry...I'm so very sorry.

Sol knew something was wrong. Gussie busied herself with unimportant, unnecessary things to avoid eye contact with him. Finally: "Something wrong?" Sol's voice quavered slightly.

"What should be wrong?" she answered evasively, angrily. And that was the end of it. Never in their lives did the subject ever surface but Gussie would forever bear the opprobrium of allowing Joey to vent his anger between her yielding legs.

Joey's letter was most unexpected, for never, in all time his was in CCC, did he write home. And now, the revenant son brought joy vitiated with worry to the Randazzo family. Joey was in Officer Training School; he had passed the entrance exam! Pete was vivified, full of pride; yet an insidious, gnawing guilt ate at him. Joey was deracinated from the family by Pete's refusal to abrogate his commitment to Sol. And now his only son was in harm's way, forced to become a soldier when he could have been home running the business. But the foudroyant revelation that his son was soon to be an officer in the American Army was the anodyne that helped Pete cope with his guilt.

Joey's prophesy that war was coming was vindicated when the Nazis rolled their panzer divisions across the Polish border in 1939 opening the gates of hell that was to be World War II. Neville Chamberlain's paean of "peace in our time" had come a sublime cropper.

Tensions ran high in both the Berg and Randazzo households. Marie could not constrain her anger at Sol; he had arrogated her son's claim to a business that had been in the family for generations. Sol no longer felt welcome at the Randazzo home for Sunday dinners. Nothing that Pete said could shield Sol from Marie's anger.

Nate Berg anguished when Nazi atrocities starting with the *Anschluss,* the annexation of Austria in March of 1938, Kristall-nacht in November of 1938 when the windows of thousands of Jewish businesses were broken and finally and most tragically for Nate Berg, the German annexation of the Sudetenland area of Czechoslavakia ; Britain and France's abandonment of Czechoslovakia as part of the appeasement at Munich; bending to Hitler's demands at the expense of the Czechs. In 1939 The Nazis invaded the entire nation. The Slovaks seceded and became a pro-German entity and the deportation and murder of thousands of Czech and Slovak Jews began. It was more than Nate Berg could bear and he went into a deep depression that required Gussie to spend time with Sonja Berg assisting her in dealing with Nate.

Sol's uxorial plans were put on hold when President Roosevelt signed the peacetime draft law in 1940. *Goodbye dear, I'll be back in a year* became the top tune on the Lucky Strike Hit Parade.

Pete's health had improved and Sol had a plan. His draft number could come up at anytime and that would mean Gussie would have to run the business by herself. Too much of a load for one woman. Was Pete now strong enough to run the stand, perhaps with help from someone in the family, he thought. This is where it got complicated: Pete had made a verbal commitment to Sol promising that the business would go to him "eventually." What does "eventually" mean Sol pondered. Sol had improved the business and built a following with the stores catering to blacks. This has to be worth something, Sol figured. Pete's a straight shooter; how much will he give me for my share of the business even though there is no written, legal agreement saying that I own any part of the business, Sol wondered. He felt his face redden at the vey thought of talking business with Pete.

Sol laid it on the line with Pete; *I'm probably going to get drafted. Gussie and I should get married— now; maybe they'll take married guys last. I want to start a business of my own—maybe a small store that Gussie could handle by herself while I'm in the army. I need money to buy a store. I've saved every penny I earned from my share of the profits, so I've got a few bucks put away. Am I entitled to some money if I return the business back to you, Pete? 100 percent. I honestly don't know if I'm entitled to anything. I'll leave it up to you, Pete.*

Sol's presentation was delivered as a fast mumble with his eyes downcast and it came across as borderline galamatias.

"For crissakes slow up and look at me so I know what the hell you're talking about.," Pete demanded. So Sol repeated his request more slowly, and this time he made eye contact with Pete.

Pete gave Sol two thousand dollars. He called it a bonus because there was no contract or anything legal between them. Pete

31

was gracious and generous and he treated Sol like a son. He walked the entire neighborhood with Sol; haggling with store owners who might want to sell because the neighborhood was changing; with hungry, fast-talking real estate agents. Pete was better at this sort of thing than Sol and he really fought hard to get Sol a good deal. Sol wanted a store in the old neighborhood that probably would be patronized by blacks because he felt confident that he understood how to deal with blacks; and there wouldn't be much competition either. Pete was concerned about Gussie's safety, running a store by herself in a black neighborhood. Sol reassured Pete that Gussie was up to the challenge and was in agreement that a store dealing with blacks would make the most money for them faster, especially since the food stamp program had come into being.

Finally they found the perfect situation; a small store with no competitors nearby and living quarters above the store that could be fixed up into a nice apartment. And they made a deal; a very good deal.

"Now when are you kids getting married?" Pete asked, devilishly. "Don't forget, the offer still holds for me the throw the party," Pete said.

"Were going to go down to City Hall and have a judge marry us. It'll be a lot cheaper and it won't put any strain on Gussie's father who's really pretty sick."

"Aw shit, kid. City Hall with some mick judge who could give less of a shit," Pete complained.

" You're going to be best man, Pete," Sol said. "Is Marie still mad at me? I want her to come down, too. Matron of honor."

" Marie has always loved you and she never stops worrying if you're eating right. Don't' you worry; we'll be there. And I'm taking everybody to Monaco's for a wedding dinner after. No arguments."

"Deal," Sol said as he hugged Pete.

They told Nate Berg that they had been married in a very simple "Jewish ceremony" to save money for their new store and to buy furniture for the apartment. Nate's disappointment that there had been no wedding at the *shul* was assuaged by the news that the couple had wisely saved enough money to buy a store. But he was not the same man he had been when he had surprised Gussie and Sol kissing on the front porch. He had gotten word that several members of his family in Prague had been taken to the Nazi death camps. Gussie would have her hands full helping Sonja take care of him as he plunged into an even blacker depression at the news.

Learning to buy merchandise to stock the store and shopping for furniture for the apartment proved to be a Sisyphean task. Pete taught them the art of *hundling* with the suppliers to get the price down. And, gently he told Sol that there was no need to buy premium quality; cheaper grades of meat and produce would help keep their prices down and that was going to be important if their customers were primarily the blacks who were moving into the old neighborhood.

They had done some good business during the Thanksgiving season of 1940 and they were relaxing in the apartment. Gussie had done a nice job of creating a cozy home above the dreary, decaying streets below. Sonja had given them her precious china that had belonged to her grandmother. It was elegant stuff and Gussie would bring it out when she had time to prepare a special dinner. Sonja had taught her well.

Their little Atwater-Kent radio was playing background music as they enjoyed their quiet moment together. Suddenly, static tore into the music and, as Sol reached for the dial an excited voice announced that the Japanese had attacked Pearl Harbor. They sat quietly for a few moments, stunned. And then she said: "Sol, I'm pregnant."

"When?"

"When what?"

"When, When? When are you due? Why didn't you say something?"

" I just found out. What do you want from me? Eight months, something like that."

"Jesus. I'll probably be in the army by then. Who's going to take care of the store?"

"The store! How about maybe worrying about the baby."

34

"I mean the baby, the store, you, everything. Excuse me, sweetheart, I'm all mixed up here."

"Talk to Pete. Maybe his sister—you know, the fat one that's always smiling—what's her name.?"

"Angie, Angie! That's a possibility. She worked down at the Terminal with Spicusa Brothers a long time ago. But she knows the business. I'll talk to Pete. Great idea, babe, Great idea!" Then his face clouded. "What about the baby? Who's going to help you with the baby while you're in the store?"

"I'll keep the baby down in the store with me. She'll be fine."

"She?"

"She, him, whatever."

"Maybe the draft will take guys with kids last. Maybe I'll be able to stay with you longer."

"Go to the army, Sol. Learn to kill Germans."

"I already know how."

Sol was gone in March, 1942, drafted into a unit of the Pennsylvania National Guard. Because he had no advanced education or special skills, he was assigned to an infantry unit and went into training in the tic-infested woods of Louisiana. There was a shortage of equipment in the early days of 1941 and Sol's unit used broomsticks instead of rifles, and old trucks, painted gray, served as tanks.

Eventually the Garand rifles arrived and the troops went to rifle ranges to learn to shoot. Sol was terrible at first, flinching and closing his eyes when the rifle fired. The drill instructors rode him unmercifully, banging on his helmet with their swagger sticks and calling him a variety of creative anti-Semitic names. A tent-mate from the mountains near the West Virginia border took Sol aside, and asked him how long he was going to take "all that bullshit from the D I.?" The hillbilly hated the army and he could not stomach the abuse that was being heaped on Sol, even though he had no special love for "Hebrews." The mountain man knew how to shoot, if nothing else, and Sol was desperate to learn; so the mountain man took Sol deep into the woods and taught him to keep his eyes open when the rifle fired and to refrain from throwing his shoulder forward. They practiced and practiced and eventually Sol nailed some beer cans from two hundred yards, and he fell in love with his rifle and the infantry. He became a damned good soldier by the time basic training was over. He was the scout for his platoon and the mountain man, whose name, incidentally, was Norbert Harper, had been made his squad leader. Whether Norbert Harper knew it or not, Sol loved him deeply and would follow him anywhere in battle.

Gussie was doing her part on the home front. The baby, Maxwell Sidney (after an uncle gassed by the Nazis) Steinberg was born on May 20, 1941, and he gave Gussie no problems at childbirth nor during the nights thereafter. He was a good eater, sleeper and pooper. And he gurgled away happily in his crib at the back of the store as Gussie and Angie did business with their mostly black clientele.

Maxwell's birth and Gussie's success at the store snapped Nathan out of his depression, and he was more than delighted to invite members of the Randazzo clan to the *bris*. Only one Randazzo aunt came close to fainting when the *Mohel* deftly executed the circumcision.

Despite the food shortages and the rationing in 1942, Steinberg's Grocery, as the store was named, continued to do decent business. Angie knew how to buy at the food Terminal and she taught Gussie, who proved to be an apt pupil. The girls always managed to get their price in the early morning haggling, though the quality was not top grade.

The blacks patronized the store in ever increasing numbers when the word got out in the neighborhood that "Steinbergs" stocked their favorite foods; the pervasive feeling was that Steinbergs was catering to black tastes and wanted their business. Pete helped out from time to time, especially in expanding the meat department. For Gussie, this phase of her learning was a calamity. The panoply of strange cuts with their esoteric names displayed in the meat case kept her stomach in a state of abject distress; chitterlings, hog maws, pigs feet, pig ears, pig skin, tripe, jowls, oxtails. But the blacks seemed pleased that the girls were knowledgeable about these items and served them up with deftness and aplomb. At the beginning, when these items were new to her, Gussie would dissemble by offering to find the customer a "really fresh piece," all the while kicking Angie's feet as a signal that she was lost.

Gussie was often asked how it was that she knew all about these southern cuts of meat, her Jewish features prompting the question; Gussie's stock reply was that she was raised by a black lady after her mother had died and she grew up on soul food. She spent hours in the library looking up recipes for hog maws and chittlins, oxtail stew and pigs feet. Angie rolled her eyes in disbelief at the utter *hutzpah* of Gussie when she had the nerve to explain that hog maws were not the pig's stomach, but rather the lining of the stomach and needed to be washed carefully.

"Damned if I ever knew that," said the mightily impressed customer.

"Jeezuus!" Angie hissed. "You're going to get caught with that 'down-home' bullshit if you ain't careful."

And it almost happened when a customer blithely requested pokeweed. Gussie, overworked and exhausted from keeping all the names straight, turned to Angie and said, a bit too loudly, "What in the fuck is pokeweed?"

The customer overheard Gussie and, utterly surprised said, "You don't know what pokeweed is, girl?"

Clever Gussie quickly recovered, saying "I'm sorry, darlin', I thought you said pukeweed!" and the store burst into gales of laughter as Angie slunk away to find the obscure green. There was a display case that contained somewhat more conventional cold cuts such as bologna, ham, head cheese and, off to the side, a tray of the traditional favorite fish, whiting. Sometimes the whiting was less than fresh and eventually this created a bitter complaint from a customer.

The customer's name was Lenore Henderson, a retired school teacher living on a small pension. She was badly disabled with arthritis, and she did not own a car nor did she have relatives who could drive her to the market to do her food shopping. She was forced to hobble two blocks from her home to Steinberg's Grocery to do her food shopping. And she hated it. She felt degraded having to shop in a grocery store she considered second-rate and overpriced for the quality of the food they sold. Gussie spotted her as she limped into the store holding a partially wrapped package. She locked eyes with Gussie and dragged herself over to Gussie's counter and got right in her face. She slammed the fish, a whiting, partially wrapped in soggy, blood stained white paper on the counter. "Would you eat this garbage?" Stunned silence, "Answer me! Would you eat this stinking fish? Would you? Cat got your tongue? Maybe I'll grab hold of you and stuff this piece of rotten shit down your greedy Jew throat, you shameless robber, you!" Everyone stopped in their tracks and stared at the furious old woman. "You think because I'm black you can sell me garbage? If I could walk I'd never step foot in this filthy store, you thieving bitch. I'm a retired school teacher, not some cotton-picking fool. I know good food when I see it. If there was another store nearby, I'd crawl to it rather than let you cheat me like I just came off the bus from Mississippi."

"That's enough, lady." Angie snatched the package of fish, checked the price on the wrapping, rang the register, counted out 89cents and slammed the coins on the counter in front of Lenore Henderson. "Now take your money and get the hell out of here and never come back."

There were hushed mumbles of reaction, some favorable, some angry, As Lenore Henderson turned to leave, Gussie spoke up. "I'm sorry you were not pleased with the fish. We got it at the food terminal the morning of the day that you bought it. There's a war going on and things don't always get to market as fast as they should. Would you like something else? Pick out anything that looks good and fresh to you and it will be on the house. We appreciate your business and I know how hard it is for you to get to the store. So please, select anything you like with our compliments." They stared each other down for several long seconds. Then Gussie spoke, loud and clear for the entire store to hear: "I can tell that you are an educated woman and I would never call you a smart-ass nigger."

"My Lord," from a black voice at the back of the store.

" So never, ever again, call me a greedy Jew. Do we understand each other? " An almost imperceptible nod from Henderson. "I want you to continue shopping here," Gussie said. Angie rolled her eyes. "Any more complaints?" Angie said, hands on her hips and her eyes black with anger, She was looking for a fight and there were no takers. Everyone busied themselves looking happily into the bins and cases as Ms. Henderson selected several cans of salmon in exchange for the whiting fish she returned.

"You're going to get a lot of that kind of lip. These niggers are getting pushy," Pete said

"I ain't taking that kind of shit from them boogies, I'll guarantee you that!" Angie spat.

"Look, you're two women alone in a store in a black neighborhood. You're the only grocery in the area. You're a soft touch for a holdup. Nobody else is taking the risk of operating down there—not Krogers, not A and P, not Food-Town! You got a right to get a premium for giving them a convenient store. What else are they going do—take the streetcar uptown to shop for food?" Pete extolled.

"So we rack up the prices…. okay, we got a right to do that. But some of the stuff we're buying at the terminal is slop. They're going to piss and moan like that old lady did." Gussie said.

"Look, Gussie, you ain't running a premium grade market. The food is good—it just ain't fancy grade. You want to give them top grade? Go ahead and you'll go broke 'cause you're going the get stiffed if they poor-mouth you into giving them credit and they skip out on you. And they'll steal you blind if you don't watch them like a hawk. You can have a good business at that store if you watch your pennies and shut your ears to their bitching. You ain't cheating them—you're doing them a favor providing them with a food store right in their own neighborhood when nobody else will. It's up to you, Gussie. Be tough, be smart or be gone," Pete lectured.

"As long as I'm there, if they get mouthy, they hit the bricks," Angie added.

Gussie got the message. She wasn't going to be a sucker…a dummy…a loser like her father; she was going to make money and pay the price of running a tough business.

Sol and Norbert remained in the same platoon in the 168th Infantry which found itself defending hilltops overlooking the Kasserine Pass in the Tunisia campaign. America's poorly equipped and inexperienced First Armored Division, "Old Ironsides," was soon to face Erwin Rommel's heavily armed panzer divisions, The battle took place from the nineteenth through the twenty-fifth of February, 1943. It was a disaster for the poorly trained Americans who were driven back over fifty miles.

In the aftermath of the battle there was a complete shakeup in the American command structure, from the platoon level to the top echelon. Sol's platoon was badly shot up, though he and Norbert came through unscathed but humiliated and disgusted with their officers. New officers where brought in to train the regiment for the return engagement with the vaunted German Afrika Corps.

New, modern weapons were brought in and the green troops were trained with harsh discipline; no way was the American army ever again to appear impuissant to the enemy. Norbert Harper proved to be a natural born squad leader, holding on to the hill his platoon was defending until forced to retreat by direct order of the battalion commander. He actually told the officer commanding the platoon to "fuck off, we're busy killing krauts from this position." The second lieutenant threatened Norbert with a court martial for insubordination but he was killed before he could fulfill the threat. As they passed the body of the young officer, his face frozen in a gaping rictus, Norbert spat and mumbled, "yellow bellied 90 day wonder, probably screaming for his mama when he got hit." Sol grimaced and shook his head violently in revulsion at Norbert's heartlessness. Still he admired the man as a killing machine soldier and a loyal comrade, overlooking Norbert's utter lack of human sensitivity.

At the rear position where every unit was being reorganized, Norbert Harper was given the rank of sergeant and made platoon leader. His only reaction was to verbalize his idee fixe that the new platoon commander would be a "a little feather-merchant, 90 day wonder college boy who would piss his pants as soon as we got into a fire fight."

How wrong he was. When the new C.O. showed up to review the platoon, Norbert whispered, "shee-it." First Lieutenant Joey Randazzo grabbed Norbert's skivvy shirt and jammed into his throat with his massive first. "That's the last shit I want to hear coming out of your chaw-bacon mouth."

Norbert brushed Joey's hand away and shoved Joey back as he snarled his defiant, "Fuck you. Keep your greaseball hands off me or I'll shove this bayonet up your ass."

With no hesitation, Joey pulled out his .45 and pushed it into Norbert's nostrils. "Give me an excuse to blow your head off right here and now," The stared their blood hatred into each other's eyes for what seemed an eternity before Sol broke ranks and pleaded for them to cool off.

"Norb, please, he's okay, he's my brother. Please, Joey, stop. Please stop; the sarge is my best buddy and he's a great soldier. Give him a break, please, Joey."

"Get back in ranks, boy, and remember my name: It's Lieutenant Randazzo and I swear I'll kill the next shit-bird that steps out of line. Back in ranks, sergeant, and remember who's in charge here. I'm regular Army, not some kid out of ROTC. You will stand inspection at 0500. After a quick, and I do mean quick, chow, saddle up with two canteens of water and be ready to soldier. Dismissed!

Sol was stunned; should he run after Joey and hug him or should he mollify Norbert?

After darkness had fallen over the desert, the temperature dropped precipitously. The men bundled up in sweaters and field jackets. Sol, shivering in the cold and full of dread as he approached Joey's tent, did not know what to expect. Who was this angry, violent person he had loved for most of his life.? Who was this creature that called himself Joey Randazzo? What had happened to him?

Joey was reserved and unemotional when Sol stuck his head inside the tent flap and asked if he could come in. Imagine, asking the guy who called himself a brother, a guy who had been everything to him; imagine asking for permission to enter his tent. What had happened to Joey? Who was he? Joey gave Sol a brief, perfunctory hug and nodded to a chair for Sol to sit. He noticed that Sol was shivering so he handed him the flask from which he had been sipping brandy. Sol took a quick swig and tried to think of how he would start the conversation. Joey's questions were flat, almost mechanical. How was Gussie? How long had Sol been in the army? Had he seen any of the Randazzos lately? Did his platoon put up a fight at Kasserine? Finally Joey got down to business: Forget the family, forget the old times, forget all that shit. People change, Sol; they grow— they become different. I'm different, Sol—I'm career army. I want you to be different too, he said. You're not my father's pet errand boy at the food terminal; you're one of my troops. I hope you come out this war alive, but I'm not here to protect you like I did when we were street-fighting the micks as kids. Then he abruptly stood up and shook Sol's hand and said, "Good luck, Steinberg. Be a good soldier and we'll get along fine."

As Sol stumbled back to his tent through darkness, his mind replayed Joey's words:

"Good luck Steinberg!" Never had Joey called Sol by his last name. Who the fuck was this guy? He was a total stranger, this stiff, cold person who had climbed inside Joey Randazzo's body. Good luck Steinberg? Are you kidding? What the fuck had happened to him?

Sol's letters to Gussie were frequent and full of longing for her and their cozy apartment. Gussie surmised that he was part of the invasion of North Africa but she was shocked when Sol told her that Joey and he had met and that Joey was now an officer, in command of Sol's platoon. Gussie could hardly wait to find out if the Randazzo's knew that the boys had met, probably in Tunisia, but the Randazzos had received only one letter, about eighteen months ago when Joey wrote to tell them he had made it through OCS and that he was now a second lieutenant. The Randazzos read Sol's letter over and over, clinging to the thin thread of attachment that the words on a wrinkled piece of paper gave them. Joey's remoteness broke Pete's heart; why had he lost his only son; what had he done wrong? Pete asked God for an answer every morning at early mass.

Anna Mae Highstreet was part of the great migration of blacks from the cotton fields of Mississippi to the northern industrial cities toward the end of the Depression. Jobs were still difficult to find and Anna Mae liked to party; cheap, high-powered "bust-out wine" was her beverage of choice. She would get high on wine and sleep half the day away trying to shake off her dreadful hangovers. Eventually she started hustling for money. One of her "johns" was a tall, light-skinned guy from Barbados and as close as Anna Mae could figure, he was the father of the baby boy she gave birth to at Mercy Hospital in 1940.

She named the baby Luther and relied on food stamps to buy milk and baby food. Eventually she found her way to the Steinberg Grocery before the food stamp program ended in 1943. Luther was a sickly baby; he just never got enough to eat. As much as Anna Mae loved him, the cheap wine often came before good food for the little boy.

Gussie raised hell with Anna Mae when she would try to check out with a half gallon of wine and very little baby food. And on several occasions, Gussie ran Anna Mae out of the store and warned her never to come back. But Anna Mae persisted and she became a fixture around the Steinberg Grocery, often drinking her wine in the alley adjacent to the store.

If Gussie found Anna Mae drunk, dragging the little boy around with her, Gussie would take little Luther away from her, bring him into the store, feed him and let him take naps on a little mattress at the back of the store. This was the beginning of a lifelong relationship between Gussie Steinberg and Luther Highstreet.

By no stretch of the imagination could Norbert Harper ever be perceived as a crybaby but buried deep in his psyche was a reflexive need to look out for the underdog; and under Joey Randazzo's tyrannical command, the men of the platoon were being abused. And the problem needed fixing. Norbert requested permission to discuss the situation with the company commander, Captain Emil Dusek, an ex-steelworker from Cleveland. Dusek was enraged when he heard about the runs with full gear in the heat of the day. He said he needed corroboration by another man from the platoon. Norbert asked Sol if he would testify. Sol asked for time to think it over; the thought of turning on Joey, no matter how radically he had changed was extremely upsetting to Sol. Norbert interpreted Sol's hesitation as fear and he called Sol eight kinds of a "chicken shit, yellow belly." Sol took it in stride; he was accustomed to Norbert's hyperbole. Sol made one of the most difficult decisions of his life when he decided to back Norbert; he owed it to the guys in the platoon to speak out against Joey's outrageous behavior.

Joey was called up for review by Captain Dusek and a group of officers from headquarters company of the battalion. He was threatened with a court martial and loss of rank if there were any further reports of improper abuse of his authority as an officer.

Sol was shocked out of the deep sleep of exhaustion when he felt the cold muzzle of Joey's .45 grinding into his cheek in the middle of the night. "Little fucking suck-ass fink, lousy Jew bastard." Joey's hysterical, sandpaper voice struck terror in Sol in the cold darkness of the silent tent.

"What do you want, Joey," Sol said, not knowing what was coming next. Joey kept the .45 against Sol's cheek.

"There's something I been meaning to tell you."

"What?" Sol whispered, his voice quavering with fear.

"Your wife is a great lay. You're a lucky man, Solly boy."

"What the hell are you saying, Joey.?"

"I fucked her on top of a pile of bananas, which is what you do with monkeys. She loved it, Sol, and I'm going to do it again when I get home, because I've got a feeling you're not going to make it home."

Rage supplanted fear in Sol and he brushed the .45 away from his cheek. "Get out of here, Joey. You're a sick man, Joey. I feel nothing but pity for you." Joey quietly walked out into the darkness of the desert night.

Marie Randazzo fell to the floor screaming and weeping, clutching the telegram from the War Department informing her that her son, First lieutenant Joseph Anthony Randazzo was killed in action against the enemy in Tunisia on March 19, 1943.

Neither Sol nor Norbert was sure whose shot killed the crazy bastard during the counterattack at Kasserine Pass. Sol said that he would have to write a letter to Pete Randazzo telling him what a brave man his son was. "Yah, you do that, Steinberg. Mention my name in the letter," Norbert said.

Sol and Norbert were together in the invasion of Sicily and later in the grinding futility of the campaign in Italy where Norbert was killed at Monte Casinno in March of 1944. Sol was deeply affected by Norbet's death, but he was now a grizzled veteran, inured to the mindless slaughter of Allied troops in their attempts to breach to German Gustav line from January 1944 through May 18, 1944. When the Allies finally broke through the German defenses, at great cost in May, Sol's outfit was pulled out of the lines and transported to England for R & R. Eventually, Sol was sent to Germany as a replacement in Patton's Third Army. When the war ended in Europe, Sol returned to the States where he was assigned to an outfit training for the invasion of Japan. He was a tired old man of thirty-one when he was finally mustered out and honorably discharged in February of 1946.

Gussie and Pete Randazzo hardly recognized Sol when he got off the bus after he had been discharged. Pete embraced Sol and wept bitterly until Gussie gently pulled him away. Pete wanted to know everything about Joey, though Sol had written several letters to him after Joey's death. Sol promised to go to the house the next day and talk to the entire Randazzo clan.

Gussie was expecting to make love on Sol's first night home, but he was strangely quiet and somewhat distant. He begged off, saying he was exhausted and needed a good night's sleep. Gussie sensed that something was wrong by the way in which Sol seemed to hesitate before answering Pete's questions about Joey.

As they lay in bed, with Gussie holding Sol and softly touching his graying temples she finally whispered: "Is something wrong, sweetheart?"

"Yes," was his shocking reply. And Gussie knew. Joey had told him.

Gussie and Sol went to the Randazzos the next morning. Marie had prepared pastry and coffee for the get together. Blessedly, bright sunlight suffused the room to lighten the heavy sorrow that had descended on the house. Pete attempted to change the mood, asking Sol what he thought of his son, now five years old, the spitting image of Gussie. Everyone fought to maintain self-control and to let Pete and Marie ask their questions of Sol. The mood was utterly antithetical to typical Randazzo gatherings; Sol could feel everyone's eyes burning into him. They asked the same questions over and over: How had Joey been killed? Where was he hit? Did he die instantly? Had he felt any pain? When did Sol first know that Joey had been killed? What did Sol do when he found Joey's body? Was there a priest present when Joey was buried? Does Sol know the exact location of the burial grounds? Will the government ever bring the bodies home so we can bury Joey in our parish cemetery? Gussie sensed something; Sol was holding something back; his answers were mechanical, casuistic. When Pete finally said, "You're my only son, now. I love you for taking care of Joey," the weeping started; quiet sobs at first, coruscating to near hysteria.

Sol settled into the quotidian routine of running the store with Gussie; Angie had retired as soon as Sol felt able to go back to work in the store. Slowly, he assumed his old persona and their life seemed to return to normal. He spent every spare moment bonding with his new son who had started kindergarten at an uptown school near the home of Gussie's aunt. Maxwell was registered as living at the aunt's address to enable him to attend the modern school in that neighborhood. Sol put him on the bus every morning, always asking the driver to keep and eye on Maxwell. This convinced Gussie that their marriage had not been irreparably damaged by her indiscretion with Joey.

Many months later Gussie asked a question that had been nagging her since that first morning when they had met with the Randazzos: How had Joey died? "Why do you want to know? Why now are you bringing this up," Sol asked.

"Was it terrible for you to see him dead? I mean, was he horribly wounded," she asked.

"No. He was killed by a bullet in his back."

"In his *back,?*" she said.

"Yes." A peremptory reply; no emotion. Sol simply met Gussie's eyes and they looked at each other for several seconds without speaking. Gussie never again brought up the subject, but for the rest of her life she was freighted with the question: could Sol have murdered Joey in revenge? It was a question she never dared ask. She hoped that the brief exchange would create a tabula rasa in their life from that point on, and that they could both forget what might have transpired.

Business was excellent at the Steinberg Grocery; everyone in the neighborhood who wanted to work was employed, and they not only bought food at the store but wine, beer, cigarettes, soft drinks and candy. Sol created a wine and beer section with brands favored by the people of the neighborhood. Drugs were not yet a problem in the community. Ever so often, Pete would slowly amble into the store to say "hello" and to check the produce to make sure Gussie and Sol were buying "right." Sol and Pete would embrace and kiss in the Italian fashion. Gussie would look closely at Sol for any signs that would indicate that he might be uncomfortable with Pete, which would certainly be the case if Sol had harmed Joey. There was nothing in Sol's face or eyes to indicate anything but love for Pete. Pete was starting to look like a very old man; he dragged one leg ever so slightly as he walked and he had developed a persistent cough from his many years of smoking Camels, his favorite brand.

After the initial greeting it was not unusual for Pete to find a box or an empty crate, and sit and watch the action in the store. One October afternoon in 1946, when there were no customers in the store, Pete motioned for Gussie and Sol to join him at the back of the store. "I got to ask you something and maybe it's none of my business anymore, but I'm going to ask anyways. For Sol, I understand...he's like a regular dago; he don't worry about appearances. But you, Gussie...you come from a respectable Jewish family."

"So?" Gussie asked, curious now.

"So, how does your family really feel about you running a store for *moolies*?"

"Moolies?" Gussie had heard the term but was never sure of its meaning.

"Moolies, moolies! Comes from the Italian name for eggplant—melanzana. It's a dago put-down for blacks," Sol said.

"See what I mean?" Pete said, "he's a regular dago."

"Pete, I remember, years ago—you were teaching Sol and me how do buy non-prime produce and telling us if we watch our pennies, we could make a good living in a neighborhood store; especially this location where we don't have competition. So why, all of a sudden are you hinting we shouldn't be doing this?" Gussie asked.

"Because it's dangerous down here now. Marie would move if she wasn't tied to the parish and our church down here," Pete said.

"You want to know something, Pete," Sol interjected, "we love this old neighborhood. This is where our people all settled when they came from the old country. And we know how to handle the moolies. We treat them with respect and if a troublemaker comes in, we 86 them the hell out of here. And I got a piece under the counter if, God forbid, I ever have to use it. And we're making a good living, Pete. What are you worrying about?"

"And Pete, we fixed up a real nice home upstairs. So why move and pay through the nose for an apartment and be in competition with those fancy stores? We've got it made down here, Pete," Gussie said.

"Hey, as long as you're safe and happy and making a good living, God bless you. Marie says I'm like an old lady with my worrying about things." Then his eyes filled with tears and he said, "I was thinking about Joey. How nice it would have been if he had liked this business and the two of you—the deuces, I called you—you could have been in business together." Sol hugged Pete until the old man's tears stopped.

"Joey was meant to be a soldier, Pete. He died doing what made him happy—a career army guy. He would have gone nuts in a store and you know it," Sol said. And, despite her determination to never think those thoughts again, Gussie's mind became clouded with old questions again.

Pete kissed them and said he was going to ride over to the Terminal where he had evolved into somewhat of an eminence grise.

Anna Mae and Luther, who was six years old in 1946, lived on the relief check she received from Social Services. She would turn an occasional trick to pick up some extra cash, and when she did, she would go in to Steinbergs and try to buy some cheap wine, which Gussie always s refused to sell her. Anna Mae would nag and beg and Gussie, in exasperation would tell her to go somewhere else; but there were no other stores in the neighborhood so Anna Mae would continue to importune Gussie until she lost patience and relented. Gussie would threaten to report her to Social Services because Luther was not getting enough to eat. The threats didn't seem to worry Anna Mae who had developed a new strategy. She would sit in the alley next to the store and wait for Gussie to leave or to go upstairs to the apartment to start dinner. Then Anna Mae would rush into the store and grab a half-gallon of wine, knowing that Sol could care less how she spent her money.

One day in mid-November, Gussie spotted Anna Mae sitting in the alley, drunk as a skunk, an empty wine bottle at her side. Gussie confronted Sol and demanded to know if he had sold her the wine, which Sol admitted he had done. "Please don't sell her wine anymore, Sol; she should be using that money to feed her little boy. He looks like a wraith."

"Sweetheart," Sol replied, "I'm not a social worker. I can't be responsible for how our customers choose to live."

"She shouldn't have a child;  she has no idea how to take care of that poor little boy. When he was a baby, I used to put him in a little crib that Angie rigged up at the back of the store. But he's getting to be a big boy and I can't do it anymore."

The weather was bitter cold  early in December of 1946.  People were stocking up on the foods they would need for Christmas dinner.  Anne Mae came into the store, trailed by tall, skinny, ravenously hungry Luther.  The usual bickering started when Anna Mae tried to pay for a half-gallon of wine she had selected.  While Gussie and Anna Mae argued, Luther stood in front of the cold cuts counter, literally salivating as he stared at a loaf of bologna. Gussie saw Luther standing in front of the meat case and her heart went out to the hungry little boy.  She took the bologna out of the case and cut off a big  slice which she put on a slice of bread and gave it to Luther.  The  child wolfed it down  as Gussie and Anna continued their debate.  Finally Sol spoke up: " Why isn't that kid in school?  Gussie, make up a package of  cold cuts and get a loaf of bread and milk  for this lady.  I'm going to let her buy the wine with the understanding that she's barred from ever coming into this store again. I've had enough of this crap. We've got a business to run; this is not a relief agency. Take your wine and get out of here." And, as an after-thought, "And feed that kid!"

It was barely daylight when Sol saw the red and blue lights of the police cruiser stopped in front of the store.  He shouted for Gussie as he ran down the steps and out the front door.  An ambulance had arrived and the medics were carrying the frozen , lifeless body of  Anna Mae Hightree.

"What happened to her?" Sol asked the officer who seemed to be in charge. The officer held up an empty half-gallon wine bottle.

"Passed out and froze to death.  You know this lady?" the officer asked.

"She comes into our store.  She's got a little boy. Does anybody know where he is?" Sol said.  Gussie had thrown on a coat over her nightgown and rushed out after Sol.

"Oh, God! We've got to find Luther. God knows where she left him," Gussie shouted.

"We'll find him, ma'm."

"Please, please, bring him here if you find him," Gussie pleaded.

"Isn't there any family somewhere?" asked the officer.

"I don't know. Just bring him here—we'll take care of him until you find some relatives," Gussie said, her voice breaking, and tears filling her eyes. Sol stared at her in amazement.

"Are you serious, Gus? We're going to take care of that kid?"

"Just until they find some relatives that look responsible," Gussie said.

"And if they don't?" Sol challenged.

"Sol don't bother me with 'what ifs'. Let me worry about it."

"We'll be in touch. I'll need your names and a phone number," the officer said as he reached for his note pad.

The police did a perfunctory search of the neighborhood and came up empty. No one knew anything about Anna Mae nor did they care to talk to the police. It was as if Anna Mae had never lived. When they returned to the Steinberg store, the cops asked Gussie to call them "if anything turnes up."

When they left, Gussie threw on some clothes and started a search in the most run-down section of the neighborhood. When she saw a familiar face, she would ask if they knew where Anna Mae had flopped. Eventually, a wino pointed a trembling finger at a wretched, falling down, flop house.

Gussie found Luther in a room that Anna Mae had in the flop house. He was shivering in a fetal position with a filthy, thin blanket wrapped around his skinny body. The room was barren and cold, strewn with dirty clothes and empty wine bottles. Gussie coaxed Luther out of his cocoon and wrapped her arms around him, enveloping his shivering body with her warmth. "Where my mama?" he cried as she cuddled him.

She carried him back to the apartment and gave him warm cocoa and oatmeal. Sol watched, wondering where this bizarre drama was going. Gussie told the frightened little boy that his mama had gone to heaven, but he didn't comprehend. "Where my mama," he cried over and over until, exhausted, he eventually fell asleep. Gussie made up the little bed in the spare room that they kept for visitors. "Now what," Sol asked.

"Now nothing. A little boy needs to sleep," a hint of defiance in Gussie's voice.

"Aw, come on!" Sol said, annoyed.

Maxie, Sol abjured the formal "Maxwell," was visibly upset by Luther's presence in the apartment. "Is he going to stay here?" Maxie asked, his lower lip protruding petulantly.

"Yes," Gussie said, "now you'll have someone your own age to play with."

"I don't like him, Mom. He talks funny; I can't understand what he's saying. I don't want him here," Maxie whined. Gussie's temper flared.

"Just get used to it, mister," she snapped, "he needs a home just like you do. You understand, Max?"

"Doesn't he have a home of his own?" Maxie asked.

"His mother died. He had nowhere else to go. Make friends with him. It'll be fun, you'll see," Gussie said.

Maxie went into a funk, locking himself in his room when he returned from school.

Months went by and the situation stabilized. The police never returned to make inquiries regarding the deceased woman's child nor did Social Services become involved. Luther Hightree, for all practical purposes was a non-person; there was no record of him anywhere. Gussie checked all the charity hospitals to see if there was a birth record or if a birth certificate had been issued. Finally, at Mercy hospital they told her that they did have some record of a woman who came in as an emergency case in 1940 but refused to give her name and left with the child without notice. In other words, Luther Hightree, if Hightree was indeed the father's name, did not exist except in the home and heart of Gussie Steinberg.

Luther had no commerce whatsoever with Maxie, who had built a circle of friends at his uptown school. Maxie, quite often, would have Gussie's aunt Frieda call to say he was staying after school to play with some friends at her house and that he would sleep over and go to school directly from her house.

Sol took it upon himself to register Luther in Central Elementary, a school close-by in the ghetto. Gussie took care of dressing Luther in presentable school clothes. At first, Luther skulked at the back of the classroom, too frightened and too shy to mix with the other kids. Eventually, one of Luther's teachers made him a "project" and began to draw him out. As the weeks went by, Luther slowly but inexorably became a normal child. When it was time for parent-teacher conferences, Gussie was thrilled to hear that Luther had developed into a quick learner and was an eager pupil.

Maxie, Sol and Gussie were told, was a brilliant student and has been advanced a full grade. When he came home from school, he would seek out Sol and question him about the war and all the places he been as a soldier. Maxie was learning to write cursive, and he took scribbled notes as Sol regaled him with stories about North Africa, Sicily and various countries in Europe. Sol noticed that Luther would sit in the hall outside of Maxie's room, and listen in on the stories. Luther sensed that he was not welcome in Maxie's room but he desperately wanted to hear Sol's stories. And he desperately wanted attention from Sol, following him like a puppy and assiduously observing everything Sol did. Sol was touched by the little boy's yearning to be close to him and he began to spend time with Luther, helping him with his school projects and teaching him how to correctly pronounce new words. To Sol's surprise, Luther was a preternaturally quick study. The street jargon that Luther had learned from his mother began to disappear. Sol began to enjoy working with Luther, concentrating on improving his diction and expanding his vocabulary. This gave Gussie much pleasure and she and Sol became closer than they had ever been. Sol was a real *mensch!*

The market for automobiles, post war, had loosened up and Sol was able to purchase the very first car he had ever owned; a two-tone, Chevy coupe. Sol would take Luther with him as he drove around town and when he went to the food terminal very early in the morning, before school started.   But there would be tense moments  when Maxie competed with Luther for Sol's attention.

When this occurred, Luther would withdraw and seek out Gussie down in the store.

The years rolled by and the memories of World War II began to fade; the nation slipped seamlessly into the sedate and prosperous mid-fifties. The boys were in high school; Luther at Central High in the ghetto and Maxie at the prestigious Country High in the suburbs.

Maxie had become exceedingly self-conscious around his new friends at the wealthy Country School, because of his home above a grocery store in the ghetto. The denouement occurred when Maxie asked to have a conversation with his parents. Is "he" around, Maxie asked, not wanting Luther to be involved. "Don't be angry, but I've got something to tell you," he said as Sol and Gussie tensed up, preparing for the worst. "I'd like to simplify my name."

"What the fuck is that supposed to mean," Sol barked.

"Sol!" Gussie admonished. " Maxie…What are you asking?"

"It's a literal translation of Steinberg; from the Yiddish or Polish or whatever, to English. I want to Anglicize it from 'Steinberg' to the English version of the same name—'Stonehill'. Stein means stone, Berg means hill; Stonehill. Not such a big deal."

"Got if all figured out, right, big shot? You want your mom and me to disappear so you shouldn't be ashamed in front of your fancy new friends? Maybe the store should go away, too?"

"Sol, wait. Wait!" Gussie knew Sol when he got hot; this was another one of those "Jew put-downs" that reminded him of his days on the streets and the fights with the Irish thugs. "You're embarrassed by your name? Your new friends never heard Jewish names before?"

"Mom, this is 1956 and you're not immigrants. This is America and I want an American name. I'm not from the old country," Maxie inveighed.

"You don't want my name then you don't want my money. Go find an 'American' to send you to school," Sol shouted, his veins bulging dangerously.

"Sol, don't talk cheap like a street person. He'll go to school and he'll go to college and we'll send him. And when he needs his own people, he knows where to find us," Gussie said. "Go and be healthy and happy, Mister Maxwell Stonehill."

"You said 'go'—I do want to 'go.' Aunt Lillian said I could live there. I can't live down here in the ghetto any longer. I'm going to move to Aunt Lillian's."

"Lillian Herzog. She's now what? Lola Henderson, maybe? You changed her name too?" Sol raged.

Maxie started to sob. "You make me feel like a rat; like a double-crosser. I just want to be a normal person, you understand? A normal person!"

"Pack your clothes. I'll drive you with great joy," Sol said.

"Sol! Stop. Leave him alone," Gussie pleaded.

Maxie's departure tore a hole in Sol's life. Luther sensed that Sol was hurting and asked if he could work in the store and learn how to wait on customers, thinking that might take Sol's mind off of Maxie. Sol was touched by Luther's offer and he told him that he would pay him a salary as soon as he "knew what he was doing."

And so began Luther's career as a grocer. Sol worked very hard teaching Luther the tricks of the trade and Luther was an apt apprentice. Before long he was waiting on trade and learning how to haggle and buy at the food terminal with Sol before he left to attend school.

After several months, Luther had accumulated enough money so that he was able to go uptown to a haberdashery and buy clothes. When he returned with his purchases, he put on his new shirt, sports coat, and shoes and paraded in front of Sol and Gussie to get their reaction. Gussie forced a smile and said, "Very nice, Luther." Sol simply looked Luther over, from top to bottom and said nothing.

"What do you think, Boss?" Luther said. He had recently taken to calling Sol, "Boss."

"Fine, if you want to look like one of those jitterbugs."

"Say what?" Luther said, suddenly embarrassed by Sol's disapproval.

"You're learning to be a businessman, not a jive-ass street hustler." Luther chuckled at Sol's attempt at black-talk.

"Sol, for God's sake," Gussie scolded.

"No, I want to know. I ain't studying to be a pimp," Luther said.

"So let's take this shit back and get some stuff that will make you look like a gentleman, okay?"

"When did you become a fashion *maven*, Sol?" Gussie teased.

"I had a great teacher," he said gesturing to Gussie.

The blue suede shoes were traded in for brown wing tips, the bold-checked sports coat for a muted grey herringbone, and the pink shirt for a blue, button-down oxford shirt. Luther looked at himself in the full length mirror, his face registering uncertainty.

"Boss, you turning me into a white man, ain't you," Luther said with a grin.

"You want respect? You got to dress the part. Trust me, kid, dressing "white" isn't going to hurt you in school with the chicks and even on the street. Don't be afraid to look like you're a quiet man who knows what he's doing." Luther thought about that for a minute and it began to make sense to him; he eventually bought the concept and he would carry it through life as the statement he wished to make to the world. *I may look like a square cat, but don't mess with me!*

Slowly, gradually, very tactfully, Sol began modifying Luther's diction.

"What are we doing here, Boss, trying to make me sound "white?" Luther said, baiting Sol.

"I don't want you to be white, Luther...I like you just the way you are."

"No shit, Boss? I could swear I was sounding like a school teacher."

"Don't be a smart ass...I want you to sound like a black guy with an education, which I was never lucky enough to get," Sol said.

"And that's going to get me respect in school, in business and even on the street," Luther said, mimicking Sol's earlier polemic.

Sol worked on eliminating the "jive talk" as he called it, from Luther's speech pattern. "You will still sound like a black man, but an educated black man, so sure of yourself that you will not be afraid to sound dignified even on the street with wise guys talking hip, black talk," Sol said. And Luther listened. And Gussie was awed by a side of Sol that she never knew existed. *Where did this stuff come from? The man was a street urchin when I found him .Unbelievable.*

The fifties embraced and nurtured Luther and Maxie, and they emerged as attractive, self-assured young men, ready to take a bite out of the world. Luther found the respect and admiration that Sol had promised; he was essentially running the store, driving Sol's new Chevy, shuffling through all the good-looking chicks, looking after both Steinbergs, dressing and speaking like a confident, educated man and feeling the itch to get out into the world on his own. He was confident that Sol and Gussie were safe and secure in the store; business was good, very good. Nothing to worry about. Luther was grateful to Gussie for her mother-love and to Sol for everything he had taught him, but—he wanted to go beyond being "grateful"…trying to conform and to please. He wanted people to please *him*. Each time he looked into the mirror he liked what he saw; a really cool dude; light-skinned, tall, handsome and different, very different from the big hitters he had been watching on the street. Sol was so right—those guys would not know how to take him. Yes, he thought, the way I dress, the way I talk…they've got to pay attention. And they're going to give me respect. He knew it was time to leave. Goodbyes would be painful; just slip away and do my thing. He had surreptitiously packed his clothes into a single, large suitcase that he had purchased at an army-navy store, and he silently left the Steinberg Grocery for the last time, locking the door behind him. It would be many years before he would return, to once again, help out.

He walked several blocks to the streetcar line and boarded a deserted car going uptown. He had no destination in mind; just someplace uptown. The lights were still on at what he was sure was a black club. He tapped lightly on the door of the service entrance, and a large, menacing black man opened the door a crack and growled, "What do you want, man?"

Luther spoke calmly and confidently. "I realize it's early, but I would like to speak with the manager. Are you the manger, sir?"

The large black man twisted his face into a look of disbelief and supreme annoyance. "You out of your fuckin' mind? You come knocking at the door at four in morning looking for the manager!" He was enjoying his role as the outraged boss man and began milking the encounter for all that it was worth. "What business you got with the manager?"

"Look, I apologize if I am disturbing you. I'm new in town. I just got in and I'm interested in working here, if you've got an opening of any kind," Luther said, his voice steady and deep.

"Opening of any kind, you say? You wash dishes? You mop floors?" a sadistic grin crawling across his rough, battered face. The punched-down eyebrows were those of an old fighter.

Luther gathered himself up and glared at the man for a few seconds and said, "Do I look like a fucking dishwasher to you? I've been a store manager for a grocery chain. Now, is there someone I can make an appointment with to talk about a job?"

"You be a store manager, huh? Walking around in the middle of the night carrying your suitcase. Listen, you already got yourself an appointment. I'm the goddam manager here. You're some kind of a fancy dude, I can see. Now what kind of work could you do in club like this?"

"Can I come inside and talk to you?" Luther said, looking steadily into the big guy's eyes.

"You better not be carrying or trying some shit with me," the big guy said as he opened the door and motioned Luther in. Luther looked around and saw that this was a plush night club-restaurant. "Can you cook?" Luther shook his head. "Can you tend bar?"

"I'm good with people. I know how to keep customers happy," Luther snapped, suddenly feeling encouraged. The guy was actually taking him seriously, now.

"Can you mix a goddam margarita?" the big guy challenged.

" I'm a fast learner. I'll work free until I learn all the drinks. I've been to school, I'm educated. Give me a chance, you won't be sorry," Luther said.

"Look at me—step over here in the light. Lemme' see what you look like in the light." He studied Luther carefully and a look of approval crossed his face. "You a cool looking young cat, I'll say that. And somebody done dressed you up nice. Yeh, the chicks are going to like seeing you behind that bar."

Luther didn't hesitate. He grabbed the big guy's hand and shook it vigorously. "Can I leave my suitcase here while I go looking for an apartment. What time do I start tonight?" And Luther's new life started at Club Valencia as an apprentice bartender under the watchful eye of the big guy, whose name Luther would learn, was Kid Foster, a well known ex-pug who owned the club and had opened the door for Luther.

Luther had to find a pad, something he could afford in the suburban fringe. He thought he had enough for the first month's rent. The blacks were starting to move out of the ghetto into some of the older suburbs and they occupied the homes and apartment buildings from which the whites had fled.

Late in the afternoon Luther found a furnished, one room apartment and managed to talk the landlady into accepting a down payment for the first month's rent. He ran back to the Club and salvaged his suitcase before returning to his new pad and collapsing on the blue, mohair sofa bed for a few hours, before he had to report for work at Club Valencia.

Maxwell had graduated *cum laude* from Country School and had applied to several Ivy League schools, hoping for a scholarship. Harvard, Brown, Dartmouth and Princeton accepted him but offered no scholarship help. He knew that Gussie would help out with tuition if he asked; but he was reluctant to ask, knowing that Sol would have things to say to him that he did not wish to hear at this point in his life.

He tried several more Eastern schools and got a favorable reply from Boston University which offered him a "full ride" work-scholarship that took care of tuition, books, room and board. His work duties were those of a "transporter," which required him to carry documents and books between departments and to assist the librarians in arranging books on the shelves.

Shortly after Maxwell arrived, representatives of ZBT, Zeta Beta Tau, the long established Jewish fraternity on campus, contacted him and urged him to pledge the fraternity. There was no way that Maxwell could afford to live in the frat house, but he accepted the pledge pin and did his stint as a pledge before being accepted as a member of the fraternity. He would stop at the house frequently to participate in activities and parties.

Maxwell was a little surprised when ZBT had the first keg party of the season. He shared the common misconception that Jews were not drinkers but he soon disabused himself of that notion. At the keg party a group of girls from Wellesley arrived, having been invited by one the more adventuresome members. The Wellesley women were cordial and polite, well-mannered and proper. After introductions they began mingling and making small talk with the boys. The women did accept beer when offered and they seemed to enjoy themselves. Soon, the level of noise grew and there were bursts of laughter and shouting. The beer was taking effect. The girls drank heartily, but there was no swilling or chug-a-lugging. Maxwell surveyed the women and came to the conclusion that the Wellesley women had a "certain look" that he could not quite define; but he was quite taken with the "look" and the mannerisms of the women. It was all new and quite exciting to Maxwell.

He had not introduced himself to any of the women; he simply observed and listened.

"Nice party. Why are you standing here all alone? We don't bite, honest." She extended her hand with beer driven brio and said, " I'm Katherine Edmunson, Kitty to my friends. Who are you?"

"Oh, sorry," Maxwell said, flustered.

"Sorry for what," she blurted.

"For not talking." he said, inanely.

"You're allowed. Do you want to talk to me?"

"Oh, absolutely," Maxwell said, realizing that he was sounding like an idiot.

"Then get me a fresh beer and we'll sit over here and get acquainted."

Maxwell dashed off and plunged through the crowd, anxious to get back to this tall blond with the aristocratic drawl. "Here we go," he said handing her the beer.

"So, who are you? What's your name?"

"Maxwell," he answered, nervous under her penetrating gaze as she looked him over.

"Fancy name, Maxwell. You must be rich to have an elegant name like that." That made him laugh; loosened him up. He gulped his beer, wanting to feel relaxed and glib around this smashing looking girl with shoulder length, lustrous hair.

"Actually, I'm poor. And everyone calls me Maxie, not Maxwell. Maxie's not so fancy, is it?" This guy's an unusual character, she thought. Delightfully nutty.

"So, poor Maxie, where are you from? You sound like Midwest, am I right?"

"You are very right." Then without realizing what he was saying, he stammered out, "You are the most beautiful girl I have ever seen."

"Well, how nice of you to say that, poor Maxie." And she kissed him lightly on the cheek. She paused for a moment, then said, "Get me a slip of paper and something to write with." Maxwell dashed off and flew back with paper and a pencil stub. She looked at him and smiled as she jotted down her phone number. "I would like you to call me, Maxie. I'd really like to get to know you. Incidentally, what's your name—your last name?"

"Stonehill."

"That doesn't sound Jewish. You are Jewish, right? Even though you look Irish or something."

"Yes, I'm Jewish. No, Stonehill doesn't sound Jewish because it's really Steinberg." Maxwell could not believe he was saying these things. This girl made him want to spill his guts to her,

"So, you're really poor Maxie Steinberg, from somewhere out in the sticks." She gulped her beer and said, "Are you going to call me, Maxie? Notice I dropped the "poor" from your name."

"I'll call you for sure, Kitty, but you better leave the "poor" on my name. I have zero money to take you out."

"So we'll sit on a bench on campus and talk. Can you manage to get to Wellesley?" she said, quite sweetly.

"I'll find a way."

"Gussie! Gussie! He's gone. Wake up—come in here!" Sol's hysterical shouts shocked Gussie out of a deep sleep and she ran to the shouts, her bare feet slapping the floor as she struggled to keep her balance.

"What happened? Sol, what happened here?" she shouted, her tongue still thick with sleep.

"Luther is gone. All his clothes are gone. He's gone, Gussie. Oh my God! Why did he leave? Sol's voice broke as he began sobbing. Gussie was now fully awake and she held the utterly distraught Sol in her arms,

"Let's sit down. Let's go have coffee in the kitchen. Let's sit and we'll talk.. There must be a reason. Something happened. Let's see what happened."

They sat at the kitchen table, stunned, bewildered and at times, angry. As daylight broke, they realized that Luther was gone and he probably was not coming back. Why had he left, without a goodbye or a word of explanation? Finally, Gussie spoke: "You know, Sol, Luther has been a non-person from birth. Remember? No records at the hospital, no birth certificate. A non-person. A ghost who disappears into thin air. He'll be fine, Sol. We did what we had to do to give him a life. Let him live and be happy wherever he goes."

Sol said nothing. He simply stared straight ahead. Then he stood up abruptly and said, "I've got to go to the terminal and buy. Get dressed and open up. We should be busy today."

Gussie's parents, Nate and Sonja Berg came to visit; they wanted to share the good news of Nate's new position as a licensed pharmacist with a major chain. He had passed the state board and his jejune position as an underemployed scientist was over. His mien and bearing reflected his sense of reborn pride. Nate's sister, Lillian, in whose home Maxwell lived while attending high school, had asked Nate to get news of his achievements in college. Maxwell had not written to her since leaving for Boston University. Gussie temporized, not wanting to admit that she too, had not heard from Maxwell. The conversation turned into vagrant badinage and finally Sol could stand it no longer. Perhaps it was to assuage his pain and humiliation, that Sol had become stolid, obdurate, when the subject of Maxwell arose. "Maxie Steinberg" he said, "is now Maxwell Stonehill. And he has rejected us and everything we stand for."

"What are you saying? I don't understand what you just told us, Sol," Nate said. He had paled and Sonja gasped and touched Gussie's cheek, compassionately.

"He changed his name when he moved in with your sister Lillian. Didn't she tell you that? Didn't you see him while he was living there?" Sol said, angrily.

"He doesn't call or write? He doesn't need money for college?" Sonja asked, her voice weak and tearful.

"Maxwell lives in another world. It is a world I know nothing about. There is nothing more to say." Sonja began to weep and she buried Gussie's face in her bosom to comfort her. Gussie had not wanted her parents to know about the loss of her son in her life but she was relieved that Sol, in his direct way, had told the truth.

As they left, the Bergs murmured meaningless words of encouragement; it was a phase, Maxwell would come to his senses and love and respect his parents again. But for Gussie and Sol, it was business as usual; grinding out a good living, running the Steinberg Grocery on Central avenue in the ghetto, and managing their grief at losing two sons.

Kid Foster crammed the various drink proportions into Luther's head, and he was impressed with his deft movements and the flourish with which Luther presented the drinks to customers at the bar. The lad was going to be okay and the ladies were going to go for him. Kid Fostser was glad he hadn't slammed the door on the nervy young cat that came knocking on the service door at 4 o'clock in the morning. All of Luther's moves did not go unnoticed by the hostess, a meretriciously seductive looker named Natasha, stationed across the aisle. She winked, she nodded approval, she gestured, wiggled and did everything but remove her skimpy, slinky, spangling dress. She really dug this tall, light-skinned, Caribbean-looking young cat, as did the female trade at Club Valencia. Luther had lucked out. He found his niche.

"Listen, learn who's who, keep your mouth shut and smile," Kid Foster had told him.

Luther studied the "who's who" of regulars at the club. He was in the thrall of the big hitters who came with their dolled up chicks. They had power, real power. They would make their lay-downs on the bar, fifties and hundreds tossed down without concern, as they sat at the bar and surveyed the scene, looking dangerous and terribly important. Luther noticed everything; their wrist watches, their diamond rings, gold bracelets, expensive hats and sharply pressed suits, glistening, two-toned shoes. They spoke in near whispers and in short bursts. Cool. So very, very cool. Kid Foster would dance attendance on them, making sure their special table was ready for them. When the "transactions" took place Luther tried not to stare. A big paw on the bar, something concealed beneath the paw. A casual sliding motion and the reception of the concealed item by the stone-faced Foster, who in turn slid a thick bundle of cash to the waiting paw. It was over in seconds; Kid Foster and the big hitter would click glasses and throw down a celebratory shot. Luther looked at the hostess station after a "transaction" and caught Natasha's eye and her know-it-all grin. She raised her penciled eyebrows and nodded her head knowingly. Luther knew he had to get to know Natasha. She knew what was happening at all times. Luther wanted to be in the know. Who were these big shots, and why did Kid Foster slide them bundles of cash...were they pushing drugs? And why did they do it right out in the open? Weren't they afraid of the someone spotting them?

Luther stayed in the club after closing watching the porter clean as he straightened up the bar. "Can I get you a cup of coffee and something to eat, honey?" It was Natasha. The lights had been turned on and Luther got a good look at her. Yeh, she had a little mileage on her; lines around the eyes and the mouth, but still very damn sexy.

They sat at a table in the main dining room and Luther had an opportunity to closely observe the décor; a swag of beige fabric billowed artistically from the ceiling. the walls papered in a deep, elegant green, complementing the plush green carpeting. The tables were ebony black and the chairs were padded and covered in striped green and black fabric. Someone had paid big bucks to decorate this place. Natasha watched as Luther studied the room. "Pretty, ain't it?" she purred.

"Yeh, sure is," Luther mumbled, his mouth filled with pecan pie. "You been here long?" he asked casually, not wanting to appear too anxious to get involved with Natasha.

"Soon as they opened, the Kid called me," she answered. Luther noticed her use of the shortened, "The Kid" in referring to Kid Foster.

"You know the boss a long time?" he probed.

"Yah, honey-bunch. A long, long time," she answered in her best, mystery lady voice. Luther read her inflection correctly...the broad was sending out signals that she was a player in the scheme of things. "The Kid's a pusher, isn't he,?" Luther said nonchalantly.

"Whoa, baby boy, you stepping in deep water now. Don't be asking question like that," she said, serious now.

"Not a big mystery, they're doing business right on the bar."

"That's 'cause I signal that it's okay, no cops in the joint. Keep your eyes on me when the heavy cats come in. I nod if the joint is clean."

"You know all the cops? What if an undercover cop comes in that you don't know?"

" Honey baby, I know them all, and if I don't know them, I can smell them a mile away. "

"You never make a mistake?"

"Never." She took out her compact and did her face, knowing that Luther was very impressed with her. " You ain't got a car, do you honey. You want a ride home?" she asked.

"Yes. That would be nice," Luther said, his street instincts telling him that more events were in the wings. And they were. When they got to Luther's building Natasha wrinkled her nose. "Man, this all you can afford? Let me see what your crib looks like."

Luther nodded his okay and they went up to his tiny apartment. "That miserable bed what you sleep on?" she said. He maintained his composure as he cleverly waited for her next move. And it came when she said, " You want to see what a proper apartment looks like? Get some clothes for tomorrow. I'm taking you home with me, pretty baby."

Her apartment was big and luxurious; how could she afford this on her salary as a hostess? Luther had had plenty of experience with chicks at Central High and he was used to firm, young bodies. Natasha was a letdown. The thighs were heavier that he expected and there was more belly fat than he was used to. But he soon forget her physical shortcomings when she starting doing her tricks; licking him and sucking him and rubbing him. She had him practically whimpering with ecstasy and begging for more before he fell into a sated slumber. Natasha was now in control of the "pretty boy" bartender. And she would soon show him some tricks that would mature him quickly into a big man in their world.

Laura, one the Randazzo twins, came into the store, and walked slowly to Sol. Before she could speak, Sol embraced her and said, "How bad?"

"You better come to St. Lucy's with me, now. He's calling for you. Everyone's there."

"I'm coming too," Gussie said, and she reached for the store keys and locked up before sliding into Laura's car with Sol.

Marie hugged Sol as he entered Pete's room and began to weep bitterly. "Go," she said, pointing to Pete, fighting for his last breath, "he always loved you." Sol caressed Pete's skeletal hand and leaned over and kissed the dying old man who had been a father to him. Pete's lips moved as he struggled to speak to Sol who put his ear next to the old man's lips. " I know," he gasped. "I know what happened to Joey. I forgive you, son. He was no good. I love you, Sal Randazzo." His eyes smiled, and he was gone. Sol kissed Pete and rose to make room for Marie who wrapped her arms around her dead husband and wailed a death knell.

The Randazzo twins, Laura and Louis, and their young children were in the room and they asked Sol if he knew that two soldiers who had known Joey had come to visit their father and that they told him they thought that Joey had been shot in the back by his own men. "Was that true, Sol? Did his own men hate him that much?" Sol met their eyes and he said nothing for a few moments. Then he hoarsely whispered, "Not true. Joey was a fine officer." Then he kissed both women and said he wished to be a pallbearer. He despised himself for the lie with which he must forever live. Pete's last words had etched themselves in his brain, "I know what happened to Joey." What did he really know?

Aunt Lillian, who had finally managed to get Maxwell's address at Boston College, wrote to him to tell him that Pete Randazzo had died. Maxwell, surprisingly, was deeply touched; he had heard the story of his father's life with the Randazzo family and he felt that Pete Randazzo had been an extraordinary human being. Maxwell Stonehill was himself maturing into a caring human being.

Edmundson, Peterson and Kahn was a classic "white shoe" Boston law firm and Kitty had importuned her father to bring Maxwell in as a part-time law clerk, to file, run briefs and documents to court and other firms and clean the offices on the weekend.

Maxwell had found his way to Wellesley after their first meeting at the ZBT keg party and he and Kitty had eventually become lovers and deeply devoted to each other.

Maxwell had arranged his schedule so that Fridays were open. That enabled him to work Fridays and Saturdays at the law firm. At the beginning, Mackenzie "Mac" Edmunson was annoyed when Kitty told him she was in love with a guy from nowhere; a Jew, as a matter of fact, named Maxwell and that she wanted him to give the guy a job at the firm. This had been the latest in a series of inappropriate suitors which Kitty had presented to him. But Kitty had always had her way with her father; she was so very much like her mother, Mac's beloved Enid, who had died of a painful cancer when Kitty was eight years old.

"Why a Jew, Kitty?" Mac had demanded. "Ten thousand guys out there from your background, and you bring me a kike. With no money, yet."

"Is that all, Dad?" Kitty refused to bite. "Can you find him a job for the weekend so he can make a few bucks and be able to take me out for a hamburger?"

"Bring him on," Mac Edmunson sighed.

Maxwell had never had thoughts of becoming a lawyer, but he fell under the thrall of the excitement and the intellectual challenge of this prestigious law firm. The firm's litigators, the lawyers that argue the cases in court, sometimes in front of a jury, were of particular interest to Maxwell. "You know, Kitty," he said after several months on the job, "I may shift to pre-law. I might try to make it into law school."

"You've got to be kidding," she said, "hasn't my Dad given you enough shit to discourage you forever?"

"Once he stopped calling me 'Abie' we've gotten along great. He even took me to lunch at the Esquire Club with all the biggies. What do you think? Can you stick with me through law school?"

"What are you going to use for money? Law school is a long haul, buddy boy."

"I'd like to go to Harvard. That's the best."

"Dream on," she said. They don't take many guys who didn't do their undergrad at Harvard. And a scholarship, yet?"

"I don't know about my father, but my mother comes from a long line of "brains.""

Kitty looked puzzled. "What do you mean 'you don't know about your father' ? What is the story on your father?"

"Don't ask," he said, forcing a grin, "just don't ask. It's a long story."

"So tell me the 'long story'…I want to know all about you, Max. There are things I don't know yet. And I want to know everything. I really, really do, honey."

"You think Mac will write me a recommendation?" he said, changing the subject.

"Stop the bullshit, will you? Someday we're going back to wherever you came from and I'll meet all your people. It's about time I did, anyhow."

"Not just yet, Sweetheart. In due time, I promise."

The following semester, Maxwell began taking pre-law requirements and doing straight "A" work in all of his classes. He began going to court with Mac, observing everything and everyone, espe-

cially the litigators, those tough, brilliant, persuasive  prima don-
nas that all law firms treat with great deference.

"Holy shit, another Jewish lawyer.  Just what the world needs,"
Mac said when Maxwell told him of his desire to go to law school.

"You've got a Jewish partner. Harold Kahn is a Jew."

"May you someday have the class that Harold Kahn has, kid."

"Maybe I will, boss.  Maybe I will, someday."

Officer Peter Supelak, a regular visitor to the Steinberg Grocery, sauntered in to small- talk with Sol and Gussie as he casually helped himself to a jelly donut. "You got something under the counter in case you need it?" he asked.

"Something what?" Sol scowled. Supelak was a constant source of annoyance and an inveterate mooch. Moreover, he had constantly made snide racial slurs directed at Luther, constantly referring to him as "boy."

"You know, a piece, a gun. There's a punk hitting stores in the area and I don't want you getting caught without protection." Sol ignored the cop's foolish prate. After a minute of embarrassed silence, the fat cop motioned to the cold cuts and obsequiously remarked that the salami looked "nice and spicey." That was Gussie's cue to cut him a chunk. The Steinbergs put up with Supelak because his presence in the neighborhood probably discouraged the punks from trying anything. Smacking his greasy lips as he walked out, Supelak advised the Steinbergs to keep their eyes open for suspicious guys. When he had gone Sol said, "That slob is way out of line encouraging me to have a gun. Intelligent police officers don't want civilians using firearms. Let the thieves take what they want. Don't risk getting killed by getting into a shoot-out."

"So why do we have a gun under the counter by the register?" Gussie asked. Sol did not answer; his mind was elsewhere. Pete's dying words left him unsettled with the incubus of guilt weighing heavily upon him in his quiet moments; and Luther's departure had both angered and saddened him. Over the years, Gussie had become inured to Sol's moods and his episodes of asperity.

It was Gussie who first sensed that the guy humming nervously as he pretended to study the wine labels, was trouble. The store was empty and the street was deserted. She nudged Sol to alert him. The guy was tall and very thin with a nervous twitch. In his ragged sweater he hardly looked like a wine aficionado. "Need help, buddy?" Sol asked.

"Just lookin'" came the high pitched reply.

"Well we're getting ready to close, so I'm going to ask you to come back when you have more time to look," Sol said, trying to sound calm and pleasant. That triggered the move by the guy. He reached inside his baggy sweater and pulled out what was obviously a Saturday night special revolver.

"You closin' alright, mother-fucker. Now go lock the door, Jew bitch, and don't yell or he a dead man." Sol nodded to Gussie to comply and she rushed to lock the door. "Now open that register and it better have plenty in there or you a dead fuckin' Jew."

Sol opened the register and pulled out the bills and spread them on the counter, all the time studying every move and gesture of the nervous hold-up man. "Sheeet!" the thief wailed, "you ain't got nothing here. Now go get the rest of it!"

"That's all we have, this is a small store…that's everything. Please take it and go," Gussie pleaded. That seemed to anger the thief and he backhanded Gussie across the face, knocking her to the floor. "You shut the fuck up," he shrieked as he looked down at Gussie. In that brief moment, Sol's nerves sparked and he snatched the under-counter gun and killed the thief with a shot into his eye. "Sol, you killed him," Gussie screamed.

"Go put some ice on your face and call the cops," Sol said, his eyes remarkably expressionless.

Sol was cleared at the inquest and the shooting made the news the next morning.

Everyone close to the Steinbergs rushed to the store; the Bergs, Nate's sister Lillian and her husband, the Randazzo girls; and they all pleaded with Sol and Gussie to sell the store and get out of there as soon as possible. "Don't get so excited," Sol said, "this store is still a good money-maker and Gussie and I have always lived here. Pete, may he rest in peace, helped us get started here and showed us how to make a good living.. This is our home, right

Babe? And there's not going to be anymore holdups. The word is already out on the street that we're not pushovers."

Nate Berg walked over and embraced his daughter. "You know, Sol, from the first time I saw you on the porch with Gussie, I thought you were a little *meshuga,* and now I'm convinced. You just killed a man. You don't feel anything? You're not upset or scared? What kind of a person are you anyway?" Nate asked.

"Nate, the most scared I have ever been is when you started questioning me the first time Gussie invited me for dinner. You remember, Gus, how you yelled at him and told him to quit cross examining me?" Gussie, chuckled at the memory of that first dinner.

"You were scared out of your wits, Sol, and you didn't know which fork to use for the salad," Gussie said. Her eyes glistened with the beginning of tears. You have grown from a wild street kid to a wonderful husband and I love you. You killed a man to save my life. So Papa, I once again ask you to please leave Sol alone." Nate Berg had to smile.

The Steinbergs were not going anywhere. Later that evening Gussie received a call that left her almost speechless. It was from Maxwell. His aunt Lillian had called him with news of the holdup and shooting and he was terribly concerned. He begged his mother to sell the store and move out of the ghetto neighborhood. Sol, noticing that Gussie was deeply engaged, walked over to her and moved his lips silently asking to whom she was speaking. She held her hand over the mouthpiece and whispered that it was Maxwell. The conversation resumed and Maxwell brought her up to date on his life at Boston University and his relationship with Kitty Edmunson. Sol brushed restraint and civility aside and shouted: "Ask him why all of a sudden he remembers we're alive. And tell him our name is still Steinberg."

"Sol, can you control your mouth for a few minutes please?" Gussie hissed. She resumed her conversation with her estranged son. He told Gussie about his plans to get into the Harvard Law School. She refrained from asking how he was going to pay for such an expensive school, instead telling him about Luther's departure and how well their store was doing. Luther is Luther…he's doing okay for a kid that had the life he had with that mother of his. No, they were not going to sell the store and move; where else could a small store be so profitable? Was he serious with this girl, Kitty? Obviously, she's not Jewish, right? Maybe you can work in a visit in the meantime? No, too busy between work and school… I understand. Take care of yourself and maybe find a nice Jewish girl? No?... Okay, Okay! Give our love then, to this Kitty. Goodbye, Mawell. Stay well, son.

Luther had developed a following at Club Valencia and Natasha had taught him how to ask the "Question": "Can I get you anything special tonight?" If the customer was a user they would nod affirmatively as a signal that they were ready to buy. Luther would then ask if they wanted a single, double or triple; coke wash for cocaine, margarita for marijuana and highball for heroin. Usually, a quick nod from Natasha in the direction of the customer would indicate that they were users. Only on a few occasions did she brush her nose with her finger to indicate an undercover cop had entered the club. Luther was making big bucks and Kid Foster let him operate without interference because he had become a polished purveyor of the product. Of course Luther had to split his take with the Kid and Natasha. Still, there was more money coming in than Luther ever dreamed possible.

Luther was careful, discreet and very much in control. His conservative, understated appearance and good diction were a perfect cover for him. His dark green Pontiac was a far cry from the pink Caddies the show-off pushers liked to drive. Luther was not about to get busted. No way.

Luther's new apartment was smartly furnished and accessorized by an interior decorator who acceded to Luther's insistence that the place not be gaudy or look like a great deal of money had been spent on the place. It was, in every respect, the pleasant, comfortable dwelling of a bartender making a decent living. Nothing more. Luther was a product of Sol's tutoring, incarnate.

Luther had matured into a fine looking twenty-four year old man; he had filled out a bit and he was no longer a youthful, pretty-boy; he had become a great looking man of substance. Women looked at him and they very much liked what they saw. Natasha was annoyed by the attention that women gave Luther; she had become possessive and  demanding.  And she was getting older, and broader in the posterior.  It was time for her to go. Luther desired firmer flesh and  more casual relationships.  Natasha however, was his spotter and had been his mentor when he was an apprentice in their enterprise.  To offend her would be a financial disaster, and would probably bring down on him the wrath of Kid Foster, Natasha's longtime friend.  Luther began to realize that it was he, not Natasha, who had to go.

The Oakdale Country Club was relatively new and its membership was essentially successful young  professionals; lawyers, stockbrokers, doctors, dentists, developers and  new-money businessmen. It was a club for people who could not pass muster at the venerable, sedate, Riverwood  Club, where the old money disported themselves.

To Luther, it was the ideal venue. The sixties "swingers" at Oakdale would doubtlessly be users of his products.

Luther's departure from Club Valencia was surprisingly uneventful.  Kid Foster had anticipated Luther's need to be his own master. He wished him well with the caveat that he not put Club Valencia in jeopardy by talking to anyone  about the operation at the club.  Natasha simply told him he was an ungrateful motherfucker who ought to have his dick cut off.

Luther's application for employment at Oakwood was vetted in a perfunctory fashion;  four years at Club Valencia indicated that he was steady and dependable.  Luther's landlord reported that he was a good tenant who had lived  in the building for four years and was always prompt with rent payments. Moreover, the  Oakdale assistant manager who interviewed Luther was a young woman who was quite impressed with him. He got the job as luncheon and cocktail hour bartender.

The bar scene at Oakwood bordered on the riotous. Fungible young swingers in golf  garb stood two deep at the bar drinking fashionable martinis, shouting at one another, bragging, flirting, showing off.  The stools at the end of the bar, where Luther serviced the table orders, had become very recherché'—chatting on familiar terms with the handsome new bartender was a much sought after status thing.

The breakthrough came when a fortyish fellow whose belly fought its way out of his golf slacks, slyly inquired if Luther had any "recreational cigarettes." Luther sensed that the guy was probing and that he was probably a blabbermouth when he got to his second martini. So Luther did his faux naïf routine and pretended that he did not understand the request.

Luther studied the bar regulars and he catalogued the people who looked promising.

During a rare, quiet moment, when the golf crowd had gone, a young couple in business clothes engaged Luther in conversation. "Ask him," the young woman said.

"You think he's okay? her escort asked.

"Sure. He looks like he knows the score," the woman said.

"Something I can do for you?" Luther asked, innocence personified.

"Have you got anything for sale, other than booze? Something that can give us a lift after a tough day in court?" the man asked.

"Oh, don't give us that virgin plough boy look. You know what we're asking for," the woman said. Luther was finally ready to make his commitment. He reached under the bar and produced two packets of the white substance the couple was asking for. And the man quickly slid a matchbook across the bar to Luther. "It's all there, trust me, partner." After a pause he asked, "Is this good merchandise?

"The very best. That's all I handle. May I ask your name, so I know who I'm dealing with?"

"I'm Evan and she's Beth. You're in good hands, I assure you. We're with the prosecutor's office, so you've got nothing to worry about. We'll be good customers."

"Evan, I'm very glad to have made your acquaintance," Luther said, as he walked down the bar to serve another customer. This was the beginning of Luther's new venture and it looked very promising.

Evan and Beth were, indeed, young prosecutors and they proved to be very discreet, and grateful to have a readily available and quite safe supply of coke. There proved to be many other buyers that Luther carefully vetted before deciding they were acceptable customers; among them, surprisingly, were doctors, dentists, public officials and politicians…people who could certainly be counted upon not to cause problems.

Luther was building the type of clientele with whom he felt comfortable and secure. He felt accepted and respected by his clientele. Luther coveted "respect" and he preferred he term "clientele" in preference to customer. Moreover. he felt that these people would follow him wherever he might relocate. The money was rolling in, but Luther demurred from the use of a checking account; he paid cash for everything and kept his money in a safe deposit box under an assumed name. There had never been a record of Luther Hightree and he was not about to create one now, especially in view of the Vietnam war draft.

Luther's mind was elsewhere when the waitress servicing the dining room came to the service bar and snapped out her order. When he looked up, she smiled smugly, supremely positive that she had stultified the "poor sap," just the way she always did when men saw her for first time. Lindy Blanc had recently arrived from New Orleans and it was apparent that she was probably an octoroon, with a mixture of Spanish, French, and African blood. "Did you hear my order? You look a little shook up," she said, a bit too flippant to suit Luther. Gorgeous or not, no broad could get away with smart-mouthing Luther Hightree at this point in his life.

"What did you say to me?" Luther asked, his voice dripping venom. Lindy paled noticeably, despite her delicate tan complexion. She instinctively knew she had read this haughty, prepossessing guy very, very incorrectly. No way was he one of her "poor sap" victims.

"I asked if you heard my order…I wasn't sure," she said, suddenly the soul of politesse. Luther had scared the shit out of her. From then on, their relationship was one of graciousness and cordiality until Luther took it a step beyond when he asked her if she would like to have dinner. He knew that "blanc" meant white and he wondered if she had adopted the name to draw attention to her light complexion. They began to relax with each other and enjoy

each other's company, with Luther, of course, in control. And before long they became lovers, with Luther making sure she always
had a little extra cash to buy clothes and cosmetics.

Luther's life had for him, reached the apogee of satisfaction
and fulfillment. His thoughts drifted back to his childhood and
the consummate humiliation he had felt when Maxwell had rejected him. He hoped that Maxwell's life was chaotic and aimless
as he indulged in the luxury of a bit of schadenfreude.

"**S**onofabitch," Mackenzie Edmunson muttered, "the kid did just what he said he would do. Summa cum laude. Listen Kitty, I'll do what I can, but I think it's a long shot for Harvard, especially—well, some people think they've got quotas…you know what I mean?"

"Jewish quotas?" Kitty asked. "That's hateful. Dad, you're a prominent alum and you're a contributor—that's got to mean something."

"I'll write everyone I know and give him a strong recommendation, but I suggest he apply to several law schools. He's from the Midwest—what's wrong with Michigan? They've got a great law school."

"He wants Harvard. Do what you can, Dad."

Something did the trick; Maxwell Stonehill received his acceptance to the Harvard Law School for the class commencing in the Fall of 1962. Now all he needed was tuition money. Not a problem…Kitty loaned him the money from her trust fund and Mackenzie Edmunson had apoplexy. But of course, Kitty had her way with Daddy.

The romance came close to coming a cropper because Maxwell literally locked himself in his room, asking not to be disturbed, at he hit his law books. He was determined to graduate at the head of his class, Kitty's blandishments, notwithstanding.

To manage her sex deprivation, Kitty took a job as researcher with Newsweek. The couple did, however, reach an accommodation that resulted in a Friday night wine and sex orgy when Kitty took the train in from New York.

Maxwell did break away from his studies when Mac Edmunson asked him to have lunch. There was a vaguely ominous tone to the invitation; Mac had something rather important he wished to discuss. Mac got right to the point: "Needless to say, I was not overcome with joy when Kitty told me she was in love with a Jewish guy. I have no issues with the Chosen People but I feel everyone should play in their own sandbox. You're a smart guy, Max—do mind if I dispense with "Maxwell?" —it's sort of a precious name—" Mac asked.

"Let's do the whole thing, boss. 'Stonehill' is really Steinberg."

"So what's wrong with 'Max Steinberg'? Are you ashamed of your name?"

"Not at all. 'Max Steinberg' is a Polish-Jewish name. Maxwell Stonehill is an American-Jewish name. I am an American Jew, not a Polish-Jew. Understand?" Maxwell asked. Mac's face showed nothing. He wanted to get beyond the name issue. He wished to continue.

"At any rate Max, you must realize there are complications to mixed marriages. I presume marriage is in the offing. What's it going to be, a rabbi and one of those what-do-you-call-ems–?

"Chupahs," Maxwell helped.

"Chupahs," Mac continued. That's not what I had in mind, though I know it's an ancient and honored custom," Mac said, dissembling somewhat.

"It's not what I want either, boss," Maxwell said.

"Oh, no?" Mac said, surprised and relieved. "What did you have in mind?"

"How about a quiet ceremony in the garden of your lovely home with a judge doing the honors? Less expensive, less angst, no headaches."

"Your folks going buy that?"

" No. But let's keep it simple, boss. My father and I are not on speaking terms so they don't need to be here. They won't feel comfortable and you won't either. I'll deal with that issue at the appropriate time."

"Why won't I feel comfortable? I'm not a goddam snob. People are people." Mac said.

"Trust me on this one, boss. It's better all the way around if we just keep it simple. I'll handle my folks."

"Jesus.You're some piece of work, Max. I guess you know what you're doing. You always do. Just make sure that my kid has a happy life. You hear what I'm saying?" Mac said, as his eyes narrowed.

"I hear you, boss."

"And pay back that money to the trust fund. It's college money for your kids," Mac said.

1965 was the best year ever for Luther's business. His following continued to grow and cocaine was the hot ticket for the young professionals whose world was getting turned upside down as the nation convulsed over the Vietnam war, the student protests and racial unrest.

He had decided it would be best if Lindy quit her job at the club; he didn't want her involved in his business. He ensconced her in the apartment and gave her sufficient walking around money so she would not become bored. Rather, it was Luther who was becoming bored. He was ready for a new challenge; a new venue in which he would be the big boss. As he thought about the concatenation of events that brought him to this successful point in life after his departure from the Steinberg apartment on Central avenue in the ghetto, he became restless. He needed something new.

Lindy asked if Luther ever got a vacation. She wanted to go down to New Orleans and have some fun in the French Quarter. The concept of "vacation" was utterly foreign to Luther. He had heard people say they were going on vacation but it never occurred to him that he, too, could take a vacation. Why the hell not. Luther asked the club manager if he could take a two week vacation. The manager graciously granted Luther a two week vacation.With pay yet! Jeezus. He and Lindy took a plane to New Orleans and she showed him a fantastic time in her old haunts in the French quarter.

The world had gone crazy as far as Sol was concerned; first they bellyache about electing a Catholic president and then they kill him. And then that corn pone Johnson takes over the presidency and he's trying to get us into a war with the Vietcong? Who the hell ever heard of Vietnam? Korea wasn't bad enough? And what's suddenly with the *schvartzes* becoming Muslims and Black Nationalists? "Gussie, I'm getting too old for all this *mischigas,*" he sighed.

"Stop moaning and take your pills so maybe you'll be around for a while. You know, Maxwell is finishing up this year, remember? A Harvard lawyer. Who would have thought?" Gussie asked.

A person named "Stonehill" is of no concern to me, Gussie," Sol said, stone-faced.

There were several Jewish families still living in the Central Avenue area; the Friedmans, who ran the Laundromat, Abe Zellman, the auto merchanic and gas station guy, Morrie Rappaport and his wife, Sylvia, still doing real estate, Sally Kahn, the spinster, who ran the little dry cleaning store, Lou and Ruth Bernstein, who had the Dollar Store, and Sam and Molly Kronenberg, the used car *goniff.*

"Why not have a good old-fashioned card party; gin rummy, poker, whatever. With a late super, after. It'll be like a 'survivor's party' for the Jewish families still living in the neighborhood," Gussie enthused. "You know, Sol, people need the company of other people. We're alone too much."

"That means you're getting tired of me. I can take a hint."

"Don't be such a comedian and help me get a group together for Saturday night," Gussie said. Sol did as he was told and made the rounds of all the Jewish business owners still in the neighborhood.

Sure enough, there was a noisy, laughing, gossiping, glad-to-be-together  mob, eating, drinking, telling Yiddish jokes and arguing politics jammed into the Steinberg apartment.  When they broke up around  2a.m. they stood at the door, reluctant to leave; still talking and promising they would all get together again, soon. Gussie was pleased; Sol looked like his old self again; the anger was gone and  his color was much better, Gussie decided.

Maxwell Stonehill did not graduate at the top of his class at the Harvard Law School; there were many, many brilliant, studious guys who were just as hungry as Maxwell Stonehill to make names for themselves so they might be gobbled up by blue ribbon law firms. Maxwell was in the top ten, which impressed Mac Edmunson. "So where do we go from here, son," Mac asked. "We'd be pleased to have you come on board with us. Only Harold Kahn came close to what you did at Harvard," Mac said, sincerely impressed with Maxwell's achievement. "Besides, you need to be gainfully employed and soon. My daughter is anxious, boy, very anxious. She's already hired a decorator to do the garden for a wedding," Mac laughed.

"Boss, I'm honored by your offer. How does it work if your father-in-law is your boss and you fuck up?" Maxwell asked.

"I simply kick your ass and we continue on. Not a big problem, son," Mac said, putting his arm around Maxwell affectionately.

"Dad's a little off kilter. I think he would have wanted a big church wedding with me in a white dress. And he misses Mom. He's really kind of lost without her," Kitty said. "But we're doing the smart thing, really. A judge is a perfect solution."

"Let's give your Dad what he wants, Kitty. I don't want to cause him any pain. I really love Mac, Kitty."

"What are you saying?"

"I'm saying let him have a minister instead of a just a judge. And an organ and bridesmaids and groomsmen and you in a long white dress. Full bore."

"Are you serious? A minister?"

"Just tell him to go easy on the Jesus stuff. Heavy on God. It makes little difference to me. I never even had a *bar mitzvah*. Really, babe, let Mac have his big day."

"You're a sweet boy, Maxie Steinberg. No wonder Dad is fond of you. If you're serious, I'll tell him tonight.

"Tell him, Kitty."

It was like an olfactory epiphany for Maxwell Stonehill as he stood under the awning, waiting for the organist to start the wedding procession; he smelled the roses, the gardenias, the faint, delicate  perfumes of the bridesmaids.  Strange, he thought, why should I be focusing on smells; look at this garden…it's like a fairy tale; the  formal white jackets,  the exquisite pale yellow of the bridesmaids' gowns and Kitty in her stunning bridal gown. The guests were mostly New England  old money with the exception of the four groomsmen, Maxwell's old ZBT buddies, trying their best to blend in. Mac was elegant, tall, imposing and gallant as the proud father of the bride.  And the silence!  These Wasps don't even whisper. So well mannered.  Goddam, they've learned how to do things.

Maxwell stood waiting for Mac to bring his beloved daughter to the rose-embowered  arch and to give her to the groom, so alien to the culture and traditions of  his  ancestry. The minister spoke beautifully, invoking God's blessing on the couple without asking Jesus for help. Maxwell was happy, far beyond anything he had ever experienced in his life and pleased that he had vouchsafed Mac Edmunson a perfect wedding for a beloved daughter.

Maxwell and Kitty found a lovely old home in exurbia, with several wooded acres and a barn.  The house would need some work and the barn would soon house two horses. Kitty pre-ferred cold-blood Morgans, all of which terrified Maxwell who felt  incapable of dealing with the required plumbing, carpen-try and stall mucking.  Kitty subjected Maxwell to a draconian training regimen designed to transmogrify a city-bred, Harvard lawyer into a country squire.  It proved to be a formidable task but eventually Maxwell learned to post on an English saddle, to counter-sink nails in the siding, and, strangely, to relish the odor of manure, a quirk that Kitty told him was terribly sick. Who was this person rising at 5a.m. having coffee with his wife before heading for the barn to feed the horses; then showering and shaving and dressing in a three-button, natural shoulder suit and a blue, oxford button-down shirt and rep tie; then being driven to the train station by a beautiful wife with a raincoat over her nightgown, for the ride to the prestigious offices of Edmunson, Peterson and Kahn? It was an out-of-body sensation for Maxwell Stonehill; it was as if he were watching someone else living that beautiful life. Could that person really be me–Maxie Steinberg? God—am I saying "God?" Thank you, God… thank you, thank you, thank you.

Mac was pleased when Maxwell expressed his desire to became one of the firm's litigators. "It plays hell with your nerves and your stomach lining," Mac warned. But it was not a problem. Maxwell assisted the firm's litigators in every way possible until Mac felt confident in letting him go to court and argue a case. Maxwell had an innate proclivity for persuasive argumentation and gut-wrenching courtroom brawling. His preparation was meticulous, detailed and thoroughly researched. Smiling in appreciation Mac muttered, "The people of the book. It comes natural."

"Bullshit," Harold Kahn replied, "I could never do what the kid's doing, and I'm one of your so-called 'people of the book.' " Maxwell Stonehill was on his way, secure at last in his own skin and graciously responding when people began calling him "Maxie." As Mac had said a few years ago, "Maxwell is kind of a 'precious' name."

The "Central Avenue Jewish Survivors Club" congregated in the Steinberg apartment over the store on June 10, 1967 and made a half-drunken attempt to dance the Hora to celebrate Israel's astonishing victory over five Arab nations in the so-called Six Day War. Everyone had brought something to eat: corned beef, salami, potato salad, strudel, wine, whiskey—the works! No one really made sense as they shouted bellicose threats to the Arabs and praised God and kissed and hugged and drank too damn much for people who were not necessarily big drinkers.

It was a night to remember, as was June 5, 1968 when Bobby Kennedy was assassinated. "What the hell kind of a name is Sirhan Sirhan, for crissakes?" Sol screamed.

"He's a goddam Palestinian, what else?" sobbed Molly Kronenberg, the New York Times *maven*.

"He would of made a great president…even greater than Jack Kennedy," Morrie Rappaport shouted.

"Listen, I ain't so sure. Don't forget he worked for that fuckin' McCarthy with that Roy Cohn," Abe Zellman added.

"He changed, he changed, for crissakes. Give him a break. He became a real human being…a real liberal. You know why they killed him? It wasn't the Arabs.

They killed him because he's a Catholic. That's why they shot Jack. They paid the dumb Arab to shoot him. It was them crazy Evangelicals," Lou Bernstein pontificated.

"Quiet! Quiet for a goddam minute," Sol shouted. Things are going on in this country like none of us have seen in our whole lives, and I'll be honest, I'm worried. I'm honest-to-God scared. Did you see those cops beat those kids at the convention in Chicago? That Daley is a goddam dictator. This country is going to tear itself apart."

"I don't feel safe down here anymore," Abe Zellman said. "I'm thinking about selling and getting the hell out of here."

Two o'clock in the morning, April 4, 1968. Sol Steinberg was standing in front of his store holding his .38 Smith and Wesson and shivering in the damp cold. Martin Luther King had been killed and fires were burning all over the town. Abe Zellman's station was a raging inferno and Lou Bernstein's Dollar Store was ripped apart and completely looted. Sol was prepared to shoot anybody that tried to loot Steinberg's Grocery. "Sol, are you crazy? They're wild —they'll kill you if they see a white guy standing there alone! Come inside—I called the police. Where is that lousy Supelak when you need him? Sol! Do you hear me?" Gussie cried.

"Lock the doors, Gussie, and be quiet. I'm alright. They won't try anything when they see my gun, when they see I'm not afraid of them."

They came down the street toward the store, maybe a dozen of them, wild-eyed and high. "Stay the fuck away from my store or I'll blow your heads off," Sol shouted.

"It's the Jew grocery mother-fucker! Who you gonna' shoot, man? You ain't gonna' do shit, you lousy white piece of shit. Let's get him!" the mob leader shouted. Just as they started to move forward, Sol fired a shot directly over their heads, and the mob stopped in its track. "The next one is for you, big mouth," Sol snarled.

"We'll come back for you later, whitey," the big mouth grumbled and the mob turned and ran toward the next victim.

"Sol! Sol! Are you alright?" Gussie screamed from the window upstairs.

"Gussie, will you shut up and stop screaming? Everything's under control. Go to bed. I'll be up as soon as it gets light."

The Steinberg Grocery was open for business in the morning and there was a lineup of frightened, grateful customers wanting to buy milk and bread to see them through the riots.

L uther was concerned; had they broken into Sol and Gussie's store? Had Sol done something crazy and gotten himself hurt? Lindy drove and Luther sat crouched in the back seat to avoid being spotted. He could not yet bear the thought of facing the Steinbergs. Was it guilt or shame or embarrassment? Luther could not unravel the skein of conflicted emotions that gnawed at him whenever he revisited the nightmarish images of sneaking out of the Steinberg apartment in the middle of the night without a word, without a farewell or an expression of gratitude for all they had done for him. *Why couldn't I have been man enough to at least kiss Gussie goodbye? What the hell is wrong with me?*

"This is the street, go real slow so I can check out the store," Luther said. As they passed the store, Luther sighed in relief… the store was untouched and they were open and doing business, "Thank God," Luther said softy. "Okay, Lindy, let's get out of here."

"What were you peering at? Why were you hiding in the back seat? What's going on, man?"

"Just drive, Lindy. And no more questions. I told you not to ask questions, didn't I?"

Luther was so well liked at the country club that the manager asked if he would like to be the maitre d'. Luther hesitated, fearing the loss of tips and especially the bar as a platform on which he could slide the packets of cocaine to his customers. He actually discussed the problem with Evan and Beth, his long-standing customers from the prosecutor's office. They told Luther that the packets could neatly fit inside the large menus in use at the club. The money could be slipped inside an extra menu which the maitre d' could conveniently carry.

Luther viewed the change in jobs as a promotion and once again, the element of respect became a factor in Luther's decision to become the maitre d'. The isolation of the maitre d's podium afforded Luther and his customers the opportunity to talk their deal in greater privacy than was possible at the bar.

The Central Avenue Jewish Survivors Club was no more; gone forever, either burned out, looted, or simply scared out. Only one business remained: Morrie and Sylvia Rappaport, the real estate people. They would scratch out a living dealing with the scavengers who sought to buy the abandoned buildings and the empty, cinerous lots for pennies on the dollar. Gussie stood in the doorway of the store, looking at the shuffling, pathetic neighborhood people, picking through the devastated landscape for anything of value. Thank God Mom and Pop didn't live to see this, she thought. Sonja and Nate had passed away within months of each other, simply worn out by life itself. Only Nate's sister Lillian, herself now an ailing widow, was still alive. She had received a call from Maxwell telling of his graduation from law school, and his marriage to Kitty. Lillian had at first hesitated to pass the news on the Gussie and Sol, knowing how upset they would be at not being invited to the wedding. Gussie wept; she was terribly hurt. Sol said nothng, his face an angry mask.

An elderly black woman walked slowly past the store pushing an ancient, rickety buggie, filled with the pitiful detritus she had salvaged. "Look what they done. Just look what they done," she said, tearfully.

"Look what who done?" Sol said, bitterly as he joined Gussie in the doorway. He was constitutionally incapable of letting the remark pass. "You people 'done' it to yourselves. You burned up your own neighborhood. What the hell for?"

" 'Cause they killed Reverend King, that's why," the old lady said, defiantly jutting out her jaw. Sol looked at Gussie and shook his head slowly back and forth, unable to find the words to respond to the old lady's prideful illogic.

"So Sol, do we stay?" Gussie said.

"Let's see what happens, kid. Don't be in a hurry to run."

"Who's running?" Gussie said, giving Sol a playful shove.

Slowly the neighborhood shoveled away the destruction and resumed a crippled tempo of living; living, despite everything that augured that life would be mean and hard in this forgotten old place. Gussie began to see familiar faces; the regulars were returning and they seemed happy that Steinberg's was still there. Steinberg's was a beacon of sanity and stability for the beaten down folks who did not have the strength or resources to live elsewhere. Business actually was holding up at the Steinberg Grocery as people began the struggle to rebuild their lives. Food in the pantry somehow symbolized normality and hope, and Lyndon Johnson's enactment of the 1964 Food Stamp Program gave people the means to keep food on the table. Sol and Gussie were not going to run away. This was their store and this was their neighborhood.

The East Coast, especially Newark, New Jersey, had not been spared the rioting and burning after Reverend King's murder. Kitty encouraged Maxwell to find out if his parents were okay; so he called Aunt Lillian, his information conduit, to inquire. Lillian painted a grim picture of what had happened in the city, especially the central city ghetto where the Steinberg Grocery was located. "Are they okay?" Maxwell asked. "Did they try to loot the store?"

"I talked to your mother," she said. "Naturally Sol stood in front of the store with a gun and kept the rioters away."

"And of course they're not going to get rid of the store and move the hell out of there," Maxwell said, unable to control the bitterness in his voice.

"I said something, but you know your parents," Lillian said.

"Yes, Aunt Lillian, I know my parents; I know my parents," Maxwell said in a tone of resignation and self-pity.

"I think we should go to see them. I'd like to meet my in-laws; I think it was totally rude of us not to have invited them to our wedding," Kitty said.

"Goddamit, Kitty, we've been over this a dozen times. Have you ever been in a rust belt, inner city ghetto? My parents run a crummy little grocery store selling garbage to blacks in the ghetto. I am not anxious to have you see the site of my childhood humiliation."

"For a tough courtroom lawyer, you're as sensitive as a maiden going through puberty."

"Kitty, I'm on the verge of saying, fuck you."

"Go ahead and say it, and I'll tell you a story that might bring you to your senses."

"Bring me to my senses, please. I desperately need your help," he said.

"My father has an unusual first name, Mackenzie. Right? That's his maternal great-grandfather's name, Mackenzie…Adie Mackenzie. Adie, I am told, is from the Hebrew Adam, meaning red earth. That's beside the point. Adie Mackenzie was a rumrunner, just like the old man Kennedy, father of a president. He was repeatedly arrested and finally did time in prison. He sired six kids, all of whom were thieves, burglars and pimps, with the exception of Dad's grandmother, who was a decent gal. Dad had five great-uncles he hoped none of his clients would ever discover. So we ain't so fancy, brother Maxie. Hardly anyone is, for God's sake. We've all got skeletons we'd like to forget about. So what's so terrible about mom and pop Steinberg?"

"Nothing. Except my father and I are not on speaking terms, because I changed my name to Stonehill."

"So change it back to Steinberg," she challenged.

" And representing the plaintive in the matter of Exxon contesting drilling rights with BP, from the esteemed, white-shoe, Boston law firm, is Mister Maxie Steinberg." He smirked and said, "Has a nice ring to it, doesn't it? I'll bet your dad would love it."

"I don't think it would matter to him," Kitty said.

"Well, it damn well might matter to the client," Maxwell insisted.

"Not if you win the case, Maxie."

"I'm going to say it: 'fuck you, smart ass.' " They always seemed to have good sex after they had bickered a bit.

Officer Supelak sauntered into the store and took a freebie can of Pabst out of the cooler without a scintilla of embarrassment. "I hear there's a Korean grocery store over on Mason Street. Why don't you give them your business?" Sol said, baiting the cop mooch.

"Too far from here. Besides, I like your hospitality." He swilled down the last of the beer and grabbed a pretzel out of the jar. "The neighborhood's starting to look decent again. Can't believe it's three years already, since the riots," Supelak said, trying to defuse Sol's annoyance.

"That reminds me, where the hell were you the night of the riots?" Sol said.

"Hey, I'm only one man. This beat is too big for one officer," he said, munching, dropping crumbs on the counter. "You might be happy to know I'm up for detective… narc squad."

"Detective, huh?" Sol huffed. "You couldn't find your ass with both hands."

"Sol, that'enough. Officer Supelak keeps the peace in this neighborhood and he's always welcome here," Gussie said, not wanting the cop to be offended in the remote possibility that they might need him.

When Supelak left, Gussie asked Sol if the Korean store was taking any of their business away. Sol said he had shopped the Korean store to check out the prices.

"That gook is a four alarm robber. You should see his prices. He won't take any of our customers away."

"So maybe we should raise our prices," Gussie said.

"What are you, getting greedy in your old age, Gus?" Sol teased. "Besides, it's too far away from here for most of our customers. We're convenient and we're cheap. Nothing to worry about. And quit being so nice to that slob, Supelak. I can live without his help."

"Sol, why are you puffing so much?...like you can't catch your breath or something. " Gussie asked, worried.

"Gus, I'm not a kid anymore. So I puff a little; so what's the big deal.?"

"So don't work so hard. Let the delivery guys carry stuff in. You don't need to be unloading trucks."

"I've got an appointment at the Veterans ...the VA. Annual physical. If there's something wrong, they'll tell me. And they'll maybe give me pills to take. Who knows? We'll see what's what."

Doctor Sheinbart at the Veterans Administration facility asked Sol if he had ever had a stress test. No, Sol said, he didn't even know what a stress test was. So the doctor explained the purpose of the test and sent Sol to a room where two technicians carefully explained how the test is administered, and asked Sol to step on the treadmill and start walking as they slowly increased the speed of the machine. They repeatedly asked Sol if he was okay as the speed was increased, and they monitored his heart functions as he walked. Finally, they asked Sol to sit down and rest while they analyzed the printout.

"How'd I do?" Sol asked. He became concerned when he did not get a direct answer. The technician rather ominously said, "We'll have the cardiologist review the results and he'll talk to you. He'll be here in a few minutes."

The cardiologist got right to the point: Sol had blockage in several arteries. He told Sol about bypass surgery being performed at NYU and the Cleveland Clinic.The doctor explained the procedure, the risks and the benefits. Sol was not remotely interested in surgery. He asked if there was medicine that could help. The doctor prescribed several medications and explained that Sol needed to exercise and modify his diet. No red meat, no cheese, no fats at all and a salt-free diet. Sol listened patiently, but he had already decided how he was going to deal with the blocked arteries. His solution was quite simple: "Fuck it." You go in for an examination and the goddam doctors are going to find something wrong. Sol felt good and he was not going to turn his life topsy-turvy because of a goddam stress test. And Gussie did not need to know about the arteries. He told her that the pills he was taking were for cholesterol or some damn thing like that.

Sol checked the life insurance policy he had taken out when he returned from the army; there would be a decent amount for Gussie if something happened to him. And they had put away a few bucks in CD's at the bank. Everything was under control as far as Sol was concerned. His exercise consisted of his normal work load at the store.

Things went along as usual. Sol puffed and Gussie worried, despite Sol's claim that he had a clean bill of health when he took his annual physical.

Sol had voted for McGovern in the 1972 presidential election and was angry when Nixon won in a landslide. When the Watergate scandal broke, Sol magisterially proclaimed that he knew all along that Nixon was a *goniff.*

Nixon's resignation speech was broadcast on August 8, and Sol wanted to celebrate, so he invited Morrie and Sylvia Rappaport, the real estate people, and Sam and Mollie Kronenberg, the used car *goniff,* who had returned to the neighborhood after the riots, for a little get-together to listen to "Nixon's bullshit." When the speech was over Sol said "Let's toast to better times now that he's gone," and he ran down the stairs to the store to get a few bottles of wine. After a few minutes, Morrie became aware that Sol had not returned with the wine. The blood drained out of Gussie's head and she almost fainted as she ran down the stairs to the store, followed by the others. Sol lay face down, in front of the wine display. Gussie knelt down and felt for a pulse. She fell weeping on Sol's body. Her beloved Sol, the tough street urchin running from the Jewish Orphan Home, was dead at the age of sixty.

Lillian came by cab to help with arrangements. She had called Maxwell and he was flying in. Morrie, the only one who belonged to the rundown old synagogue in the ghetto, called decrepit Rabbi Hershberg to preside at the funeral, in the Jewish section of

Memorial Cemetery. It was a pathetic, lonely little group clustered together at the grave site as Rabbi Hershberg rattled the ancient Hebrew prayers for the dead.

Maxwell ordered the traditional delicatessen tray for the little group that gathered at Gussie's apartment after the funeral. Everyone ate in silence, struggling for the appropriate words of praise for Sol. After awhile they left, one by one, and Gussie suddenly was alone, with only Maxwell to comfort her. And he hardly knew what to say to his mother. Finally Gussie spoke: "We should sit *shiva*. Can you stay for a few days?"

"Of course I can stay," Maxwell said. "How many people can we get to sit with us for the—" and he struggled to remember the word, *minion*.

"Morrie and Sam. That's all that's left down here," Gussie said, sadly. "They're busy guys; they can't sit for the whole ten days. It doesn't make any difference. Sol could not care less. A couple of days. That'll be enough."

"Then what, Mom? You can't stay down here alone. Let me find a nice nursing home place for you. I'll move you in and I'll take care of closing the store and the finanacial arrangements," Maxwell said.

"Sweetheart… Maxie. Don't be in a rush to stick me in a nursing home. I have a store to run. Angie—you remember Angie from the Randazzos—she'll come and help me."

"Mama, please! Please don't stay here. Let me help you." Maxwell was on the verge of tears.

"Maxie, you can help me by letting me live my life like a person; not an invalid in an institution. Sit with me quietly for a few days and then go home to your nice wife."

"At least let me give you some money to tide you over."

"Sol ,God bless him, took care of money for me. I'm alright, Maxie. I'll be just fine."

And that was that. Nothing more to be said. Maxwell had never reconciled with his father and he felt a deep sadness because of that. After three, painfully silent days, Maxwell kissed his mother goodbye and left the home which he had rejected as a child for the last time, freighted with guilt and worry and an unrelenting sadness..

And Gussie was alone, in the darkened store, sitting *shiva.* The young hoodlums taunted her, rapping on the windows, calling her a dirty Jew until Luther came.

Gussie let the hot water of the shower beat on the back of her neck. She was overcome with the compulsion to get clean; to wash her hair and rinse her mouth with undiluted Listerine. She was in a state of anomie; she did not know what she would do next. Luther's reappearance had unsettled her; had he really come back? What had he said to her? She had forgotten what he said. People had knocked on the door of the store downstairs; they probably wanted to know when and if the store would reopen. Gussie had forgotten Angie's phone number and she could not face the task of looking it up in the phone book…that damn fine print. Things were rotting in the store; stuff needed to thrown out and fresh merchandise brought in. Gussie didn't have the strength to tackle the job. Maybe it was time to sell out.

She had hoped she looked presentable when she walked into Morrie Rappaport's dingy real estate office.

"*Bubbkas*" Morrie said. "That's what I could get for the store, Gussie darling, I couldn't give it away. Take my advice, hand the keys to the bank and walk away. Your taxes are more than the store is worth."

"Walk away? Are you crazy, Morrie? Sol and I sweated blood to make a go of that store and you want me to walk away? That kind of advice I can live without, Morrie." Her anger got her blood flowing and her head began clear. She'd hire a couple of black kids to help clean up the store and she'd find Angie and get the store in shape again.

Luther and Lindy walked in as Gussie and two teenagers from the neighborhood were in a frantic cleanup mode. "Gussie, what's going on here?" Luther asked. "I asked you to lock the doors and stay upstairs until I got back to take care of the store."

"So—you really were here," Gussie said.

"What?" Luther said, confused.

"Oh, excuse me. Gussie, meet Lindy Blanc, my lady." Lindy put on her smiley face and took Gussie's hand, warmly.

"Forgive me, say your name again, young lady," Gussie said, straightening her hair.

"Lindy. Lindy Blanc."

"And you and Luther are—you're together?" Gussie asked.

"Yes Gus, we're together as you say. Are you okay? You look exhausted."

"I'm fine, I'm fine. My, such a beautiful young lady, Luther. So tell me something—where are you now? What's going on with you?—you look so handsome and...and ...grown-up."

"Gus, I'm thirty-eight years old. I better look grown-up."

"Thirty-eight–my God in heaven. Where did it go? A lifetime. "And tears come to Gussie's eyes. Lindy put a comforting hand on Gussie's shoulder, and handed her a tissue to wipe her eyes. They sat at the back of the store reminiscing; Gussie struggling to reorient herself to the timetable of Luther's life. Gussie had questions and Luther answered some of them, but temporized when Gussie probed into sensitive areas. Gussie insisted that they go upstairs and have something to eat. Gussie's little boy had come back and he needed to be fed properly. Lindy wanted only coffee but Gussie ignored her and began frying eggs and bacon and buttering toast. Lindy began to warm up to the situation; she sensed that this old, Jewish lady loved Luther and would probably do anything to make him happy. The conversation eventually turned to Gussie's plans for the future; was she really planning to reopen the store? Luther averred that Gussie could not possibly operate the store alone, even with the help of Angie. Gussie told them about Maxwell's plans to place her in a nursing home. "A fucking nursing home, if you'll pardon my French." Gussie had reddened with anger. Lindy giggled and looked at Luther for his reaction to the old woman's profanity. Luther took it in stride; he knew how much Gussie must have detested Maxwell's suggestion. "And that idiot Morrie Rappaport tells me my store is worth *bubbkas* if I go to sell," Gussie fumed.

Luther knew that Lindy was bewildered by "bubbkas" so he translated: "It means the store ain't worth a shit, babe. So, you can't sell, and I say you can't run the place without Sol; then maybe the great Maxwell is right... a nursing home."

"Don't be a comedian, Luther. A better solution is, I shoot myself. Sol left me the gun," Gussie said, kidding on the square as the wise guys would say. Luther could not be sure.

Luther was fishing, letting out line slowly, skillfully.

"I've got a better solution, but I want to wait a few days unit *shiva* is over."

"What did you do, become a rabbi while you were gone? I already sat a long enough *shiva.*"

"You're supposed to sit *shiva* for ten days. I know that much, Gus. So keep the doors locked until I come back. Then I'll tell you my idea."

"Is this going to be another ten years?" Gussie said.

"I'm here with you from now on, Mama," Luther said. And Gussie began to cry again.

Luther, striving to be a punctilious businessman, wrote a proper letter of resignation to the management of the country club. The club was terribly disappointed but they knew that a quality guy like Luther would eventually be moving on to broader challenges. Luther made it a point to give all of his cocaine customers his new business card:

*"Discovery Foods"*

**Prime Steaks and Seafood**

**Imported Wines and Beer**

**Olives, Cheeses and Gourmet Soups**

Not listed, but abundantly clear to his customers, would be the availability of top quality cocaine, packets of which would be subtly wrapped up with the steaks. Discovery foods would be bargain priced because it was a destination store located in the inner city in order to keep prices low. The store would appear to be a faddish "find" for upscale customers in the know; a great place to buy wine and great steaks. The presence of many white customers would, therefore, appear to be normal. A brilliant concept, everyone agreed....except, of course, Luther's putative partner, Missus Gussie Steinberg, yet to be informed that her quaint little grocery store was to undergo profound changes.

Luther had befriended the food and beverage manager at the country club and had gotten a list of suppliers for all of the prime quality products he planned to stock in the store. He had met with all the suppliers and had negotiated favorable prices for everything. Feldman Bros., was the produce purveyor, Schulte Inc., meats, and Dupree of the Sea, was the seafood supplier. All of the purveyors would deliver by truck at five a.m. He was ready.

Luther abjured the bowels of the underworld; the slimy, murderous creatures that populated the drug trade. He was comfortable with cocaine; the drug of parties for people of wealth or substance with the means to indulge themselves in episodes of temporary escape from the mundane, the quotidian. Was it because cocaine was essentially the drug of choice of well-to-do whites? Whatever the basis of his casuistic rationalization, Luther gave much thought to his selection of a source for cocaine. He settled on a rather picaresque character with the unlikely handle of Bluestreak, called Blue, by those who were in the know. Like Luther, Blue was a conservative dresser and a consummate businessman; prompt, circumspect and dependable, despite his adventuresome soul.

They would liaise at Luigi's, an out of the way, little known Italian restaurant with a quiet bar. The cops had not yet discovered the joint and the boys felt very secure meeting there. Luther outlined his scheme for the operation at the store and Blue was impressed by the abstruse construct. They estimated that Luther would probably move about thirty, one-gram packets a day. Luther usually got eighty to one hundred bucks a packet. They determined that Blue would transfer one K of product to Luther every month. This was dangerous business; getting nailed with that much powder could mean a long visit to the joint. They needed to devise a foolproof plan for transferring product. Blue suggested a courier that he had used successfully in the past. A guy dressed as a mail carrier would deposit mail and a few packages on the counter. The packages would of course, contain the cocaine. Luther asked where Blue had obtained a postman's outfit to which Blue grinningly replied, "Don't ask." The easy part of the plan was handled; now for the hard part....selling this complicated plan to Gussie.

"Are you *meshuga?*" Gussie screamed, choking on the wine Luther had given her to prepare her for revelation of his plan for the store. Lindy daubed the wine off Gussie's chin and made easy-easy gestures with her hands. "In my old age you want to turn me into a junkie?"

"Gussie, a junkie is a heavy user," Lindy said, trying to be helpful. Luther signaled her to stay out of the discussion.

"Listen to me, sonny-boy, Morrie tells me the store is worth *bubbkas* and Maxwell wants to put me in a nursing home and you, you suddenly come back into my life and turn me into a—a what? A junkie seller? This, I can tell you without anymore discussion, I absolutely, ab-so-lute-ly will not do. You should be ashamed to talk to me about such a thing, Luther." Luther, sat silently, patient and controlled.

"Drink your wine, Gus. Take it easy. I did not mean to insult you. I would never do anything to make you unhappy. If you would just hear me out. Okay? Just hear me out."

"Right now, honey, my head is spinning. This is not a good time to talk. You'll forgive me, please. Maybe tomorrow we'll have coffee in the morning. My head is clear in the mornings."

"I'll bring the bagels," Luther said.

Gussie's nights were a torment; life without Sol was meaningless; cold, vacant, bloodless. What was she here for? To wake up alone in the morning and make coffee for herself? Thoughts. So many thoughts. Sol. Sol, the crazy kid running the streets so they couldn't stick him in the Orphan Home. Gussie, what fork should I use? Let's open a store down here...there's no competition. Afraid of nothing. The holdup...Oh, my God. Killed to protect me. Even Joey.

Luther and Lindy arrived very early. They knew Gussie would be up. "Where did you find bagels?" Gussie asked as she served the coffee.

116

"Speigelman's next to our motel." They sipped their coffee quietly, hesitant to reopen the conversation. Gussie looked at Luther for a long time before she spoke. He felt the blood drain from his head.

"We won't get caught?" she asked. It took Luther a few seconds to realize what he had heard. Then he jumped up and hugged Gussie.

"No way. Believe me, Gus, only people I know and absolutely trust will come here for coke. And they'll walk out with wine and steaks and groceries. It's foolproof. I would never put you in any danger."

"One thing—I want good stuff for the neighborhood customers at decent prices. I want to die with a good name."

"Die? Die? Gussie you're starting a new life. With the money we make you can do whatever you want for the folks down here."

"Luther, remember, Sol will be watching."

Discovery Foods, Sol Steinberg, Proprietor, would have a dual personality. There would be the uptown section with the imported wines and gourmet foods and the neighborhood section with the traditional down home foods. Only now the produce in the neighborhood section would be prime-prime and the meat counter would have ham and pork chops and super-fresh chicken at regular low prices because Luther planned to sell it as his exact cost. In the uptown section, the steaks and wines would be discounted in keeping with the concept of making the operation a destination store because of the bargains. They would be the loss leaders; but there would be profit not only in the cocaine at one hundred dollars a gram bag, but in the cheeses, olives, imported canned soups and French pastries. Luther had a business plan worthy of the Harvard Business School. But first, the store had to be torn apart and cleaned up.

Luther had not lost his neighborhood street smarts. Early in the morning he walked the thirty-eighth block of Central Avenue rousting hungover winos and junkies. It was deathly quiet on Central Avenue at this hour of the morning; only the susurration of the leaves in the scabrous, old sycamore trees, those hardy urban survivors, disturbed the fetid air. Luther gently pushed his brown wing tips into the ribs of a sleeping drunk with a Yankees cap pulled over his eyes. Luther talked to the drunk as he awakened and pointed him toward the store. In an abandoned store front, Luther next found a neighborhood fixture, a mountain of fat called Three Hundred Pounder. When Pounder lurched into consciousness, Luther calmed him with a pint of sweet lucy which the monster instinctively thrust into his mouth like a baby grasping for its bottle. A drunk covered with a torn, yellow slicker lay on top of a steam grate. After Luther had conversed with him, he lumbered off to the store. Once at the store they fell under control of their task masters, Lindy and Gussie. And they worked; scrubbing, carrying, mopping and holding their noses as spoiled food was retrieved from the bins and boxes. Periodic swigs of the cheap wine was their fuel. Luther had promised them some money and bottles of wine for their labors. "More rags," Yellow Slicker called, as he fought with the embedded grime of the front window. "This window ever been washed before?" he moaned.

Three Hundred Pounder made his contribution: "The goddam street is cleaner than this floor." Eventually the cleaning and dumping phase of the operation was completed and it was time for new shelving to be installed. Luther had a source, courtesy of his contacts at the country club. And finally it was time for the sign to be painted on the front window. "A sign? What kind of sign?" Gussie asked, somewhat alarmed. "Steinberg's Grocery it always said on the window."

"Gussie, we're going to call the store, Discovery Foods."

"What?" Gussie's eyes narrowed.

" Discovery Foods, Sol Steinberg, Proprietor. In gold letters," Luther said, totally mollifying Gussie.

An elegant gold lettered sign was painted on the front window and the ancient door replaced with solid oak with brass trimmings. Luther was willing to spend his accumulated cash on a total restoration of the store.

Discovery Foods opened for business one month later, bright, clean and fully stocked. Luther was positioned at the uptown section, in front of the imported wines and next to the meat counter where the prime steaks were appetizingly displayed. Luther would man the register and would take orders for the coke packets, delivered in the arcane code he had developed with his customers at the country club. Lindy and Gussie were at the back of the store where the down home foods were displayed. And so began a new epoch at the location where Gussie and Sol first began their business careers on Central Avenue in the ghetto.

The first one through the door on opening day was that swaggering nitwit,, officer Suplelak, the detective manqué. He sniffed around, greeted by a ponderous silence and the glaring eyes of the staff. It was impossible to embarrass Supelak; he simply ignored the cool reception. "Fancy operation. Real classy," he sneered.

"Take one last look and get out. You are not welcome here unless you intend to buy something," Gussie barked. Luther was stunned at her bravado and Lindy smirked in appreciation. Supelak gave her a supercilious look and shuffled out without responding. Gussie recognized Willa Simon when she walked in. They had had a run-in several years ago when Willa, drunk or high on something, had complained about the high price of an item she wanted to purchase and shouted that the "Jew robbers should get out of the neighborhood and quit cheating poor people." Willa walked around the store, checking everything out. Finally, she took one of the shopping baskets and started selecting items. When she checked out, Luther announced the total. Willa counted the money in her purse; she was short. And embarrassed. She looked to Gussie who was watching, and said, "I'm a little short. Can you trust me 'til tomorrow? I won't stiff you, honey. You know me for a long time." Gussie got that certain look that she had when she was about to attack.

"Sure I know you. I'm the Jew that used to rob you... the one you wanted to get the hell out of the neighborhood." Everyone stiffened up. Lindy and Luther looked at each other. Willa glared at Gussie with anger and started pushing items aside.

"Take back some of this stuff so I got enough to cover it," Willa huffed. Gussie ignored her and began loading all of her items into bags.

"It's okay. I trust you. Pay when you can," Gussie said, now hatefully calm. Willa said nothing as she took her several bags and walked out without looking back. Neither Lindy or Luther said a word. The tension was reduced when the first white customer walked in. It was a stockbroker from the country club, a fairly heavy user. Luther greeted him and engaged him in small talk about people at the club. The man slowly relaxed and began checking the wine display. He finally settled on a Bordeaux and went to the register to pay. He casually laid three fingers on the counter as Luther selected  a nice bag for the wine. With preternatural speed,  Luther had reached under the counter and placed three, one-gram packets of cocaine into the bag.  The man paid with four, one-hundred dollar bills and Luther gave him his change. When the man left, Luther put the three, one-hundred dollar bills in a special place in the register.  Gussie had observed the transaction while pretending to arrange some items on the shelf.  Just like that, Gussie thought.  Fast as lightning. Three hundred bucks in a box.

She was happy when a black woman came in and looked around, stunned by the display of prime steaks and  huge scampies. Lindy quickly reacted to the woman's bewilderment and shouted, "Come on back here, m'am. We've got some beautiful pork chops and real fresh chicken.

So this is how it goes, Gussie thought.  This was going to be a very happy place. If only she hadn't snapped at that Willa woman.

And so it went, that first auspicious day for Discovery Foods. Two white customers and several down home shoppers, all of them obviously pleased by the fine quality and reasonable prices. Gussie presided over the scene like a benign monarch. She was pleased that her neighborhood customers were pleased. Everything felt different, nicer. The sun even managed to shine through the sparkling clean front window, suffusing the store in a warm, yellow glow.

Willa Simon came in and walked straight to Gussie's counter. She spoke defiantly to mask her embarrassment. "I'm still short," she said, slamming down her money. It's all I've got. You get the rest when my check comes in from the welfare. She stood there, waiting for whatever grief Gussie was going to administer. "That's fine. I'm not worried—you're a good customer," Gussie said softly. Whatever animus that existed between the two women suddenly was gone. Willa leaned on the counter, wanting to talk.

"You've got such nice stuff now that you've got white folks coming back down here to shop," Willa said in a conciliatory tone.

"The whites come down for the fancy wine and prime steaks at cheap prices. Our main business, Miss Simon, is neighborhood people. Like it always was." Gussie had stated her mantra, and Willa Simon would be a courier of the news throughout the neighborhood.

"Come here, Miss Simon."

"Willa. Call me Willa," she said following Gussie to the wine display. Gussie pulled down a bottle of expensive Pinot Noir. Luther almost choked.

"Want to try some of the fancy stuff?" Gussie asked.

"Hey! Let's not be messing with the inventory," Luther shouted, only half kidding.

"Willa should taste something besides Wild Irish Rose," Gussie replied.

"I'll probably choke on this Frenchy stuff. Besides, I'm broke, as you well know," Willa said.

"On the house. My treat," Gussie said, beaming.

"Jesus, Gus!" Luther whined.

Willa was deeply touched by Gussie's largesse and she wondered how she could have ever accused this lovely white woman—yeh, she's a Jew I guess, of being a robber. No way, bubba…she's a real sister.

"Goddam it," Maxwell muttered. "Goddam it" he shouted, louder as he crumpled a letter and threw it across the room. Kitty walked in the room in the middle of his outburst.

"Are we having a temper tantrum? Do you want mamma to send you to your room? What's the problem, Maxie?"

"She and that fucking Luther are in business together. They've reopened the store and turned it into some kind of gourmet operation. That rotten sonofabitch is trouble. Goddam it! Why can't she let go of that bastard?"

"Easy boy, easy. Who's doing what to whom?"

"Luther. Can you believe it? He reappears from nowhere after all these years and he talks my mother into reopening the store in some crazy new format. God only knows where he's been and what he's been doing. My guess is he's been a pusher. His mother was a wino for crissakes. Died in the goddam alley—froze to death full of cheap wine."

"Who is Luther? And what's so terrible about them reopening the store?" Kitty asked, utterly bewildered by Maxwell's excoriation of the revenant, Luther.

She got him a drink and was able to calm him down. She wanted to know about the store. "Who is this Luther guy? Who froze to death in what alley? When did you find all this out?" Kitty asked.

Aunt Lillian had written him a letter. She was alarmed when she heard about what was going on at the store, he told Kitty. The drink was a heavy duty blast of scotch and it hit Maxwell hard. He launched into phantasmagoria of his early life above the store in the ghetto. He told Kitty about the black woman wino, Anna Mae or something. How Sol sold her a half gallon of wine that she drank in the alley until she passed out on a cold night and froze to death. The police cars and their red and blue lights in the middle of the night. How it terrified him. And how Gussie ran through the ghetto looking for the little boy...the wino's son. How he was always hungry because she didn't feed him, so Gussie would give him baloney sandwiches. How Gussie lied to the police who were looking for the kid so she could keep him and care for him. How miserable it was to share a room with that black kid who was barely civilized. And his decision to get out of the ghetto and live with Aunt Lillian in a decent neighborhood and go to a good school where he got a scholarship to Boston U.

"Is that when you changed your name?" Kitty asked, pointedly.

"Yes, Kitty. Yes. I changed my fucking name, okay? I changed my name. I wish I could have changed everything about my life."

"So the last time you saw this Luther person you were a little boy."

"Yes. He lived with my folks until he was fifteen or maybe sixteen, I'm not sure, and then he disappeared in the middle of the night." Maxwell said.

"And now he comes back. Right after your father died. Luther redux. And he is helping your mother run the store. What's so terrible about that? How do you know he's trouble as you said? Are you perhaps obsessing about this guy—like maybe he's come back to haunt you and remind you of your troubled childhood?" Kitty asked, as she tried to help Maxwell understand his disquietude.

"Kitty, quite playing psychoanalyst. I've got a gut feeling. This is not going to be good, Kitty."

"You've been essentially estranged from your folks all these years. Why all of sudden are you sticking your nose in your mother's business?" Kitty asked, seeking a précis.

"Goddam it, Kitty, she's my mother."

"So why don't we go and see her?" Kitty asked. Maxwell did not answer. His mind was a conflation of frightening scenarios.

Luther kept the store open until one a.m. Lindy would stay up waiting for him, watching anything she could find on television. They weren't getting much sleep because they wanted to be back at the store around eight a.m. Nerves were getting a bit taunt. "How long am I going to be playing the role of a smiling grocery clerk?" Lindy sniffed.

"Guess what?" Luther said, sensing Lindy was looking for a fight. "You're going on vacation. Back to New Orleans for a couple of weeks."

" Then I'll need some new clothes for the trip," Lindy riposted, not giving ground. Luther was not in the mood to take a lot of guff from Lindy. "Don't be giving me a lot of shit, girl. You've got a closet is full clothes. Expensive clothes." He stared her down. "We're working here to build a boodle so we'll be set to go down to the islands and cool it for a long, long time. If you're that unhappy, just stay down in New Orleans and hustle yourself a mark. I've got something going here that's too good to mess with. Hear me, girl?"

"Sometimes I get to feeling like you're doing this for that old lady more than for me," Lindy said, pouting. Luther did not bother to respond. He had sensed that Lindy was jealous of his love and concern for Gussie. It was just another variable that he would need to juggle to keep his scheme going. There were plenty of Lindy Blancs out there.

In the morning they did not have much to say to each other. Luther had his coffee and that would hold until mid-morning when Gussie might make him some eggs upstairs in the apartment. Luther told Gussie that Lindy would be taking a vacation and Gussie agreed that Lindy should take a break from the store; that she had been working very hard. Pretty young women should not be on their feet all day long. Luther began to think about the future. How would he break it to Gussie that he would be leaving her again. He would tell her that she finally had the kind of store she really wanted…quality food at fair prices so she would be well respected in the 'hood. Sure, she would not be making much money; much of the food was being sold at cost. But she would be able to make a living and to pay for someone to help her in the store; maybe Angie or someone like that. Enough of the items had a decent markup so she would still be able to make out. Still, he would be abandoning her again. This bothered Luther; Gussie had always been like a mother to him. But she had lived her life, hadn't she? Wasn't he entitled to live his life? Surely Gussie would understand and she would not hate him for leaving; and she would understand that he couldn't run his scam indefinitely. He would be leaving her a very wealthy woman. Wasn't that a payback for all she had done for him?

More and more of the country club users were coming down to the ghetto during the daylight hours and a few of the braver souls ventured down at night. When the word got out that it was safe to come down at night, that part of the business would pick up. People partied at night and that's when they would want something for kicks. Luther would continue to stay open at night, waiting for business to build. The daytime business had already netted them a hefty profit.

Lindy left for New Orleans and Luther began taking his evening meals with Gussie.

They had much to talk about; Sol. Maxwell and those painful early days. Luther wanted to learn more about his mother and Gussie tried her utmost to recall everything she could about Anna Mae. "What was she like when she was sober?" Luther asked. "Was she educated? How did she speak? Did she have a deep south speech pattern?" The truth of matter was that Gussie had never spoken to Anna Mae when she was sober and it troubled her not to be able tell Luther what he wanted to hear. Little boys never get over their mothers, Gussie thought. Gussie, on the other hand, had many questions she wished to ask Luther: Why had he left so abruptly? Didn't he realize how much Sol cared for him; how much Sol had enjoyed teaching him how to speak correctly and how to dress?. Did he remember how Sol attended the parent/ teacher conferences at school to make sure Luther was doing well in school? Where had he been and what had he done all those years when he was gone? As Gussie asked her questions, Luther agonized over his mixed feelings. Why did Sol want to teach him to speak and dress like a white man? Why did Gussie rescue him and decide to raise him as if he were her son? Was it guilt feelings because they had sold his mother the wine that killed her? Would they love him if he dressed and talked like a black man? The endless hours of vagrant reminiscing was both painful and cathartic for them both.

Finally Gussie asked a pointed question: Was he going to marry Lindy? What were his plans for the future? God, Luther thought, she wants to know—the future! The future. Does she know I might be leaving? What do I tell her? Luther temporized, not daring to face the reality of telling Gussie he was going to leave. To break the spell, Luther decided on an anodyne; they would do an accounting of the coke sales and split the take. Gussie was stunned when Luther handed her thousands of dollars in one hundred dollar bills. He asked her where she kept her money. In a checking account? "Don't do that, Gussie. Get a safe deposit box. You don't want the feds to know how much money you've got." "Okay, now I'm a tax cheat," Gussie said, smiling at her own black humor.

Supelak had gotten the word, he was now a detective assigned to the narcotics detail. And he was all puffed up with new found self-importance. He could barely wait to get to Ludvina's, the cop joint where the uniforms went to unwind with shots and beers. "Look who just strutted in wearing plain clothes!" a big bellied uniform cop taunted. "The narc squad will never be the same." Supelak ignored the jibe and plopped down on a bar stool. "Give the guys what they're drinking," he said, magisterially.

"What do you know, the narc dick is springing for drinks for us poor beat cops," the big belly said.

"Kiss my ass," Supelak retorted. "You're buying the next round, wise guy."

"Pay raise and all you can steal. You're the man now, Supelak. You gotta' be feelin' good for a change," a rookie cop added.

"Yeh, I'm feeling good 'cause now maybe I can square a few old beefs that have been eating at me," Supelak said. "There's this old Jew broad with a little grocery store downtown with a smart-mouth nigger working for her. Love to know what kind of shit they're into there."

"Watch it man, the skipper just gave us a lecture on hassling our black brothers," Big Belly warned.

"I'd like to hassle this nigger's ass into the joint," Supelak grumbled, ominously.

Luther was thinking about closing when the headlights of a car stopping in front of the store brought him to full alert. The din from the car could be heard through the front window. Suddenly, a young woman, champagne bottle in hand, staggered through the front door. Luther was frightened; this was the sort of thing he had hoped to avoid, because it was certain to attract unwanted attention. Luther gestured for the woman to cool it. She did not look familiar and that bothered him. He asked the woman how he could help her. She identified herself as the wife of Doctor Michelson, one of Luther's regulars from the country club. Luther asked where the doctor was and she told him that the good doctor was shit faced out in the car. She offered to take Luther out to the car so he could see for himself that the doctor was indeed there. Luther tried to quiet the woman down and to get her out of the store as soon as possible. He asked her what she wanted and she replied that she wanted six packets of the best. Luther reached under the counter and fingered six packets. He told the woman that she needed to buy something; wine or steaks or seafood. She cavalierly asked for a bunch of strip steaks, giggling that they would have a midnight cookout. Luther again motioned for her to quiet down as he wrapped six steaks with the six packets included. He held the wrapped package, waiting for the woman to produce seven hundred dollars. Whispering through his teeth, he told her the price, holding out his hand so she would get the idea that she had to produce the cash. It suddenly dawned on the besotted woman that she had no money with her. She put the champagne on the counter and lurched out to the car to get the cash. Luther could hear the laughter and noise as the occupants of the car fumbled for the needed cash. The woman returned, childishly clutching seven, one hundred dollar bills which she plunked down on the counter. Luther handed her the package and sternly told her not to draw attention to herself nor to let anyone open the package until she got home. She grabbed the package and departed, remarking that Luther was a cute guy. Luther put six hundred in the special section of the register, and one hundred with the cash for store sales. He breathed a sigh of relief when he heard the car pull away. He would have a talk with Doctor Michelson warning him to never again come to the store drunk.

As the Michelson SUV screeched around the corner, a police cruiser going in the opposite direction made a wild U-turn and pulled the SUV over. A swaggering cop approached the now silent car cautiously, hand on his holster. The cruiser was from another district and was not on patrol; it was merely passing through the ghetto. The cop tapped on the window and motioned for the driver to lower it. He surveyed the interior of car, packed with partiers, one of them passed out in the back seat.

"Somebody chasing you folks?" he asked. "You were going sixty in a thirty-five zone. License and registration, please." The cop looked at the picture on the license and then shined his flashlight onto the face of the driver, which happened to belong to Alderman Frank Brennan of Canyon Oaks Township. The cop was impressed and his tone changed.

"Mister Brennan, you folks really shouldn't be driving around down here at night," he purred, as he courteously returned the license.

"This part of town suddenly off-limits, officer?" Brennen asked, his voice conveying authority and power.

"No sir, but…well it's dangerous down here. What brings you folks down to the neighborhood late at night, anyway?" the cop said, starting to regain his balls.

"A store that sells great steaks and wine at a discount," Brennan said, nonchalantly. "You about through with us, officer?" The cop grinned nervously.

"Just slow it down a bit and let's keep that wine corked until you're home safely," the cop said, now sounding very coppish.

As Luther feared, there were repercussions. A cruiser with two uniformed cops stopped in front of the store. The cops entered the store and the mostly black shoppers were suddenly silent as everyone stopped what they were doing and watched. The cops asked for the owner and Luther identified himself and introduced Gussie as his partner. That immediately got the cops' attention; a strange partnership. The cops told Luther that they had gotten a report of a Mercedes SUV full of people who looked like they had been drinking. They were stopped for speeding and they said they were down in this neighborhood to buy wine and steaks. Why would white people be buying steaks down here in the ghetto late at night? The officers seemed incredulous. Did Luther know anything about it? Luther assumed a casual, matter-of-fact posture and calmly told the cops that he did a lot of business at night. Again, in a probing, somewhat suspicious tone, the officer leaned forward and whispered into Luther's ear so as not to offend the black shoppers: "White folks? Dressed for a party or something?"

Luther was now at his coolest as he told the cops that he did a nice white trade because his wine and steak prices were discounted; that white folks are willing to travel to find real bargains. And he laughed, solicitously. The cops' antennae were up. The lead cop took out a pad and pencil and asked for Luther's full name, just for the record. As they left, the cops told Luther to be careful to whom he sold; if customers seemed to have been drinking he should refuse to sell to them. As the cops left, the black customers exchanged knowing looks and begin gossiping. Gussie said nothing; but her face reflected bewilderment and concern. Luther began to revisit his basic concept: would the police continue to buy the explanation that white customers traveled to the ghetto, day and night, because they had heard there were great bargains to be had for imported wines and prime steaks and seaford? Had he overestimated his own cleverness and assumed that all cops were fools? This question would freight the coming months with anxiety and episodes of self-doubt which the fast flow of cash would alleviate.

Things were not peaceful in the Stonehill household in Massachusetts. Maxwell continued to agonize over Gussie's association with Luther. Finally, Kitty had had enough: "Why the hell don't you go there and see if this Luther guy is the bet noir of your imagination? Why don't you confront the guy and get to know him? Maybe he's a decent guy helping your mother make some money in that store. And for crissakes, either do that or stop pissing and moaning. You're making the horses nervous," Kitty said, as she kissed him on the cheek.

"Does your father know you use language like that?" Maxwell said. He paced the room for a few minutes and then he slapped Kitty on her butt and said, "Alright, goddamit, I'm going back to the ghetto from which I sprang. Or sprung. Whatever. And I hope to God that Luther is the benign creature you think he is."

"And if he isn't?" Kitty said, extending her lower mandible.

"I will use all my legal training and guile to throw him in the fucking slammer."

Maxwell arrived in town the next afternoon, checked in to a motel on the fringe of the inner city and casually sauntered into the Discovery Foods store. "You must be Luther," he said, extending his hand to Luther who forced a smile of recognition.

"Maxie, I'd know you anywhere. Great to see you again after all these years."

"Yeh, it's okay for you to call me 'Maxie' ," Maxwell said, dripping sarcasm.

"Your mom's upstairs. I'll buzz her. We've got an intercom now."

"Cool," Maxwell said as he pulled a wine bottle out of the display. "You sell a lot of these *Montrachets* at eighty bucks a copy?" Maxwell asked, abandoning the pretense of comity.

"Gussie just signaled that she's coming down," Luther said. Then he grinned and said, "Matter of fact, it's a big seller."

"That's got to use up an entire welfare check, doesn't it?" Maxwell said, getting hot.

Luther stiffened up and his eyes blackened. "What are you trying to say, Maxie? You know I've got white buyers coming down here." Just then Gussie burst through the door from the apartment. "Maxie, my God! What a wonderful surprise." She ran to Maxwell and hugged and kissed him, her eyes tearing up. "Did you guys recognize each other? This is wonderful after all these years," Gussie said, her voice betraying her tension.

"Nothing's changed, Mom," Luther said, calling Gussie "Mom" to get under Maxwell's skin.

"Why not? Why not, I ask you after all these years. You're both grown, beautiful men and I'm an old lady. Why can't you give me a little joy at seeing you both?" and she began to weep. Luther went to put his arm around Gussie to comfort her and Maxwell brushed his arm away and embraced his weeping mother, as he glared at Luther. Finally Gussie regained her composure. Her voice was flat and angry as she said, "What's going on here, Maxwell? What's the reason for this visit?"

"I want to find out what kind of scam brother Luther is running here, before you wind up in jail with him," Maxwell said.

"There is no scam. No jail. Why are you causing bad feelings? You should be happy that I have a beautiful store and people in the neighborhood don't call me a robber anymore," Gussie said.

"What's paying for the fancy store, the imported wine and big steaks? What else is he selling? Mama, something is very not kosher here," Maxwell said. Gussie took a breath and started to explain as Luther held up his hand to interrupt her.

"Look man, I'm going to take you through this one last time. Either you buy it or you don't. I couldn't care less. You grabbed a bottle of *Montrachet* and you figured it sells for maybe eighty bucks. Well, we sell it for sixty-five. That's a real bargain, right Maxie? Do you eat porterhouse steaks? I mean prime beef. What do you pay? Four bucks a pound? We're at three bucks a pound.

A bargain, right? Damn right it's a bargain. Want me to go down the list?"

"So you're selling at cost. How do you make a living selling at cost? You've got to be selling something else to make money, Luther. What are you hustling, wise ass?"

"Max, that's not fair. Just stop. Right now," Gussie shouted.

"No let him go, Mom. I'll give him a lesson in food merchandising."

"Suddenly you're a business school grad? Food merchandising yet," Maxwell scoffed.

"Ever hear of loss leaders? The wine and steaks are loss leaders. We sell them at cost. But when people from uptown come in to the store, they buy other stuff—imported soups, cheeses, beers, olives and so on. And we make good money on those items."

"And the regular stuff like collards, okra, pork shoulder— the stuff the neighborhood people buy, we sell mostly at cost. I want to make it up to these people," Gussie said.

"Luther, level with me…you're used to big bucks. I can tell by the clothes you wear. Are you going to be satisfied grinding out a living in a grocery store? Doesn't make sense to me," Maxwell said.

"Maxie, I didn't go to Harvard. I'm a street kid. I was a bartender at a black club and later at a white country club. The food buyer there taught me how to buy and how to price. He had been with Kroger. That's where I learned about loss leaders. And Sol taught me a lot. I'm making a good living as long the whites keep coming down here for bargains."

"Maxie, the police already are starting to bother him. They can't understand why whites would come down to this neighborhood," Gussie interjected.

"Bother him, how?" Maxwell asked, his lawyer's sensitivity to miscarriage of justice, activated.

"They're probably going to start questioning my customers or searching their packages," Luther said, hoping that Maxwell would swallow the bait.

"Bullshit. If they so much as breath on your customers, call me and I'll have their badge," his suspicions now subsumed by his protective instincts.

"So you understand what we're doing here, honey? You know we're not—how do you say it—scamming? And you'll help us, darling?" Gussie pleaded.

"If you're making a living and you're both happy, then I'm happy. Stay well and keep in touch. He kissed Gussie and gave Luther a quick handshake and he was gone.

Business was booming. More and more of the country club users were flocking to the store, day and night. And they bought the profit items as well as the loss leader steaks and wine. It was the neighborhood people however, that gave Gussie a sense of pride and fulfillment. She would study their faces as they picked up bunches of greens, sprayed with water to keep them fresh and appetizing, smelling them, obviously pleased with their bouquet. The whiting was same-day fresh; if only Lenore Henderson would return and see them now, Gussie thought. Gussie relived the painful confrontation with Missus Henderson of years ago. People shook the honeydews and squeezed them lovingly; they were ripe and fragrant. And of course, Luther saw to it that there was an adequate supply of fresh, pink chitterlings and maws for the buyers that still requested those deep south morsels. The chicken, chuck, ground beef, turnips and okra...everything was attractively displayed and blindingly fresh. Luther had an artist's knack for display; everything invited the eye and the sense of smell. Never was the paper under meat allowed to get bloody; Luther and Gussie changed the paper frequently. When the beautiful oak and brass front door opened and closed so smoothly and silently, she recalled the old warped door that rubbed and stuck and squeaked. Gussie was frequently reminded of the engine that drove this wonderful store when she would force herself to glance at the register area as Luther, with the deftness of a magician, slipped packets of the powder that the country club set craved so avidly; then she would return to watching the neighborhood folks to assuage her fleeting sense of guilt.

Late one afternoon as the early winter darkness descended, the door opened slowly and to Gussie's delight, in walked Lenore Henderson, the aging school teacher, leaning on her cane as she

slowly walked. Gussie walked over to greet her and she was granted a brief smile by the reserved, dignified teacher. Gussie prattled
on nervously, pointing out all the features of the new store. Henderson would nod slightly in appreciation as she looked about.
Gussie prayed that the whiting, the cause of the old confrontation, would be fresh and appealing. Henderson was interested
in ground beef, which she smelled and to which she nodded her
approval. Gussie ventured a question: where had Lenore Henderson been shopping all this time? Lenore answered that a neighbor
had been driving her to the Korean store. Gussie felt emboldened
enough to ask if she had been satisfied there, but Lenore Henderson saved her the trouble. She admitted the Korean's prices
were higher than what she was seeing now, at Gussie's store. Finally
Gussie took Lenore Henderson's hand and welcomed her back
and apologized for the not quite fresh whiting that had once upset
her. Gussie, sensing that Lenore was loosening up, led her to the
fish display and pointed out the glistening fresh whiting which
pleased the elderly school teacher.

Willa Simon, now a regular customer, brought many new customers to the store. Recently, Vera Deering, a member of Willa's
church became a frequent visitor. Gussie could not read Vera
Deering; she rarely spoke and her face revealed nothing. Gussie
treated her with the deference due a friend of Willa Simon, but
she was never sure if Vera Deering was a friend or a silent critic.

Pete Supelak, newly promoted to detective in the narcotics squad, was obsessed with the activity at the Discovery Foods store. Luther had smart-mouthed him and Gussie had barred him from entering the store unless he intended to buy something. His reputation as a mooch continued to haunt him. He strongly suspected that drugs were being sold in the store. Why else would white people be driving down to the store at all hours of the night? Supelak's new duties took him to various parts of the city and that prevented him from observing the store around the clock. So he importuned a patrolman named Emil Siwinski to park his cruiser in an alley near the store at night and observe the activity. Siwinski demurred at first. Lieutenant Matt Carney, the district commander was the only one who could authorize a stakeout and Siwinski was not about to run afoul of Lieutenant Carney. Supelak argued that it would not be an actual stakeout if he simply stopped near the store as he was making his rounds and watched. Supelak lied, saying that Carney also was suspicious of the store and would probably reward him if he spotted any illegal activity there. Siwinski eventually acquiesced after Supelak plied him with drinks and flattery. He would park in the alley for a short while as he made his rounds and observe the store.

A few nights later, as Willa Simon and Vera Deering were walking Vera's mutt, Vera suddenly tensed up and nudged Willa. "Did you see that?" Vera whispered.

"See what?" Willa replied, annoyed. Vera could be melodramatic at times.

"That police cruiser hiding in the alley. I'll bet they're watching the grocery store and I know why," she huffed. "They're selling drugs, that's why. And that's what paying for the fancy food they're selling us."

"Vera, you are so full of shit at times. You just love to bad-mouth people. You should be grateful we've got such a nice store in the 'hood. Don't be spreading rumors. Just mind your own goddam business for a change," Willa blasted. Just then, a Lexus pulled up in front of the store and woman got out and walked into the store.

"There!" Vera gloated. "A white woman at this hour? Is this a normal shopping time for a woman all dressed up in business clothes?"

"She's a businesswoman coming from her office to buy wine or shrimp or something. It's worth her while to come down here. They're selling stuff way below other stores uptown. Quit being such a busybody, Vera Deering," Willa said.

"We'll see," Vera said, primly.

A few days later, Supelak cornered Patrolman Emil Siwinski at the bar at Luvina's. He wanted a report on what Siwinski had seen while parked near the grocery store at night. Siwinski innocently replied that all he saw was "a broad driving a Lexus who went into the store around nine-thirty. Not much else." Supelak blew his top, calling Siwinski a stupid Polack. Didn't he think it was unusual for a rich broad to be coming down to the ghetto at night, Supelak bellowed. Siwinski shrugged and started talking to his buddies at the bar. Supelak was determined to put the store under his personal surveillance. He would need to convince Lieutenant Carney that it was worth spending time to keep an eye on the store.

Matt Carney came from of family of cops. He looked as though he had been sent out from Central Casting. He was lanky with gray, buzz-cut hair and narrow blue eyes that seemed to see everything around him all at once and his flat, gravelly voice told people that he brooked no nonsense. There was no way that a clown like Supelak was going to bullshit him.

"Listen, Dick Tracy, you are way out of line requesting surveillance of a legitimate business just because you've got a bug up your ass that they're selling drugs. What do you base it on? You saw a few white people in a black neighborhood?"

"Skipper, there's a steady stream of expensive cars pulling up there all hours of the night and all day long. What brings them down to Central Avenue at night? Supelak whined.

"Other than drugs, what do you think brings them down there?" Carney asked.

"I asked a few niggers in the neighborhood—"

"—That's a no-no, you moron. You do not use that word, especially when you are on duty, you understand?" Carney barked.

"Sorry, Skip. I checked the store out when they reopened and it was real high-end. Imported stuff. Wine, big shrimp, prime steaks. The works. And the neighborhood people that I know from my beat duty days told me their prices are way low. So how are they doing it?"

"How? I'll tell you how. They're in a low rent area. Their overhead is low so they can sell cheaper. And white people will travel to get bargains. It's a fad. After awhile it'll wear off and the white trade will drop off. In the meantime, you let them run their business without being hassled," Carney said, reasoning with the pest across his desk.

"Can I at least watch the place for awhile? No hassling. And if I see some really unusual activity—can I give you a report?"

"One thing about you bohunks, you're stubborn. Watch the store but don't forget you've got other responsibilities," Carney said.

"Thanks a million, Skip. I'll be careful out there," the obsequious cop simpered.

"And stop calling me 'Skip.' I'm Lieutenant Carney, to you."

Willa Simon sauntered into Discovery Foods and shopped very slowly, feeling the produce and sniffing the seafood. This was unusual because Willa was an in-and-out shopper, always in a rush. So why was she loitering today, Gussie wondered. Gussie watched Willa, unobtrusively, and suddenly she realized that Willa was observing Luther at the cash register, doing his magic with the coke buyers. Three buyers had come and gone while Willa lollygagged around the store. "Can I be of help to you, Willa? Are you looking for something you can't find?" Gussie probed.

"No, but I think I can maybe be of help to you," Willa answered suggestively.

"Come on, Willa, spit it out; what's on your mind?"

"Can we talk private?" she asked.

"We can do go upstairs to my apartment if you want to be real private. You're starting to worry me, Willa."

"I think you've got something to worry about," Willa replied cryptically. As they walked to the door that opened to the stairs leading to the apartment, Gussie caught sight of Luther whose face was registering a worried, what's up expression. Gussie nodded and smiled to indicate that all was well. Gussie poured Willa a cup of coffee as they sat at the homey kitchen table. "So tell me, Willa, what should I be worried about?"

"We keep seeing a cop car hiding in the alley across Central Avenue. He sits there at night. I took my walk on the other side of the street and I could see the cop; he was peering right into the store," Willa said.

"So why are you peering at Luther? What are you looking for?" Gussie said.

"None of my business, Missus Steinberg—"

"For God's sake stop with the 'missus', my name is Gussie."

"Like I said, Gussie, it ain't none of my business, but I think the cops are looking to see if you're pushing shit—drugs in here. While I was watching, three white, uptown customers grabbed wine and some packages of cheese and stuff and checked out real fast. And I could see hundred dollar bills flashing by real fast. Looks like something's going on. What's worrying me is somebody like that holy-moly Vera Deering could come in and maybe spot those big bills changing hands at the register. She's seen the cop car several nights when we walk the dog. You got to be careful with her. Well, maybe I talked too much, Gussie, but I really love the way you're running the store for the folks down here and I'd hate to have something happen to you." Gussie said nothing for a long time. Then she kissed Willa on the cheek.

"I'll be careful when Vera comes into the store." Nothing more was said but it was mutually understood that Willa knew what was going on. And Gussie knew in her heart that Willa would never talk.

"Vera is a mean kind of gossip and I know she's spreading rumors. I'll do my best to convince people that she doesn't know what the hell she's talking about," Willa said. And that was that. Nothing more to say.

As Willa checked out, Gussie walked over and told Luther not to ring up her package. "On the house," Gussie said as she and Luther exchanged knowing looks. That evening Luther told Gussie that things were starting to heat up a little. Nothing to worry about yet, but whenever Gussie wanted him to cut out all she had to do was give him the word. This upset Gussie; she never wanted Luther to leave. She loved her life and she loved her store. She would take her chances and ride things out as long as they could. "Let's be real careful when that Vera woman comes in. I'll point her out to you. She's seen the cruiser in the alley and she knows they're watching us." This was Gussie's answer to Luther's offer to cut out.

Supelak knew he was doing more than Lieutenant Carney had authorized, but the afflatus driving him could not be controlled. He walked the length of the thirty-eighth block on Central Avenue, shining his flashlight into the empty storefronts, looking at the comatose winos and potheads. He was looking for a stoolie that could be controlled, somebody who could be his eyes and ears until Carney okayed him to put the store under surveillance.

Then he spotted him; his street name was Three Hundred Pounder because of his massive bulk and his childlike malleability. He was sleeping on the ancient swimming pool float that he dragged around from location to location. No one knew from where he had come; it just seemed that he had always huddled in some abandoned storefront on this block. Supelak shined his light into Pounder's face and he awakened with a start looking straight into Supelak's Glock, jammed into his face. "What's goin' down, man?" he gurgled.

"You know me?" Supelak snarled. Pounder squinted into the light.

"Yeh. You're the beat cop. I ain't done nothin'."

"I ain't no beat cop anymore, you tub of shit. I'm a narc detective now," Supelak said, not realizing how ridiculous it was to brag of his new status to a besotted half-child.

"Yes sir," Pounder whimpered, as he extended his arms to show he was not a druggie. "I'm a wine man. Don't mess with no shit, sir."

"Drink," Supelak growled as he pushed a pint of cheap port into Pounder's face. Pounder took a long swig and then Supelak yanked it away. "Now take your choice, Sweet Lucy or" —and he jammed the Glock into Pounder's mouth, grinning sadistically at the wino's terror. "From now on you're my eyes and ears. I wanna' know everything that goes down in that store over there. Everything that nigger Luther does. Anything you hear about the store in the 'hood. You hear what I'm sayin'?"

"I hear you—I sure do hear you. I be watchin' real good, detective."

"An nobody knows you're talkin' to me, ain't that right?" He tosses the pint at Pounder.

"Right. Nobody." Supelak struts away to his unmarked car, sexually aroused at his power.

Lindy looked rested and happy when Luther picked her up at the airport when she returned from New Orleans. She was loaded down with packages and boxes in addition to her luggage. Luther nodded toward the packages as the cabbie loaded the trunk. She sheepishly admitted that she had done a little shopping on Michigan Avenue in Chicago during her layover. Luther sarcastically mimicked "a little shopping" and said she better be ready to go back to work in the store to pay for all the shopping. He was being facetious; he was genuinely happy to have Lindy back. And she demonstrated her appreciation that night in bed. She knew exactly what gave Luther the most pleasure. She had his number, or so she assumed. She was wrong.

She was back on the job the next morning and Gussie noticed the tight designer jeans that Lindy had wiggled into. "Can you breathe in those pants?" Gussie asked, smiling broadly. Lindy did not respond. Gussie was starting to get on her nerves. Lindy resented the fact that she had to work in a grocery store to help Luther make their getaway boodle. She had been the cynosure of the club scene down in New Orleans. Plenty of heavy hitters wanted to get next to Lindy Blanc with the pale skin. Yet her dreams of social mobility drew her to Luther; Luther of the conservative clothes and white boy's diction. No flashy, wide brimmed fedoras and suede shoes for him. She would sweat the grocery gig until they were ready to split with a big bankroll.

Gussie had gone up to bed and Luther was handling the white trade. Business was brisk most of the evening and when things slowed down a bit, Lindy went outside for some air. As she sat on the steps of a four-suite apartment, smoking a cigarette, a big car loaded with whites pulled up. She watched the buyer go in and come out a few minutes later, carrying a big package. The buyer entered the car and she could hear the laughter of people in the car as they sat at the curb momentarily. Then Lindy spotted a group of toughs moving in. Lindy knew what was about to happen and she rushed to the car screaming, "Lock your doors! Lock your doors— they're going to hold you up!" The lead tough rushed for the car as it lurched forward and sped away. The punk, in frustration, slapped Lindy and knocked her to the sidewalk. Lindy screamed for help and Luther rushed from the store carrying a pistol. He looked back and forth down the darkened street and saw Lindy lying on the sidewalk, bleeding from the nose. Luther spotted the knot of thugs pressed against a wall across the street. He ran toward them and they dispersed in all directions. Luther fired at them several time but missed. Then he ran to Lindy as lights went on in several apartments. Gussie came running out, pulling a robe over her nightgown.

"What happened?" Gussie shouted. "Oh, my God, she's bleeding!"

"Nosebleed," Luther panted. "Take her inside and put ice on it." Siwinski heard the shots being fired and came roaring out of his stakeout position, siren blaring and bubble lights flashing. He screeched to a halt in front of the store and jumped from the cruiser with his weapon drawn. "Freeze!" he shouted, his voice quivering with fear, "Do not move! Drop your weapon! Drop it now!" Luther complied and stood there stoically. Siwinski approached, shining his flashlight in Luther's face.

"Did you fire your weapon? Who did you fire at?" he demanded.

"I am Luther Hightree and I own this store. There was an attempted holdup of my customers," Luther said, calmly.

"Customers? What customers?" Siwinski rambled.

"They were just getting into their car. My clerk was sitting there, having a cigarette and she saw the punks go after the car and she screamed. They ran and I came after them," Luther explained, laying everything out explicitly for the rattled Siwinski.

"You fired your weapon at the suspects? How many shots?" Siwinski was now in a take-charge mode. "You cannot be firing your weapon on a public street in the dark. I could cite you for that," Siwinski said; he was the big cop now. He then demanded I.D. and proceeded to question Lindy, asking if the customers were Caucasian or black and if Luther or Lindy had ever seen them before; the make of the car and the number of passengers. He then asked what they had purchased, commenting suspiciously that it seemed quite unusual for white people to be shopping in this area, especially at this hour of the night. Luther then went into his usual spiel about his place being a destination store for white bargain hunters seeking the big values he offered on imported wines and foods. He invited officer Siwinski to stop in sometime and take advantage of the low prices on the great steaks. Luther temporarily befuddled the poor benighted Siwinski who could only mutter that Luther should let them know if he heard anything.

They closed the store and went up to the apartment to unwind over a few glasses of wine. Lindy's nose was a bit swollen and her blouse was badly bloodstained. Gussie felt the fabric and said that she could get the stains out and that Lindy should bring her the blouse tomorrow. Lindy nodded a bored assent. Luther studied Gussie; did this incident shake her up? Did the cop's suspicions worry her? Was she ready to call it quits?

"This was just what we needed, huh, Gussie?" he probed.

" You answered the cop's questions. They'll eventually get it through their *goyisher kops* that it is normal for white people to shop down here at night. And we can prove it if they would come in and see for themselves what bargains we've got."

"What's a goysher?" Lindy asked, mangling the Yiddish word.

"A gentile. Jews think some gentiles are stupid," Luther proudly pontificated. "Sol taught me that," he added in response to Gussie's quizzical look.

"I wonder if our good friend Supelak is buying our story?" Gussie wondered..

"His absence is starting to worry me. I like it better when I can keep track of that mooch," Luther said. Then, continuing his probe of Gussie's mental state he added, "So you're still feeling secure about our operation, Gus?"

"I'm cool," she said, twisting her face into a "tough-guy" look to Luther's immense amusement.

But Lindy had reservations: "When the word gets out uptown that they can get mugged at our store, there goes our nighttime business."

"You want to know something, babe? If they want the coke, they're going to come down here regardless," Luther said.

"Are they that addicted that they would risk getting killed?" Gussie asked.

"They're addicted to partying…to getting their kicks coming down to the ghetto."" Like Park Avenue folks used to go slumming in Harlem," Gussie added.

"As I keep saying, Gussie, coke is a rich man's toy."

There were some major changes in the neighborhood; some good, some bad. Abe Zellman, whose gas station went up in flames, was reopening a new station with a mechanic's garage at the corner of 30th and Central. He had called Gussie and said he'd like to get together. Abe had been alone since he lost his beloved Margie. What did he mean "get together?" Gussie wondered. She had always liked Abe; in some ways he reminded her of Sol. He worked with his hands and was a strong guy…nice and tall with a good build and a head of a red hair. Did he still chew that disgusting wad of tobacco? She'd make him spit it out before she'd let him into the apartment; that was the deal. I hope he calls; I'd like to see that rascal, Gussie thought.

So, one of the old-timers was returning and another was leaving. Louise Randazzo, one of the Randazzo twins came with the unhappy tidings: Marie Randazzo had died. Her emphysema had finally got her. People had been nagging her to stop with those Pall Malls for years. She'd stop for awhile and then she'd start sneaking them again.

Gussie sat through the church services; the incense thing always got to her. They buried Marie next to Pete's grave in Memorial Cemetery after a sad graveside ceremony. After the ceremony, Gussie walked over to the Jewish section to visit Sol's grave.

The twins, Laura and Louise, had matured into handsome young women. They were married with kids and living in Oak Park, a very nice community. Laura had talked to Morrie Rappaport about putting the big old Randazzo house up for sale. It was a sad thing; so many memories in that house. What a clan; Joey and Sol running wild and Pete at the stand in the produce terminal. Happy memories. Then that memory that had always haunted Gussie wormed its way to the front of her brain; Joey acting like an animal, throwing her on sacks of bananas and tearing her clothes off. She had actually been thrilled by the whole ugly thing. What was wrong with her? Why hadn't she screamed and fought him off? She loved it. Every second of it. And Joey was killed. Had it been because of that?

Gussie and Sol had had a robust sex life and Gussie would think about it at night. Sometimes she stood nude in front of the full length mirror on the bedroom door proud of her body, still pretty firm for a woman of her age. She was a tall, green-eyed, very attractive woman albeit thoroughly disguised in her "practical" Enna Jettick shoes and Sol's bulky, shapeless sweaters. Yeh. I hope that crazy Abe Zellman calls me. I'd like to get dressed up and go out on a "regulation date." Sol wouldn't begrudge me a little fun, she thought.

Abe did indeed call and asked Gussie if she still liked ribs. There was a new black-owned joint down on twenty-third with ribs to die for. It's safe. They get lots of white people and they make sure you're comfortable. Gussie was game and she still had a taste for ribs with that special sweet hot sauce the blacks made. Gussie got herself up in her best pair of formfitting beige slacks and a nice top. Her best bra showed her off to good advantage and in heels she was a damn good looking woman. Luther looked her over, bug-eyed at the mind boggling transmogrification of Gussie

Steinberg. "That's what you call getting all Gussied up. That Abe Zellman is going to cum in his pants when he sees you."

"Luther, don't talk crazy. We're going to get some real down-home ribs. Be home later." And she walked out to Abe's snazzy, rebuilt Jaguar.

The rib joint was a winner! Best ribs Gussie ever had. And the owners fussed over her when she revealed that she was the owner of Discovery Foods. Everybody was talking about the store, the rib people said, and they promised to come and buy some of those great steaks. Abe had other things on his mind and his hands were busy; touching Gussie frequently and everywhere. She finally had to playfully slap his hand and admonish him as though he were an obstreperous teenager. Suddenly, the episode began feel like opera bouffe. Abe however, got the message—take it easy, act your age. Everything in due time. Abe was not about to blow his chances with this very desirable woman. So he settled down and kept his hands to himself. After the ribs, Abe suggested a quiet little bar that he knew a short distance uptown where they could have a nightcap and talk about old times. This suggestion suited Gussie's mood perfectly and away they went for brandy and conversation which lasted into the wee hours of the morning. The ride home in the Jag was wonderful and Gussie agreed that they should do this again. A very successful first date.

As Gussie got ready for bed, she began to think about her life. She was happy, and she was making money; and she was realizing a dream in being able to deal generously with the people in the neighborhood who were now holding her in high esteem. But was this a real life or a simulacrum that could suddenly end and disappear. It was, after all, a life based on mendacity and cunning.

The purple capillaries on Carney's drinkers' nose looked as though they might burst as he chewed Siwinski out. "I don't give a rat's ass that you aborted a holdup. You had no business being on stakeout down there without my permission."

"We heard there was drug action in that store," Siwinski said, gulping in fear.

"You take it upon yourself to put a legitimate place of business under surveillance? Without authorization? Are you a goddam moron? You realize what a jackpot we could be in with City Hall? …get the hell out of here before I bust you," Carney roared. As Siwinski turned to leave Carney said, "Wait a minute…who told you there was drug action in that store?"

Siwinski temporized. "Rumors. You know, you hear stuff from people."

"Give me a name," Carney bore in.

"No name in particular." Siwinski's color drained.

"Don't fuck with me or you're going up for review," Carney said.

"Supelak," Siwinski choked out.

"Do yourself a favor, just patrol your area. No more stakeouts unless I okay it and do not, I repeat, do not take orders or even suggestions from that idiot Supelak." Carney warned.

"I got it, Skip."

"You got it, huh?"

Supelak's idee fixe gained momentum after Siwinski's report to Carney about the putative holdup and the shooting, but Carney did not share his enthusiasm. Carney had him on the carpet and warned: "No questioning, no surveillance, no nothing. Casually watch the place but do not, under any circumstance annoy, interfere and or obstruct their ability to do business." As far as Carney was concerned, Discovery Foods was a legitimate business, and he wanted no trouble with the mayor.

But Supelak was looking for trouble; he simply could not constrain himself. He went looking for Pounder, his "eyes and ears."

He found Three Hundred Pounder asleep in his favorite storefront, across Central Avenue from Discovery Foods. Supelak shined his flashlight into the big man's face and kicked him in the ribs to awaken him. Pounder awakened with a start, furious at being tormented again by Supelak. "Why you gotta' do me that way—kickin' me like a sleepin' dog," he whimpered.

" 'Cause you are a sleeping dog, you fat mound of shit. You been watching things for me?" Supelak bullied. He tossed Pounder

149

a pint of cheap sherry. "Here. Mother's milk. What's going on in that store? You see any pushers you recognize going in there? Anything unusual?" He prodded Pounder with his shoe. "You hearing me?"

Pounder bucked up after being kicked again. "Damn man! Stop kickin' me if you want me to tell you stuff."

"Speak to me, asshole" Supelak snarled.

"Rich dudes...big cars...fancy chicks."

"Doing what?" Supelak pressed.

"Buying groceries. Late at night. Just don't seem natural, is all" Pounder said.

"What about people from the 'hood?" Supelak said.

"Hardly ever at night. Just during the day when the Jew lady and the black chick be waitin' on trade," Pounder said.

"So it's just Luther who's dealing with the white trade at night?"

"'Bout it," Pound shrugged.

Supelak wanted more. "Can you see anything through that store window? Are they buying packets of shit? Can you tell from where you're laying?"

"They all comin' out with bags of groceries, is all I can tell."

"Groceries, huh," Supelak muttered, his suspicions still eating at him.

Several days later as Luther was returning from the market, he spotted detective Supelak walking down Central Avenue, explicitly following Lieutenant Carney's orders; just looking around as he walked. Luther could not resist the urge to heckle the pompous cop.

"Well, good afternoon, officer Supelak. Oops! I made a mistake. You got promoted; you're a detective now. How come you're walking a beat? You should have a car, shouldn't you?" The arrogant black guy's sarcasm was too much for Supelak's onion-skinned vanity and he lost control. He stopped in his tracks and headed directly for the store just as Beth and Evan, the couple from the prosecutor's office, came into the store. He signaled them to cool it while Supelak was in the store. "You here to hassle us again?" Luther asked the cop.

"Easy boy. You see anyone hassling you?" Supelak emphasized the word boy.

"You're in the store—that's enough for me," Luther said. Beth and Evan watched with interest.

"You got any objections if I buy a couple of them steaks everyone talks about? Maybe a nice bottle of wine. I'm a shopper, boy, a regular shopper."

Gussie got right into the cop's face. "You get the hell out of here. You're no shopper. You never paid for anything in your life." Beth and Evan burst out laughing at the flummoxed cop. Supelak tried to recover by talking to the couple. It was another of his blunders.

"Find everything you were looking for? You come here often for these prime steaks?" suddenly Supelak was playing the clever detective.

"Are you questioning me, flatfoot?" Beth said, glaring at the cop.

"Who you calling 'flatfoot,' lady? I happen to be a narcotics detective."

"And I happen to be an assistant prosecutor, and you are way out of line, officer. Who is your is your district commander? He needs to know about you," Beth went on, looking her fiercest. Then Evan jumped in.

"It's Carney. Matt Carney. This is the fifth district, right?" Supelak smirked idiotically, trying to look unconcerned.

"Would it be alright if I called him?" Gussie asked.

"Absolutely. He likes to hear how his officers are performing. His number's in the phonebook. By all means give him a call," Evan counseled.

"Yeh…well maybe I'll call the prosecutor's office and tell them you're shopping in a place under suspicion." Supelak's biggest blunder.

"Just keep talking, officer," Beth said, grinning spitefully and scaring the hell out of Supelak, who had reason to be scared because Gussie was determined to talk to Lieutenant Carney.

"Wait, wait, wait, madam. Just go slowly and tell me exactly what happened and what the officer said," Carney pleaded when Gussie called to report the incident.

"I have a better idea," Gussie said, "could I come in to see you in person?"

"Certainly, certainly, Missus…?"

"Steinberg, Gussie Steinberg. I've been at my location for thirty-five years and I've paid my taxes for police protection."

"I'm looking forward to meeting you, Missus Steinberg." That fucking Supelak, Carney thought, grinding his tobacco stained teeth.

Gussie pushed her way through the forest of lumbering blue coats as she searched for Lieutenant Carney's office. A desk cop, bemused at the sight of the elderly woman wandering around the precinct, asked if he could help her. He then directed her to Carney's office. She rapped on the glass door and Carney bellowed for her to enter.

"Captain Carney?" Gussie ventured.

"Thanks for the promotion, ma'am, it's Lieutenant Carney." He grinned his most charming Irish grin as he rose to greet Gussie. "You must be Missus Steinberg, right? Please have a seat. How can I help you?" And Gussie let go with a litany of Supelak outrages going back to when he was a patrolman mooching cold cuts. When she got to his confrontation with the two prosecutors the previous day, Carney's antenna and his blood pressure went up. "He came into the store yesterday and starting questioning customers and they got into an argument?" said the incredulous Carney, thinking of condign punishment for the blundering cop. "Who were these people? Did you know them?" he asked.

"Friends of Luther's… he's my partner," Gussie answered. As Gussie continued describing the situation in detail, Carney's mind was processing Gussie's words: *Friends of Luther's.* White customers. He gently started a faux-naif line of questioning: "Does Luther generally deal only with the white customers?"

"Yes."

"Does he seem to know them by name?"

"Yes."

"Does Luther operate the register?"

"Yes." With his white customers. *His white customers?* Carney's mind was racing.

"Do the same white customers come back fairly often?"

"Usually."

Then Gussie wondered where the questions were going so she redirected the conversation to her demands to know what could be done about Supelak. She said the couple said they were from the prosecutor's office and that they were very annoyed at Supelak. Carney quickly assured her that Supelak would not enter her store again. He gave Gussie his card and encouraged her to call him whenever she had any questions or problems with any of his officers.

When she left, Carney began to process the various elements of the Discovery Foods story. He began to feel that perhaps there was something kind of "cute" about the whole operation. If only Supelak had a scintilla of judgment and self-control he could be of help. Maybe there was something to the rumors. *Strange dance partners this old Jewish broad and a slick black guy at the register with only white customers.*

Supelak started blabbering his defense before Lieutenant Carney could say a word. "That smart nigger used abusive language to me on the street and I couldn't let him get away with it, so I went into the store and said I was shopping for some of those great steaks people were raving about. Just to worry him, that's all Skipper."

"Alright, I don't blame you for getting hot, but you gotta' stay out of that store for now," Carney said in a shockingly understanding tone. Supelak felt his sphincter relax.

"I want you to continually watch the store as you drive through that block without drawing undue attention to yourself. There may be something to the rumors about that store. But for shit's sake don't cause any confrontations. I'm on top of this and I'll tell you what your next move will be. You hear what I'm saying to you?"

"You have got it, Skip," Supelak said, emphasizing each word in a moronic cadence.

"And stop calling, me 'Skip.' "

Maxwell and Kitty were at it again. Lillian had mailed Maxwell a squib from the paper about the attempted holdup and the shooting at the store. He was livid. The "N" word was used every other sentence as Maxwell denounced Luther in a prolix diatribe. Kitty listened patiently before telling Maxwell that Gussie was a big girl and that she should be inured to holdups in that neighborhood. Maxwell told Kitty about Sol's killing of a holdup guy years ago. But this was different. Luther contended that it was his customers, in a car, ready to leave the store that the punks attempted to hold up.

Kitty still did not understand his disquietude. "Who were these customers, late at night in an upscale car? What the hell were they buying at that hour of the night?"

"Goddamit, Max, we've been over this a dozen times. They might have gone down for some good wine at a discount. Or any of that high-end stuff they sell. People like to slum; they like to be in the know where you can get big bargains. Give Luther credit; he's got himself a clever format and if there's a little danger, Luther and your mom know how to take care of themselves. I'm really getting sick and tired of this conversation , Max. Sick and goddam tired. Let it go. We've got a life. Let's enjoy it, for God's sake. You went all those years just worrying about being Maxwell Stonehill without giving your folks a thought. Why now, all of a sudden? Is this some kind of delayed Jewish guilt trip?"

"Kitty, shut the fuck up… Please. I'm sorry. Don't shut up. I'm an idiot. I know. I've got a lot of baggage I've been schlepping around for a lot of years."

" I still think I'd like to go and meet your mother."

"Just don't get shot."

Luther and Blue Streak met at Luigi's, their favorite little Italian joint to discuss terms for a new shipment. Blue felt that the mailman delivery gig was the best bet for getting the product to Luther's store. Blue was pleased that Luther had increased his order and that business was good. The old buddies had a few grappas, the very strong Italian brandy, and relaxed a little from the pressures of their respective enterprises before going their separate ways.

Blue's faux mailman made his delivery to Discovery Foods without incident at eleven a.m. Supelak noticed the mailman delivering mail to Discovery Foods as he drove down Central Avenue, making his rounds. He thought nothing of it. But the true mailman made his normal delivery at one p.m. as Supelak was making a final pass through his territory. He saw the mailman and again he processed it as routine, normal. Only later did it occur to him that there was only one mail delivery a day. Or could there be two on certain days? Thoughts began to percolate in Supelak's brain. *Two mail deliveries within a couple of hours of each other?*

Supelak stopped at the big post office that serviced the area and made an inquiry. No, there is only one mail delivery a day; usually around one p.m. Supelak did not dare go into Discovery Foods and ask why they got two mail deliveries in one day. He decided to discuss it with Lieutenant Carney.

The information tantalized Carney; could the early mailman be a phony? Did he deliver something to the store? What did he deliver? Carney's mind was in high gear.

He complimented Supelak for being a good observer and told him to stay cool, that he would be told what the next move would be.

The store had been open about an hour and there were quite a few black women shopping. Gussie was busy with a customer when she heard a hushed murmur as the store became silent. Pounder had come in and motioned to Luther who quickly went to him. Pounder's face was bruised and grotesquely swollen. "What's happening, big man? Luther whispered.

"Got to talk," Pounder said frantically.

"Who done your face?"

"Let's go outside, I need a little taste."

"You got it bro," Luther said, comforting the big man. Luther signaled Gussie that everything was okay as he grabbed a bottle of cheap port from the wine rack and left with Pounder. The women shoppers exchanged looks and continued their conversations. Luther and Pounder walked down Central Avenue until they came to Pounder's empty storefront. Pounder plopped down on a battered canvas stool that he had salvaged from a dumpster, and it sagged under his weight. Luther handed him the pint of port and Pounder wrestled with the cap until he got the bottle open. He took a healthy swig and then closed his eyes as the port hit bottom. Now he was relaxed.

"What's your real name, Pounder? Luther asked.

"Bird."

"Say what?" Luther asked.

"Bird—Bird. You know—" and he flapped his arms to illustrate. My momma give me that name 'cause I used to jump out of my crib or sumpthin'."

"I'll stick with Pounder, okay? Talk to me, man."

"That cop. Supelak."

"What?"

"He out to bust you, man."

"How do you know?"

Pounder began to sob. "He make me do it."

"Do what, Pounder? Don't cry. Just talk to me," Luther said.

"Spy on you."

"How do you spy on me?" Luther asked, calmly, not wanting to frighten Pounder "From where I Iay at night I can see into the store."

"And?"

"He make me tell who I see comin' and goin'.'"

"And who did you see coming and going?" Luther coaxed.

"Rich  folks. Big Cars. Chicks in fancy clothes. Late at night. Too late to be buying groceries."

"You tell that to Supelak?"

"He stuck a gun in my mouth, man!"

"But now, you're talking to me. How come you're telling me all this stuff?"

"I hate the pig. Kicks me awake at night. If I don't got nuthin' new to tell him he pistol whips me."

"Is that why he done your face like that?"

"I don't care. I hate snitchin' on a brother. I know you be nice to folks in that store."

"Here's what to do, big man. You just string him along. Tell him you see lots of little old black ladies at night  buying yesterday's greens and bread.  Bargains, you know. And tell  him that the whites are just browsing around— looking at the wines and buying steaks. Nothing suspicious."

"I'll try, man. But he a smart devil. He gonna' know I'm lyin'.'"

"No. Don't worry. He'll buy anything you tell him about the store. He's  hungry for information. And it'll take a little heat off. Let me know what he says. Luther then stuffed a few bills into Pounder's pocket. "Be careful. If he gets mean, I'll find you another spot to sleep where you'll be safe."

"What happened to that big fellow? His face, my God!" Gussie said.

"Supelak scared him into watching the store at night to see who comes in."

"Supelak again?  I talked to his Lieutenant and he said he would keep him away from us. I'll call him again. He gave me his card just in case this would happen," Gussie huffed.

"No, it's okay, Gus. He's just stringing Supelak along. If he approaches our customers we'll have his ass. Don't worry. Everything is cool. Business as usual, Gus."

Pounder was frightened. He was afraid to lie to Supelak. He decided to come off the street and check into the shelter for a few weeks.  He loved the freedom that living on the streets afforded him and he felt confined and restricted in the homeless shelter, but he would tolerate it for awhile,  hoping that Supelak would forget about him and go away.

Supelak searched the streets for Pounder and was frustrated when he could not find him. The big man had been his eyes and ears. Supelak desperately wanted to report new information to his lieutenant, but there was nothing new to report. Everything was now quiet on the thirty-eight hundred block of Central Avenue and business roared on at Discovery Foods. And the money rolled in. More money than Gussie had ever seen in her entire life. After her last settlement sit-down with Luther, as she sat there inundated with hundred dollar bills, an idea crept in to Gussie's head. She would seek out Willa Simon and ask her for help.

A few days later, Gussie spotted Willa Simon at the cabbage bin. Gussie casually asked her if she was a strong church lady, a question that Willa thought was a bit weird. She wanted to know why Gussie asked. Gussie told her that she was planning to do something for the church but she didn't know the rules or how to go about it. Willa jokingly asked Gussie if she had suddenly found Jesus. Then she told Gussie that she was not what one would call a true believer, but she did show up for church on Sundays.  As Willa hefted a cabbage for closer examination, she became serious and asked Gussie what she was fixing to do. Gussie told her that she wanted to give some money toward a recreation center for the neighborhood kids. Willa then told her that the church was indeed planning a Boys and Girls club, but so far it was bogged down in discussion. Gussie said that that was exactly for what she wished to donate money. "Bless your heart," Willa said and told Gussie simply to attend one of the planning meetings and tell them what she wanted to do.

Gussie quietly made inquiries and was given the date of the next planning meeting at the Resurrection Baptist Church . She softly walked into the church as a planning meeting was apparently in progress. Reverend Amos Graylock, a tall, gracile man in a black suit, with graying hair and rimless glasses was conducting the meeting. Gussie, unobtrusively took a seat at the back of the church. As she listened, the Reverend passionately proclaimed, "We've got to do better. We owe it to our young people out there on the streets." This is exactly what Gussie wanted to hear. She was taken with the quiet dignity with which the meeting was conducted. She had imagined there would be shouting and hand clapping. A church lady wearing a large hat had stood and reported that the quilts were just not selling; that people simply could not afford them. The Reverend reluctantly acknowledged her statement and asked if there were any other ideas for raising money.

An elderly man, leaning on a cane rose and suggested that sidewalk barbecues are always an option but he was told that barbeques had been done to death.

At this point Gussie felt it was an opportune time for her to speak out. She rose and stepped into the middle of the aisle and said, "Excuse me, please. Can I say something please?" All the heads in the church, perhaps thirty people, turned to look at Gussie, some registering surprise, others anger and annoyance. The elderly man with the cane shouted, "Who the hell is that white woman?" and he was quickly shushed.

"Yes, madam," the Reverend spoke politely. "Did you wish to say something?" Willa, shocked and pleasantly surprised, jumped up and shouted, "Gussie, my heavens come on down in front here, where the folks can see you. Reverend, this is Gussie Steinberg from the grocery store we all go to." Reverend Graylock stepped down from the platform on which he stood and walked forward to shake Gussie's hand in a welcoming gesture, as the churchgoers murmured to each other. "What brings you to our meeting, Missus Steinberg," he asked, most cordially.

"I would like to make a contribution of five thousand dollars for the center with one condition, please...that the center be called the Anna Mae Hightree Center. Everyone was stunned by Gussie's proclamation and the noise level rose as the congregation spontaneously broke up into many little groups heatedly discussing what they had just heard.

The Reverend felt emboldened to add, "Madam, we are perfectly capable of managing our own affairs, much as we appreciate your concern and generosity." Gussie reddened, noticeably, suddenly feeling lost and embarrassed.

Vera Deering rose, spewing invective. "She's being generous with her drug money. It would be sinful to take her blood money." Gussie glared at Vera, wanting to tear her head off.

The Reverend jumped in, adjuring: "If what Miss Deering says is correct, I must tell you, Missus Steinberg, that I consider drug money to be blood money…money made by exploiting some unfortunate souls in this community." He stood there, as if a numinous glow had suddenly enveloped him. Graylock, a holy voice in an evil world.

But the numinous glow was shattered by the strident voice of one Willa Simon: "Reverend, with all due respect, get your head out of your ass!" There were shouts of outrage at Willa's sacrilege.

The Reverend maintained his dignity as he looked at Willa and said, "Quiet, please. Let's hear what the lady has to say."

"She's a blasphemous whore…don't let her speak," someone shouted.

"I asked for silence, please. I wish to hear what this lady has to say."

Willa gathered herself up, narrowing her eyes at the person who had called her a whore. Putting her arm around Gussie she said, "This lady runs a fine store and she charges us fair price, a lot lower than that Korean guy on Grand Street. There ain't no exploitation or whatever, as far as I can see." She looked directly at Vera for several tense seconds and continued, "How come you call it blood money, Reverend? You ever shopped in her store? She's got her reasons for wanting to help us. What right to we have to insult her like this?"

"I say again: who is this Anna Mae Hightree?" the Reverend asked.

Willa's face hardened for her acerbic reply: "She's five thousand bucks, that's who she is. When is the last time you saw five thousand bucks come through this church? Let the lady name the center—it must mean something important to her."

Gussie slowly made eye contact with congregants on either side of the aisle and spoke: "Anna Mae Hightree froze to death in the alley just down the street, dead drunk on a jug of cheap wine that she bought in our store instead of buying food for her little boy. You're probably thinking that I feel guilty for selling her the wine when we knew she was drunk. Maybe you're right, Vera. But take the money and let me worry about the reasons."

Many in the congregation were moved by the story. Reverend Graylock looked over his congregation; the mood had changed. "Thank you, madam," he said softly, "your desire to remember Anna Mae has touched our hearts. We will do our best to grant your wish."

Kitty sat at her marble kitchen table, sipping her morning coffee as she stared with amazement at the tiny kitchen television set. As Maxwell walked in, freshly shaven, reeking aftershave lotion, she ominously said, "Are you ready for this?"

"Lay it on me," he replied, lightly.

"Your mother was a short feature on Morning Exchange. The humanitarian of the week."

"My mother was what?" he said, in utter disbelief.

"She donated five thousand bucks to a black Baptist Church in your home town in memory of a woman who froze to death after drinking a jug of wine that your parents sold her in their ghetto grocery store. A very touching story. People in the audience had tears in their eyes."

"Certainly, this is not happening," Maxwell croaked.

"What rings my chimes is, where did she get five grand? We should plan to visit that store fairly soon. Perhaps your worst fears have come to pass."

Supelak, emboldened by his presumption of Lieutenant Carney's subvention in the Discovery Foods surveillance, glided down Central Avenue, again searching for Pounder, his prime stoolie. He shined his light at all the empty storefronts until he spotted Pounder, propped up against the wall, sipping Wild Irish Rose. He parked his unmarked cruiser and walked slowly toward Pounder. "Where the hell have you been, boy?" he asked, in his most intimidating tone of voice. "You been hiding from me? You're supposed to be watching the store for me."

"Been in the shelter, getting' cleaned up. I'm back watchin' now. For sure." Supelak squatted down trying to duplicate Pounder's point of view as he looked at Discovery Foods. "Can you make out that nigger Luther at the register at night?"

"Yeh, when it's real dark I can see into the store," Pounder said, anxious to provide useful information to Supelak, lest he be pistol whipped again.

"Can you make out his hands—can you see what's in his hands when he's doing a sale at the register?"

"No sir, detective. Too far away for that." Supelak peered at the store for a long time, then he shoved Pounder and told him to find another location for the night. The frightened, confused Pounder gathered up his belongings and ambled away, not knowing what to expect next from the agitated cop. Supelak moved the cruiser down the block, out of sight of the grocery store. Then he slowly walked back to the storefront, carrying a small pair of high-powered binoculars and a canvas campstool. He opened the folded stool and sat down, focusing the binoculars on the cash register in the store. He grunted in satisfaction; he could clearly observe the area around the register. He waited patiently for Luther to walk into the frame while waiting on a white customer. What would Luther do with his hands? What kind of money changed hands? It had to be hundreds of dollars. "Please, God," he prayed, "let there be packets of cocaine for me to see." He thought his prayers had been answered when a red sports roadster pulled up in front of the store. It was Ann Rudmann, a smartly tailored, thirtyish woman. She got out of her car and walked directly into the store. She talked briefly with Luther who walked to the wine rack and selected a bottle for her, which he placed on the counter. She picked up the bottle and read the label, then she walked out of the frame when she went to the meat counter and selected two steaks. Supelak could see both of them clearly. It was time for money to change hands. The woman reached into her purse and withdrew money. She placed it on the counter covered by her hand, and she slid her hand to Luther who quickly took the bills from under her hand with the deftness of a magician, and deposited them in the register. "Shit," Supelak, muttered. He was unable to see the money. The wrapping paper was on the counter. Luther wrapped the wine bottle and placed it in a paper bag. Then he placed the two steaks on the wrapping paper and, lightning fast, reached under the counter and placed something on the steaks before wrapping them up and placing them in the bag. "Sonofabitch." Supelak hissed, he never saw any packets of cocaine. Luther's hand had covered them. But he did see Luther reach under the counter and then place his hand on the steaks before he wrapped them. That's where he put the packets, Supelak was positive. He became excited and quickly lost control of his actions. He would make a bust and nail that smart ass Luther. He saw the woman pick up the bag and turn to exit the store. He jumped to his feet and rushed across the street, bursting out of the darkness like a madman. Ann Rudmann screamed, as she looked arourd for help. Supelak quickly produced his badge. "Police officer, lady. Please remain right where you are."

"What the hell do you think you're doing?" Ann's fright quickly turned to anger.

"I need to ask you a few questions."

"A few questions? You lunatic, you scared me to death running at me out of the darkness."

"I didn't mean to frighten you." He reached out to touch her grocery bag, which she withdrew from him. "What do you have in the bag?" he demanded.

"None of your goddam business."

"Now look, lady—"

"No, you look, officer. I'm Ann Rudmann and I'm an attorney."

"Answer my question," Supelak commanded, in a tone of voice that further exacerbated the situation.

"Look, I'm with Mooney and Moskowitz. Go on," she threatened, "just touch that bag again and we'll have your badge, your pension and your ass. Do you understand the consequences of an illegal search?"

"This ain't illegal. I have reason to believe you have drugs in your possession.

"You need more than that, Captain Midnight, to stop and search nonthreatening people."

"Don't tell me my job, lady."

"You're in the fifth district, right?"

"That is not your concern."

"I am well-acquainted with your commanding officer, Matt Carney. I suggest you call him for guidance."

"Don't be throwing names around. I'm not impressed." But he was impressed and his face revealed the doubts that had crept in.

Ann Rudmann's eyes became flinty hard. She was quite sure of herself. "I'm going to get in my car now, and I strongly advise you not to intimidate me any further."

"Go on, get out of here. We'll be watching you, lady," said the defeated blunderer.

Ann Rudmann got on the phone as soon as she arrived home and got Carney at his residence. He was a paragon of comity as he graciously told Ann that he did not in the least object to receiving a call at home from an honored barrister. Ann asked what the story was on this cop, Supelak. Carney said that he had already received the report on the incident. Ann counseled that Carney had better reign Supelak in before he generated a major lawsuit. Carney laughed the threat off, and said that the reason Supelak stopped her was that he was watching Luther Hightree with binoculars, and he saw him put what looked like packets in a package that he wrapped for her. Ann scoffed contemptuously asking Carney if he really considered that probable cause. Carney pretended to share her view that it was a foolish stop. He forced a laugh as he told her that Supelak was a new narc detective, and that he just got carried away, because he was so sure they were selling coke at that Discovery Foods place. "We owe you an apology, Ann. Tell Dave Moskowitz not to get excited. We'll cool Supelak off, I promise."

The tenor of the conversation suddenly changed as Ann asked, "How's the family, Matt? You've got a kid in Saint Joe's, don't you?"

"Thanks for asking, Ann. Everybody's fine. You take care… uh, one quick question," he asked, ala Columbo, "now don't get mad…but why do you go down to Central Avenue to shop?"

Her answer was the default précis: "I don't know how they do it, but they've got really nice imported wines at terrific bargains. Worth driving down there for, really. And steaks! Great porterhouse steaks to die for at dynamite prices. Take your wife and go down there," she warbled.

Later she was on the phone with Luther: "I cooled off that Lieutenant Carney from the fifth district, but you've got to know that crazy narc dick has you under surveillance through binoculars. I saw them. Can you believe that?"

"He tried to search your grocery bag, didn't he?"

"You're lucky it was me. I scared the hell out of him."

"How do I keep him away?"

"He'll get the word from his lieutenant, but if you see him in front of the store, threaten to call Mooney and Moskowitz. You can use my name. And warn your customers. Tell them he can't legally search their packages."

"Thanks Miss R. Hope this won't scare you away."

"You ought to know that I don't scare easy. Just don't you get scared. As long as you're careful, you'll be okay."

"How was the stuff?" Luther asked.

"Heavenly. Really good stuff."

Luther's confidence was shaken. Things were getting hot—out of control. How long could he go on before his concept is picked apart. Was it time to take the money and run? And what about Gussie? He needed to lay things out for her so she doesn't get blindsided.

Carney reviewed the incident with Supelak and he was surprisingly patient. "Did you actually see Hightree put some packets in the package as he wrapped up the steaks?" Carney asked.

"No, I didn't actually see no packets that I could make out, but he definitely reached under the counter and then he put his hand on the steaks and wrapped, real fast so I couldn't make out what he had in his hand. But I know he had something in his hand—he definitely grabbed something under the counter. I'm positive."

"Okay, you're probably right. And you were smart not to have opened Rudmann's package if you weren't absolutely positive she was carryin'. They know you were looking into the store with those binocs. So they are going to be super careful now. Knock off the surveillance for a while. Let me hash this out for awhile and I'll tell you what I want you to do next."

"Right, skipper."

As he turned to leave the office Carney said, "And Pete... you did good staying with this thing. Being a stubborn bohunk isn't such a bad thing after all." Supelak's feet never touched the ground as he floated out of Carney's office on a cloud.

Lieutenant Carney arrived at Discovery Foods first thing in the morning. As he walked in he spotted Luther at the wine rack. Gussie and Lindy were arranging produce at the back section. "Good morning, Missus Steinberg—Lieutenant Carney," he shouted.

"And you're Mister Hightree, right?" as he extended his hand to Luther. "Had a little dust-up last night, I understand. Would you like to tell me exactly what occurred?" Carney said as he learned against the counter, totally relaxed and pleasant. Gussie walked over to join the conversation.

"Let me tell you about your officer Supelak before we go any further. He's been a pest in this neighborhood for twenty years at least.  For no reason at all he would strut into the store and help himself to soda, to pastry, to a beer—just like he was entitled.  Now he's scaring our customers.  You promised me like a gentleman, when I came to your office that you would control him.  So where is the control?"

"I'm not happy about his bad behavior in your store. He had no business helping himself to your merchandise without paying. He should have been reported. But what happened last night is understandable, if you'll just hear me out. Officer Supelak is now a narcotics detective and he's been doing a nice job keeping those pushers off the streets down here.  So when he noticed all that activity at night—nonresidents dressed like they are out for an evening's entertainment coming and going,  it naturally aroused his interest.

And this activity has been going on for over a year now, so naturally he became suspicious. I'm sure you can understand his position," Carney crooned.

"Well his suspicions are crazy, just like him. We're running a legitimate business here and people travel here from all over the city because nobody can beat our prices. Should we be persecuted just because we're successful business people?" Gussie argued.

"Absolutely not, Missus. Absolutely not! " Luther had remained silent during Gussie's oration. Carney's submissive posture gave him an opening.

"You may be wondering what my role here is. Me, being a black man.  I was raised here by the Steinbergs.  They took me in when my mother died and treated me like a son.  I am not a drug pusher or anything like that. I've held legitimate jobs and I can give you references.  But after Mister Steinberg died I brought my know-how in high-end food merchandising to my mother—Missus Steinberg, and we invested all our savings in refurbishing this store and making it a destination for fine food buyers. We're working day and night to make a go of it.  This store is our life and we'd like to be left alone to make a living here."

"I wish you the best, Mister Hightree.  Call me if there are anymore problems. I'll keep an eye on the situation." When Carney left, Gussie and Luther exchanged knowing looks; they had given it their best shot and they felt they had presented a credible story to the head cop and that he was sold. They were wrong.

Luther called Ann Rudmann and after apologizing gratuitously for disturbing her at the office, he asked if the police could come in and search the store. She explained the fine points of probable cause and said they would have to get a search warrant, probably from Judge Kaufman. If they tried that, she said, her office would know about it. "We are very close to Judge Kaufman. Not to worry; they are not going to search the store."

Luther and Gussie hoped that everything was under control for the moment; but Lindy's street instincts told her otherwise. "He was just so honkie polite. Cops don't talk like that unless they're fixin' to mess with you," Lindy said.

"Yeh, you're right, babe. He smells something but he's watching his ass—trying to do everything by the book."

"So what's going to happen?" Gussie asked.

"They've got nothing yet, Gus. But they know something's going on. It's getting touchy, Gus; I've got to be honest with you.

"They can't come into the store and watch you work, can they?"

"Nope. Not without a search warrant and we'll get tipped off if that happens."

"And they can't search customers."

"No. You saw what happened last night."

"So?" Gussie said, defiantly.

"So it's getting riskier. You need this headache, Gus? Maybe we call it quits and bug out of here.

"Luther darling…I don't think I want to bug."

"Can you live with all this heat?" Luther asked.

"I've got a beautiful store and customers who respect me. And we're all making money. That I can live with. What have I got to lose? A nursing home?"

"Let's roll the dice, Gussie old girl."

They rolled the dice and the money rolled in. The Ann Rudmann episode had no legs in the user community; they continued to frequent Discovery Foods with bold impunity. Gussie had made her commitment; she knew exactly what she wanted from life. But Luther didn't. Who was he, really? He called Gussie "Mama" when the situation warranted such a locution, but in his heart he knew it was a device, a mechanism to give him an anchor. But it was, in reality, nothing but a simulacrum of a life. What lay ahead? An island in the Caribbean with this Creole girl who meant nothing to him? What had he done with his life? A bartender at Club Valencia? — a cocaine dealer at the country club? He had meant something to Sol when they went to the food terminal together in the middle of the night, when Sol was his mentor preparing him for something that neither of them could define. Wasn't he a person then? But he ran from Sol and Gussie so that part of his life had no meaning for Luther Highstree. And what did this clever scheme that he had devised really mean? It would end soon and Discovery Foods would disappear like smoke; like Anna Mae's life. His life was a solipsistic existence—everything was Luther. There was no room for anyone else.

Doctor Michaelson parked directly in front of the store, and as he started in another car pulled up behind his car. Michaelson and Luther greeted each other; apparently the good doctor had something on his mind. He was embarrassed by the behavior of his wife the night she came in swigging from a bottle of champagne; the night that the car driven by Alderman Frank Brennan was stopped by the police. The doctor has passed out and was unaware of this wife's behavior. Everyone in the group that night had been drinking heavily. Luther, as model of punctiliousness, suggested that the doctor and his wife perhaps should come to the store during daylight hours; the police were watching the store closely at night. Luther assumed they were more apt to be sober during the day and less apt to bring attention to the operation.

Doctor Michaelson glanced outside and saw officer Supelak, foot on the bumper, apparently writing down the license number of his car. "Looks like they're watching things during the day also; that cop is writing down my license number." Luther lost his cool and rushed outside to confront Supelak. He did not notice the woman who had parked behind the doctor; she was an interested bystander to the confrontation.

"What the hell are you doing now, Supelak?" Luther barked.

"Just what my Lieutenant told me to do. And you watch how you speak to police officers. I'm jotting down license numbers of suspicious cars."

`"Suspicious cars?" Luther was outraged. "This car belongs to a doctor—one of my best customers. You got him all upset."

"I don't care if it's the Popemobile…I got a right to record license numbers," cocky Supelak replied.

"But you don't have the right to scare my customers away."

"What are they scared of? If they're within the law, they got nothing to worry about."

"What about my car?" the woman bystander joshed, a slight grin on her face. Supelak ignored her; he could see that she was driving a rental car.

"He's just here hasslin' me, that's all he's doing," Luther said.

"Just doin' my job," Supelak muttered, superciliously, hatefully.

"Well, I must admit, it is somewhat frightening to find a police officer recording you license number with no explanation," Doctor Michaelson said.

"Just doin' my job." Luther would have liked to choke him.

"Don't give it a thought, doc. This guy's an idiot. He's just trying to scare people away. When I call his boss, they'll chew his ass out." Doctor Michaelson shook hands with Luther and drove away. Luther, still fuming, went back into the store. Gussie had never seen the attractive lady with the streaked blond hair before, but she was glad that she was a daytime customer and that she was not high or anything. Luther didn't know what to make of her; she was not one of his regulars from the country club. He took a stab at it. "Can I be of service to you, ma'am?" he asked, observing her carefully. Could she be a plant—and undercover agent? Her answer shook him.

"I'm looking for the boss lady of this establishment," she said. Her accent was unusual; she was not from around here, Luther surmised.

"What do you want with the boss lady? Are you selling something?" he asked.

Gussie approached the woman. "Can I help you? I'm Missus Steinberg." A smile crossed the woman's face and she held out her hand to Gussie. "So am I," she said.

"So you are what?" Gussie thought the broad was maybe a little screwy.

"I'm Missus Steinberg, also."

"You're Missus Steinberg? What a coincidence," Gussie said, humoring the blond. "Funny, you don't look like a Steinberg." Gussie said. "Who are you, really?" Gussie smelled a rat. Could she be a cop?

"I'm your daughter-in-law. I'm Kitty Stonehill, of the Stonehills that were formerly Steinbergs."

"Oh, my God," Gussie wailed as she ran to Kitty and embraced her, rocking her back on her heels. "Is Maxie here, too?"

"Nope. This is a solo visit. Maxie knows I'm here and he is having a nervous breakdown—not a serious one, just one of his regular, minor breakdowns. I am so glad to meet you at last, Missus Steinberg."

"Gussie, please."

"Okay. Gussie it is. And this handsome dude, I take it, is Mister Luther Hightree."

"That is correct," Luther replied, taking in the blond with obvious approval. "Maxie sure lucked out this time."

"No offense, Luther, but I need to talk with Gussie privately," Kitty said.

"No offense taken. I'll get Lindy to help me while you're upstairs, Gus."

"Lindy is his lady," Gussie explained. as she led Kitty to the upstairs apartment.

Kitty dispensed with the niceties and dropped the hammer. "This place is a time bomb ticking away and ready to explode. That smart aleck Luther thinks he's outsmarted the police and has a foolproof scam going here. The cops are taking license numbers and they'll start leaning on your customers who will most certainly spill their guts and get you five to seven in the penitentiary."

"Whoa, whoa, whoa!" Gussie pleaded, "take a breath, Kitty. You're jumping to conclusions."

"He is an arrogant jackanapes, nothing more." Kitty had taken an instant, visceral dislike to Luther.

"A what? A jackanapes?"

"My father's favorite word for impudent wise guys. You raised him like a son, I understand. Well, he's going to pay you back by getting you busted. Poor Maxwell! He was so right."

"You don't give us a chance to get acquainted…to have a cup of tea or something and already you're sending me to jail."

"Get rid of that guy. Out! And all his drugs with him. You've got a beautiful store. If you insist on running a business down here in the central city, sell food, not cocaine or whatever he's peddling."

"Alright, darling. If you're so sure we're selling drugs I'll make sure he stops. I don't want trouble."

"Gussie, don't talk to me as if I were a child. I am deadly serious. Sure I want to sit with you and have a cup of tea and get acquainted. I've got so much to tell you, but I can't think about anything else but that cop taking license numbers and that doctor scared shitless. Is that the way you want to live? Playing cat and mouse with the police? Trust me, the cops always win!"

"I am so happy that Maxie found a girl like you. You're beautiful but you're also strong and you'll keep Maxie from acting *meshuga*".

"I'm also pregnant and I know it's going to be a boy, and we'll name him Solomon Mackenzie Steinberg. They'll call him Sol, just like your Sol. And we will have a regulation *bris* with a *moel* and the works. But first, you can't go to the slammer."

Gussie was in tears and through her sobs she managed to get a word in edgewise: "Kitty, God bless you, you make me so happy I can't talk. But you're the fastest talker I've ever met. When are you due? You'll name him Sol? You're an angel. You're not Jewish are you? Where did learn from *bris* and moel? Kitty, you make me crazy! You're a whirlwind."

"What about Luther and the cocaine, Gussie? It's got to stop."Gussie's face changed. The tears and sobbing stopped. She had to be honest with this remarkable girl.

"He's ready to stop. His lady, Lindy, wants to go to an island. He'll be gone soon. And God willing, nothing will happen in the meantime. And we'll have a cup of tea and talk about the moel. The Randazzos fainted when the moel worked on Maxie."

"The Randazzos?"

"When things quiet down, I'll tell you the whole story. Go home now, and stop worrying. I'll be out of the cocaine business the next time I see you, I promise. What are you, Irish?

"I'm not sure. English and Scottish, I think."

"A nice mixture."

Luther was waiting for Kitty as she exited the store. "How about a nice *Monreshay* he asked, trying his best to give Montrechet a perfect French inflection.

Kitty stared him down for a moment, then said, "Nice try. Close, but not quite there. Soften the T and roll the R more."

Gussie's head was bursting with countervailing scenarios for her future, but before she could calmly evaluate her options she had to chew Lieutenant Carney's ass out.

"You gave me your card so I guess it's alright to call you. So I'm calling you," Gussie said when she got Carney on the phone. He was not at all happy to hear from her, but he was an avatar of civility. "Problem, Missus Steinberg?" Carney asked.

"You ordered that maniac Supelak to write down license numbers, right?"

"I beg your pardon," he temporized, caught completely off-guard.

"Right in front of the store…he puts his foot on the bumper and writes down the number. A good customer—a doctor. What new kind of *mishigas* is this?" she demanded.

"A what?"

"A *mishigas*—a craziness."

174

"It's not a mishigas as you call it, Missus Steinberg. It's perfectly legal."

"Legal-shmegal, is it necessary to scare away my customers?"

"Detective Supelak was instructed to record license number of any unusual vehicles."

"Doctor Michaelson is your idea of unusual? To me it looks like harassment."

"It is certainly not our intention to drive away legitimate customers."

"Well, your good intentions frightened Doctor Michaelson. Get some new intentions.

"Missus Steinberg, in the future detective Supelak will park his car severals doors away from your store and he will remain in his vehicle."

"Wonderful. That's really wonderful, lieutenant. Can you tell me why you must take down license numbers?"

"No, I cannot. Police business. Is there anything else I can do for you?"

"Yes. Take your police business and—never mind." She slammed down the receiver.

Gussie wanted to distance herself from everyone; Luther, Carney, Supelak, Kitty, Maxwell, et al. Her head was cluttered. So, despite the ingrained, girlish embarrassment she felt by calling Abe Zellman for a date, she did, indeed, call Abe and asked to be taken out to dinner. Abe immediately started scrubbing his oil blackened fingernails and demanding that the drycleaner press his suit, then and there. Abe had concluded that Gussie was beyond a decent mourning period for Sol and that she needed to be with a man; a healthy man that still had some lead in his pencil, as the saying goes. Why shouldn't they get married? They were a perfect match. Same background. Same *mama-loshen..* And he was going to tell her that she should stop doing whatever it was she was doing with that smooth black guy before she got busted. If she needed money, Abe could support her in style. He was making a good buck with his collision service. He planned to tell her all these things.

They made a striking couple; mature, yes, but handsome, healthy, full of life juices. No rib joint this time; Abe took her uptown to Maison Henri, a white tablecloth French restaurant. They both remembered enough of their high-school French to navigate the menu with a degree of *sangfroid,* shocking the haughty waiter out of his French phlegm. Gussie had acquainted herself with esoteric wines at the store and she suggested a very elegant Bordeaux that duly impressed the wine steward. The evening was a success and Abe was planning to bring up the subject of marriage but he first wanted to dispose of the subject of Gussie's questionable activities at the store. Unfortunately, that was the last thing Gussie wanted to discuss. She changed the subject and suggested that they go to her apartment for a nightcap and maybe some coffee and her famous homemade Czech strudel. Abe was no amateur in these matters and he knew he was going to get laid. He delivered a bravura performance in Gussie's bedroom and for the moment Gussie forgot about the decisions she had to make. The subject of marriage was put on hold for the nonce.

The next morning, Luther exchanged knowing looks with Gussie, and for the moment she reveled in the dewy freshness of everything she would be presenting to her customers; the delicately greenish-white scallions, the burly collards and the faintly purple turnips. If only this could go on forever; if only there was no price to pay for the happiness that the store brought her. Reality burst the bubble of tranquility when an undercover cop tried to outwit Luther. Luther made him instantly; the cheap suit and the scuffed-up shoes. With a pitiful attempt at nonchalance he said "Gimme' three of those strip steaks, about fourteen ounces each." Luther complied, laying the steaks on the wrapping paper as he usually did with his coke customers. He looked the cop straight in the eyes, saying nothing, waiting for the cop's next move. The cop was hoping for an overt move by Luther that would produce packets of coke. This was the MO Supelak had coached the cop to expect. When Luther did nothing, the cop was discomfited and at a loss of what to do next. Finally, he asked, "What kind of wine you got?" Totally awkward and a dead giveaway. "What kind do you wish, sir?" Luther was playing him like a fish.

"Lemme' see that one over there," he said pointing.

"The pinot noir or the Bordeaux." The names threw the poor cop.

In desperation he said, "The white, the white."

"Ah! A lover of the white Burgandies. A man of taste willing to pay eighty dollars for an exquisite Montrachet."

The cop blanched. "How much for the red?"

"The pinot noir is a good value at thirty-nine dollars." Do you wish to switch?"

"Yeh, the red will go better with the steaks, won't it?"

"Actually, maybe something with more body like a cabernet would work better with the steaks."

"Yeh, let's do that." Luther took the bottle from the shelf and placed in on the counter next to the steaks. And he stood there, waiting; smiling at the cop who desperately wanted Luther to reach under the counter for packets of coke.

"Will there be anything else, sir?" The cop tried to bluff his way to a showdown.

"You know what's next. Gimme' three."

"Three what, sir?"

"Goddamit Luther, quit fucking with that cop," Lindy muttered to Gussie. "Quit playin' games with me. You know what I'm saying," the cop spat.

"Do I know you? Have you shopped here before?"

"You remember me, I came with Doctor,,," he snapped his fingers as though the name has temporarily escaped him.

"Nice suit you're wearing. Armani?" Luther teased.

The cop's eyes turned black and his face curled with rage; he knew he had been made from the get-go. He brushed the steaks off the counter with a sweep of his beefy arm and stalked out. Luther turned to his audience, expecting applause for his virtuoso humiliation of the cop. Instead, Lindy was weeping with anger. "You're crazy, ain't you, man? Just silly-ass, little-boy crazy," Lindy raged.

177

"Hey, I made him as soon as he walked in with those clodhopper shoes," Luther bragged.

"So did I, but you don't see me playin' games with cops. We gotta blow this place. And I mean soon. They're wise to us, man. I'm getting nervous. Let's get out of here."

"Soon, baby. Soon." Gussie had taken in the entire scene; and she was overcome with sadness at the thought that everything would soon be coming to an end. She was not ready for things to end. Everything smelled so nice and fresh this morning.

For those who had read the *Legend of Sleepy Hollow,* Martin O'Donnell would have reminded them of Ichabod Crane. He was tall, stoop shouldered, stringy and of gentle mien. He was a product of Catholic school education and the Duquesne school of law and he had a deep, abiding love of the Jesuits. He was in his second term as the elected county prosecutor and was very well liked by his colleagues, the police and even skuzzy defense lawyers of the Dave Moskowitz ilk. He was a boy scout at heart; he really wanted to send the bad guys to jail.

He sat commiserating with Lieutenant Carney over their failure to convince Judge Morton Kaufman that they had established probable cause and that they should be granted a search warrant for Discovery Foods. "What the hell is it going to take to convince Kaufman," Carney said.

"Matt, I want to nail that guy—that Luther whatever his name is. He's making a fool of us and it sticks in my craw. But we're going to need an actual transaction, a confession. Hard evidence. That officer you sent in to make a buy was ill-prepared, Matt. You can't blame him; he did the best he could. You need to find someone from the cadre of Luther's typical buyers and send him in to make a buy. But you've got to drill him thoroughly."

"The bastard is too slick. We'll never put one by him."

"He'll make a mistake; they all do, Matt. Just be patient, you'll get him. And I'll put him away for a long, long time. I don't want to be an underpaid prosecutor all my life."

"Got your cap set for governor, eh Marty?"

"It's possible, Matt.

Lieutenant Carney and detective Supelak sat, pouring over the printout of the license plate numbers they had run through the record bureau. Carney had taken to speaking respectfully to Supelak, who could hardly believe that he was no longer a moron or an idiot. "You did a good job reading those license plates...just laying back and avoiding contact with the drivers. See...when you use your head, you get results without creating a jackpot," Carney intoned. "When we started running these plates I could hardly believe my eyes. Just look at this—money people. Doctors, dentists, advertising executives. Here's a bank president. Christ, I hope he's not handling our pension fund." A perfunctory snicker by Supelak. The boss had made a funny. "And look here, that bitch lawyer that gave you so much shit." Ann Rudmann was on the list.

"How did a punk like Hightree get a client list like this?"

"He's smart, Pete. He goes for well-known, respectable players; people that have to be discreet because they've got a lot to lose if they're involved in a public scandal. Nobody's going to shoot off their mouth."

"But where does he find them?"

"My guess...these people all have something in common; a club, an organization, a certain neighborhood or subdivision. Keep tracing those license plates. I've got a feeling  they're all from the same cut of cloth.

Business was slow; the night action had dried up, and the day-light customers were being scared away once it became common knowledge that their license plates were being recorded. By ac-cident, Carney had found a method for  defeating Luther's co-caine trade.  Still, there had been no arrests; Luther Hightree had won the game; he was still at large and would soon devise another method for pushing the powder.

Supelak, basking in the glory of his newfound cachet as a non-idiot, decided to ride as a passenger in Siwinski's cruiser making rounds in the Central Avenue area near  Discovery Foods. A con-catenation of events would strip him of his cachet.  Ann Rudmann had dashed into Discovery Foods in the early evening and emerged with a package that Supelak was positive contained packets of co-caine. He asked Siwinski to tail her car, for reasons that were not yet clear to him. Rudmann pulled into the driveway of what ap-parently was her home and rushed inside.  The lights went on and music blared. Cars began arriving and people poured into the house. A party was in progress and the excitement, Supelak surmised, was fueled by the cocaine Rudmann had purchased at the store. It was a brilliant piece of detective work and Supelak could hardly contain himself. He needed to report this event to his lieutenant, who, upon hearing the report, nearly wet his trousers. "Did anyone see you there? Did Rudmann know you had tailed her?" he shrieked. Supelak was sure he had not been seen. But of course, he was wrong. Several of Rudmann's guests had spotted Siwinski's cruiser, idling at the curb, with parking lights on. What's a police cruiser doing in front of Rudmann's house?

The Barristers Pub was a hangout for lawyers, cops, bail bondsmen, and hangers-on, all of whom were flattering each other and bragging about their courtroom exploits. Lieutenant Matt Carney, pale with dark circles under his eyes, was seated at a table with Dave Moskowitz, Art Mooney, Martin O'Donnell, and a big-belly cop. Ann Rudmann blasted through a standing group of drinkers, spewing booze everywhere on her dash to the table.

"You dirty, lying, two-faced Irish bum, you! How dare you put a tail on me!" The joint was suddenly quiet and all eyes were on Carney.

"Watch how you talk to a police officer, young lady." Someone snickered and Carney reddened. "Ann, please calm down and let me tell you. what happened. Sit down, please. Order her a drink, Dave, please."

"What the hell is going on? You're tailing Ann? What the hell for? She's a lawyer—an officer of the court. And you're tailing her?" Moskowitz ranted.

"It was a mistake by an overzealous officer. Ann's had trouble with him before. They're observing every car that visits that store on Central Avenue."

"What store on Central Avenue? What are you talking about?" Moskowitz's veins were popping.

"A store that's under surveillance as a drug source."

"So now you're calling me a junkie?" Ann hissed.

"Ann, absolutely not. Supelak just—"

"—Just what? What did she do that justifies humiliating her like this?" Dave shouted ominously. Carney was angered now and he had regained his composure.

"What in the hell is she doing down in the heart of the ghetto at night? That's a piss poor time to be shopping for groceries!"

"That's your basis for putting a tail on me?" Ann said.

"It was poor judgment by an officer who makes poor judgments, I'm sorry it happened, but you can understand why we're watching people who visit that store at night."

"Matt, I am sorry, but I do not understand why you would put a tail on someone like Ann Rudmann," Mooney said.

"If was a mistake. A fucking mistake in judgment by an over-reacting officer, alright?"

"Don't make any more mistakes where Ann is concerned," Moskowitz warned.

"Don't threaten me, Dave." Carney had had enough.

Luther received a call from the obviously agitated Ann Rudmann. The cops have gone crazy in their attempts to get a search warrant, she said. They have gone to extremes—they actually tailed me to my home after I had been to the store. The best thing to do is to shut down the operation until the heat is off and the cops find something else to focus on. I will tell your customers at the club to stay away. Take a vacation and rest up. Let us know when you are back in town and that you are back in action, if that's what you decide to do."

It was decision time….Luther would once again deracinate himself from an environment he had come to love. He had dreaded the conversation he would have with Gussie. He had gone over the words he would use during the many sleepless nights when he was tormented by the thoughts of what would happen to Gussie when he would once again leave her.

He had carefully planned the mechanics of the separation. Luther made a deal with Blue, who had agreed to take Luther's stash and give him credit for it. Luther had not wanted to carry the stash across state lines and he had faith that Blue would give him a start-up stash of like value, if and when he returned. The head chef at the country club who had guided Luther in selecting suppliers for the prime meats and seafood, would  purchase the inventory from the store at a discounted price, including the gourmet soups, cheeses and olives. The funds would go to Gussie. But would she have a desire to continue operating  the store? Would she have the psychic energy to restock to store and totally commit to serving the black community?  Could she continue to offer prime grade produce, meats and fish at the present price levels? Could she survive on the tiny mark-ups?  Who would help buy and stock the merchandise?  How old is Gussie now—sixty-two?  Could she manage to be on her feet for twelve hours a day?  Would that selfish Maxie finally man-up and act like a real son?  No way could Gussie operate the store alone. Who would help her?

Lindy had done her share of planning, also. Luther eschewed Lindy's jejune day- dreams of a paradisiacal life in the Caribbean. The money they had accumulated  from the cocaine operation, while substantial, would not last them a lifetime. Luther would have to get back in action at some point. Lindy had decided that they should buy a condo on Grace Bay in the Turks. The secluded, endless white sand beaches and chic restaurants and shops had completely captivated her. "Fine," Luther agreed, "the Turks are fine. I've got other things on my mind…things I've got to take care of before we can leave." There were times when Lindy got on his nerves and he envisioned  the annoyances that would  be part of the package of his uxorial  duties, should he decide on a permanent union with Lindy. Then he would revisit all that they had been through together…her willingness to exchange her Saks Fifth Avenue party dresses and the all- night raves for working jeans, for the endless hours on her feet as a grocery clerk, dealing with vagaries of serving poor black customers. Lindy had paid her dues; she was entitled to the Turks and she had earned Luther's love and devotion. They would soon be leaving the Central Avenue ghetto for the white sands of Grace Bay.

Luther closed at nine o'clock and went upstairs to the apartment and knocked on the door. Gussie opened the door and sat down at the kitchen table which was set with coffee and strudel without saying a word. Luther sat, knowing that an emotional scene awaited him.

"So," she said as she poured the coffee, "when are you leaving?"

"Well, let's talk about that, Mom. Lot's of arrangements have to be made."

"So, arrange."

"I think you ought to put the store up for sale, and find a nice little place down in Florida and take life easy for a change."

"Florida? That's where old Jews go to die. I'm not ready yet."

"You want to keep running the store?

"Who else is going to do it? Sol's gone and you're leaving. That leaves Gussie Steinberg, proprietor."

"And who else, Mom?

`"Stop with the 'mom,' already. That's always a sign you're going to give me grief." She cut him a piece of strudel and put it on his plate "I'm not helpless, I'll find someone I can rely and Sol's store will go on." She took a sip of coffee and said, pointedly, "Without cops."

"You know the suppliers? The guys that deliver at five a.m. want me to call them?"

"What am I, blind? Feldman is produce, Schulte the Nazi is meat, and Dupree of the Sea is fish. And I'll *hundle* the prices if they get cute."

"You got to be okay with money. But if you keep your prices where they are, your margins are going to be tight. You may be working for almost nothing."

"If I make a few pennies it will be enough. I love this store, Luther. I'll be grateful for what you did. You've got a good head on your shoulders. Too bad you use it to sell cocaine. Maybe now you can find something else to do."

"Mom, I'm the one who will always be grateful for everything you and Sol have done for me. And my mama, wherever she is, is so proud to have the rec center named after her. God bless you for that, Gus."

"There's no more fancy sales? You're through with the powder? Please go before they find a way to arrest us." And she cried.

Luther got up to comfort her. "Will I ever see you again? Will Lindy be with you permanently?"

"Mom, and that's a no-bullshit 'mom,' I swear I'll be back when things cool down and after Lindy gets a belly full of laying on the beach. But you've got to promise to stay well and pretty until I get back."

"If it's less than ten years time, maybe I'll be here." They embraced and they both wept softly.

There was one last instruction Luther had for Gussie; he wanted Supelak to pay for the terrible abuse he had heaped on poor, child-like Pounder. He told Gussie to call Willa Simon and for them, together, to go and talk to Reverend Amos Graylock and tell him everything that Supelak had done to Pounder; the pistol-whipping, the gun jammed in Pounder's mouth, the bullying and constant kicking and tormenting as Pounder slept in the doorways. Tell him about the lumps and bruises on Pounder's face. Ask the Reverend to take Pounder and Willa and a few other black women as a witnesses, and tell the entire story to Lieutenant Carney. "Remind the Reverend that the cops are very worried about charges of brutality to us black folks," he said, grinning wickedly.

Reverend Graylock, ordinarily a gentle and kindly man became enraged when Pounder, Willa, and other women who had witnessed Pounder's bruised face, recounted the story of Supelak's sadism. When he had called Lieutenant Carney for an appointment, Carney became tense and concerned. "What is the nature of your problem, sir?" Carney asked, nervously.

"Police brutality," was Reverend Graylock's devastatingly succinct reply.

"Could you be a little more specific, Reverend?" Carney asked, his voice quavering.

"You have an officer, his name is Siplak or something like that?"

"Did you mean, Supelak?" Carney said, he anger rising at the mere mention of the name.

"Yes, Supelak, that's it. He is an animal, Lieutenant. I will give you details when we see you." An appointment was immediately set and Supelak was summarily called to Carney's office.

Reverend Graylock along with Willa Simon, Vera Deering, Pounder and several other women who had witnessed Pounder's suffering, descended on Carney's office and confronted the cowed poltroon that had once been the swaggering bully named Supelak. When the evidence was presented to Carney he went into a vertiginous rage and immediately announced that Supelak would go up for review and would probably be discharged. Pounder breathed a sigh of relief; he did not want Supelak looking for him at night, ever again.

Kitty could hardly believe her ears, it was Gussie at the other end of the line. Kitty asked how she had gotten their number. "You heard of information?" Gussie answered. A long-distance call from Gussie was totally unexpected, but there she was, sounding strong and happy. The news was good; Luther's business was over, he was gone. The cops had stopped watching the store and the porterhouse steaks and extra large scampies had been replaced by pork shoulder, spareribs and nice, fresh fish. Gussie had enlisted Angie, who gave her a few hours a day. Gussie wanted to put Kitty's mind at ease; the drug business was a thing of the past. Kitty wanted to ask if Gussie had ever considered retiring, selling the store, or just closing up. But she did not want to endanger their inchoate relationship by being too forward. So she simply asked if business was good. Business was good, Gussie said. Then Kitty told her that she had had a miscarriage but that they would keep trying. They really wanted kids. Gussie was saddened by the news but she agreed that they should not give up. Maxie was doing fine, and the news of Luther's departure would eliminate his outbursts of temper and facial tics. The more they talked, the more comfortable they felt with each other and the call went on and on, a vagrant prattle of small revelations and confidences. Then Kitty said something quite surprising; she said that Maxie should some day face up to who he is and from whence he had come. "The Midwest is sort of a nice 'even' place; not high-powered and hysterical like the East Coast," she said. Gussie was pleased but she did not respond; she simply told Kitty that she would keep in touch. When the call ended, Gussie had come to realize that Kitty was indeed, a very unusual young woman.

Abe Zellman had rather enjoyed the look he had achieved when he had taken Gussie to dinner at the fancy French restaurant; he had scrubbed his oily, black fingernails until they were pink-white and he had gotten a blow-dry haircut with the result that he emerged as quite a good-looking dude. He enjoyed putting on a lightly starched white shirt and his cashmere sport coat. Truth be known, Abe was getting tired of the greasy coveralls and the rusty junkers he patched together for the folks in the neighborhood. Sure, the gas station and the collision repair garage had made him a very good living, but what the hell, he was set financially. He had worked hard all of his life and he was ready for a change. He would put the station up for sale and see what kind of offers he got. If he could get a decent price for the station, he would be out of there.

Gussie had called Abe and had invited him over for Friday night dinner; soup, stuffed cabbage and her special strudel for dessert. When Gussie told Abe that Luther had departed and that the "goofy" stuff was over, a light went on in Abe's head. Was Gussie going to keep the store open? Who would help her? He decided to wait and see if he got any offers for the station. If he could unload the station, maybe he would approach Gussie with a suggestion. He decided to drop a few hints. He brought up the subject of their backgrounds; where had Gussie's folk emigrated from? Czechoslovakia? Abe's family had come from the Ukraine where they had a small farm, he told Gussie. They settled in New Jersey where they became truck farmers, growing the famous Jersey tomatoes, cucumbers, celery, eggplant, squash, onions, parsley and sweet corn which they trucked to market throughout New Jersey. Abe decided to strike out on his own and eventually enrolled in a trade school where he learned auto mechanics. Abe worked for several auto repair garages and finally was able to open his own, small shop. His business grew over the years and he eventually decided to open a station in the ghetto where he knew there would be a steady demand for repair work and not a lot of competition. He talked about his days as a young truck famer and he made sure that Gussie was aware of his knowledge of all types of produce.

Abe didn't get a lot a action on the ad he had placed in the newspaper and he and his longtime assistant, Calvin Watson, discussed the situation. One afternoon, as they sat on a rickety little picnic table behind the garage eating their pulled pork sandwiches from Hickson's BBQ, Calvin began talking about all the years they had been together and how much he knew about the business. Damned if he couldn't run the place by himself. If he had the money, he said, he'd sure as hell buy the place. Abe picked up on where Calvin was going in the conversation. As he washed down the last of his pulled pork sandwich with his Orange Crush soda, Abe asked Calvin if he had any money in the bank. Calvin had put away a little over two thousand bucks over the years. They danced around the subject for quite awhile and finally Abe asked Calvin if he could put down the two thousand and pay off the rest at two hundred a month. Two hundred a month, every month without fail! Until the whole balance was paid off. Did Calvin honestly think he could do that? Calvin swore on his mother's grave that he could and that he would. And they solemnly shook hands on the deal. And Abe was no longer a grease monkey. It was time to have a conversation was Gussie Steinberg.

Gussie was dead tired when she closed up at seven o'clock on Saturday. Angie had been there as usual at five in the morning to let the vendors in and put away the stuff. But Angie had to leave at noon and Gussie ran around like a madwoman taking care of business on a busy Saturday. But Abe had said he had something very important he had to talk to her about so she made a pot of coffee and put out some pastry and waited, in her bare feet, for him to arrive. Those damn shoes had to come off. Well, he did have something quite important to discuss and they talked almost 'til daybreak. That crazy Abe Zellman had sold his business and he wanted to move in— to move in! And help Gussie run the store. Just like that! He wanted to move in and of course they would be living together. He couldn't run to the store every morning from his house, he said. He had to live there. At first Gussie thought he was kidding, then she was convinced he was crazy. But the man was serious. And Gussie had to make a life-changing decision. Abe was a very attractive man and God knows, she needed someone to help her. Another day like today would kill her, she was sure. But what was he saying? Move in—one, two, three-. Like the kids do today? Were we going to sleep together? Was this a marriage proposal? Sure, they had slept together that one night and it was quite successful. But this was every night! They would be living together, there was no other way of looking at it. Gussie had asked for more time and Abe said that she was a grown woman and that she could make a decision.

"We're not kids anymore," he said, "time is running out for both of us. You want to keep the store and have some kind of life? Decide tonight. Now! Starting Monday, I'll be the guy that meets the trucks at five in the morning. And you know I'm a *maven* when it comes to produce. And if we are happy together, of course we should get married. You want to die alone? Sol would approve of me. I'm the kind of guy that will look after a woman and take care of her and—"

"Abe, will you shut up, please?" Gussie got up and rooted through a drawer until she found an old pack of cigarettes. She lit up, puffing heavily as she stared at this man who quite possibly might be insane. "Abe, bring whatever stuff you want to keep and move in tomorrow. I'm closed on Sunday. And let me get a little sleep. You wore me out. You simply wore me out. My head is going round and round. Tell me the truth, are you a madman? I've never met anyone like you. Do you know how to use a modern cash register? Forget it. Just forget it. We'll talk about these things when my head stops spinning. Good night, Abe. Go pack your stuff."

Sol's clothes were still handing in the spare bedroom closet. She had been unable to dispose of them after Sol had died. But Abe would need the closet for his clothes. She heard Abe making room for his favorite lounge chair and a fin de siècle settee that would be an interesting addition to the living room. He also brought several nicely framed paintings and space was found for them in the various rooms. Abe was very efficient and the move went smoothly on that Sunday afternoon. Except for finding room for Abe's clothes. Abe suddenly became aware that Gussie had disappeared after they had successfully found available wall

space and hung Abe's paintings. He called her several times before he heard her in the spare bedroom. She was sitting on the
floor. Abe stood in the doorway as Gussie sat looking into a closet
full of Sol's clothes. "He's gone, Gussie. He's resting peacefully
somewhere and he won't be needing all these clothes. Why don't
you donate these clothes to that church down on Central Avenue.
I'll bet they'd love to have them," Abe said, his voice thoughtfully
soft.

"It'll be like I'm forgetting him forever," she said through her
sobs.

"Gussie, look at me. I know what you're feeling. But I've got
to tell you—I won't live with ghosts. You know what I'm saying?"
She wiped her eyes and nose with the sleeve of Sol's old sweater
that she always wore when she was doing heavy housework. "You're
right, Abe. We can't live with ghosts. Help me pack up the clothes
and we'll donate them to Reverend Graylock at the church."

At five o'clock the next morning, Gussie introduced Abe to the
drivers from Feldman Bros. and Shulte, the Nazi meat guy. Dupree of the Sea would not arrive until the end of the week. "You
going to keep that name, "Discovery Foods?" Abe asked.

"Sure, why not? It says 'Sol Steinberg Proprietor" underneath,
in nice gold letters." And a new era had begun at the Steinberg
Grocery on Central Avenue in the ghetto. Abe wondered if she
would ever change the sign and add his name along with hers.

"Who in the fuck is Abe Zellman?" Maxie screamed, when
Kitty had hung up the phone after her conversation with Gussie.

"I am going to put you back on Zoloft if you don't stop screaming," Kitty threatened. "He's probably going to be your stepfather
one of these days. Abe is an old friend and he has moved in with
your mom. She wants to keep the store open and Abe will be a
godsend for her. Besides, by today's standards, she's still a young
woman and she should not live alone. I. for one, am very happy for
her."

"You and my crazy mother have developed quite a thick relationship. Please keep me posted if the two of you have make any a
major decisions that will shatter my nerves. I am your father's key

litigator and I need peace and quiet in my own home in order to continue my brilliant career as a courtroom giant."

"Gussie and I would never think of shattering your nerves. How do you want your eggs, today?"

"I'm not hungry."

Lindy Blanc blended right in with the French tourists on their island in the Turks. And of course she needed a new, tropical wardrobe. She was going through their boodle of cash with alarming speed and Luther finally had to give her the word that she needed to slow up. This annoyed Lindy and she was cool to Luther for several days. She was no longer the cowed cocktail waitress who dared not annoy his majesty the maitre d'. She felt that she had Luther very much under control; that her seductive, pale-skinned Cajun beauty had him in her thrall. There were endless days on the beach and repetitive cocktail hours on the veranda where she had become a favorite amongst the French tourists longing to be au courant. The twee badinage annoyed Luther and a cloud of depression descended on him. He needed some action. He longed for his familiar stateside haunts and capers that would keep the cash rolling in. But he had to wait before he could once again assume the role of the welcome revenant . Things had gotten too hot at Discovery Foods for him to contemplate a reprise of his coke operation. He soon made contact with some louche Cubans who turned out to be heavy movers of cocaine from Colombia. They were a minatory group but they were more than happy to have a skilled operator able to move their product among the European tourists in the chic, new Caribbean resorts. Luther was perfect. He was far from those typical, wild man dealers swathed in gold chains with silk shirts open to the waist. With his good diction and smartly tailored tropical clothes he would never be mistaken for a character from the demimonde.

Lindy pouted when she learned that Luther was back in action; she did not want to lose her cachet as the wife of a wealthy American businessman among her new friends on the island. Luther left her with some cash and took a boat to Saint Martin, followed by a shadow, a guy names Carlos, that the Cuban mob had assigned to him. Carlos would stay in the background but he was there to make sure that the mob got their share of cash from Luther's sales. Saint Martin is divided into French and Dutch sections and both proved to be productive for Luther. Huge yachts from all over the world lay at anchor in the harbor and their young captains were ideal conduits for big sales to the billionaire owners and their international pleasure seekers. From time to time, Dutch police from the mainland made a pass through the island on the lookout for drug traffickers. Carlos could spot them instantly and would keep Luther out of trouble. Other than those brief sweeps by mainland police, things were lax on the island and Luther made a killing before returning to the Turks. He and Carlos divided the take, and temporarily parted company, while Luther rested up.

Luther kept the cash in a safe that was a steel case covered in leather to look like a small suitcase. This case in turn, was kept in the hotel's safe. Lindy had often watched as the concierge retrieved the case from the safe for Luther. Both Luther and Lindy were held in awe by the hotel staff which was very responsive to the couple as a result of Luther's generous tips.

Luther had to go to the harbor for a meeting with Carlos. Lindy said that she had been invited to join a couple who were going for a long spin in their specially outfitted cigar boat. She would return in time for dinner. And they went their separate ways. Lindy, however, made a stop at the concierge and said that Mister Hightree had requested his case from the hotel's safe. There was a brief moment of hesitation by the concierge; it was a bit unusual for the missus to ask for the case. "Please hurry," Lindy said, smiling sweetly, "Mister Hightree is in the middle of an important business deal."

"But of course, madam." And he gave her the case which contained all of Luther's money. Luther never saw Lindy again. When he asked the veranda cocktail clique which couple had invited his wife to a ride the cigar boat, puzzled looks were exchanged. No one owned a cigar boat. Madam Hightree had boarded the inter-island shuttle to go on a shopping trip. Was there a problem?

Indeed there was. Luther confronted the concierge and demanded to know why they had given the case to his wife. "But
Mister Hightree, she is your wife, is she not?" Luther had no answer. He knew he had been taken by the bitch. And he was nearly
broke. He didn't have the stomach for another tour of duty on
Saint Martin with that thug, Carlos. How long had it been since
he left Gussie's store, he wondered. Almost a year, he figured. He
was heartsick and suddenly exhausted. And Lindy's departure had
left a hole in is heart. He really loved Lindy but he could never
express his love for fear of being vulnerable. To anyone. And now
she was gone. Forever.

Luther thought long and hard before deciding to make the
call to Gussie. He knew she would be shocked to receive an international call from him.

He spoke calmly to Gussie; he wanted her to think that he was
merely touching base, keeping in touch to be sure she was in good
health and that all was well with the store. He would wait for an
appropriate break in the conversation to casually suggest that he
was thinking of coming back to the states and would like to see
how the store was doing. It was Luther, not Gussie, who was the
shocked person. When she told him that she and Abe Zellman
were living together, Luther knew there was no chance for him to
reestablish his operation at Discovery Foods. He was broke, lonely
and adrift in the Caribbean in a symbiotic relationship with a murderous Cuban mob.

The mob used first names or mob monikers only. Luther, for
the first time in his adult life, did as he was ordered. The boss of
the three man team was a wiry, twitchy guy with a short fuse, called
Che. He was the avatar of an explosive, unpredictable mob boss.
Carlos and Jorge were your standard Latino gorillas; big bellied,
swarthy, dull-eyed monsters. One didn't fuck with them; one merely listened and did what they instructed. Luther did what he was
told; he was new to the island operation, he was broke and desperate to make a buck. The mob's arcane Cuban underworld jargon
kept Luther in the dark. He knew this was a parlous undertaking
but he had to take chances. Che peremptorily declared that he

handled the money and he would decide what Luther's share of every deal would be and he would give Luther his end when the deal was complete. Luther hated his diminished situation but he would go along with these gorillas until he had accumulated sufficient cash to strike out on his own. Far away from the Cubans.

They would give St. Maartin a pass; Luther and Carlos were overexposed as a result of their recent activity there. The Leeward Islands, St. Barths, St. Kitts, Antigua and Saba had been developed into hot spots for the European tourists and yachtsmen. A no-name black guy skippered the high speed cruiser the mob used to island hop.

The first stop was St. Kitts and Luther was sent ashore to check into the hotel and work all the hotels and yacht basins. Carlos, as usual, was Luther's pertinacious shadow, guarding the stash and supplying cocaine to Luther as needed. Carlos's percipient eye for police enabled Luther to operate with impunity. When a sale was made, the cash went directly to Carlos who saw to it that it got to Che in its entirety. Luther was given operating cash for entertainment…picking up the tab for dinners and for drinks at the sophisticated hotel bars. Che kept track of Luther's expenses. Luther was on a tight leash and he felt like a consummate lackey. He was, however, very successful in making contacts with bartenders, bell captains, maitre d's, tourist groups, yacht captains and other influential pushers and sybaritic users. He was making money for the combine and he looked forward to a hefty settlement when the operations came to an end. Che was impressed with Luther's perspicacity and he loosened up on Luther's walk around money. Luther quickly established himself as a big spender. This was the anodyne for Luther's depression and anxiety.

At the Plantation Inn he struck up a friendship with an unusual beauty, a tall, thin, very pale Irish woman with a bosky of flaming orange hair. The vestiges of an Irish brogue still clung to her rapid speech. At first, she struck Luther as merely an interesting oddity, but she proved to be a very interesting conversationist. And similarly, she found Luther's unusual persona to be of interest to her. She was the manager of the hotel dining room and she dashed about barking orders and making sure everything was absolutely perfect. Just before midnight, she finished her work and was ready to relax with a triple shot of Jamison's Irish whiskey. They met in the bar one evening when Luther was at loose ends and killing time. Luther had offered to buy her a drink and she told him her drinks were free but she would happily buy him a drink provided he would join her in belting down the straight Jamisons. Which Luther did. And as the Irish booze did it's work, they began to tell their respective stories, with, of course, discreet bowdlerization.

Her name was Cara, which she said meant "friend" in Gaelic. The name Luther tickled her; it sounded like a pig farmer name, which Luther found hilarious. She had come to St. Kitts as the stewardess on a big, private yacht which her Irish boyfriend captained. "The drunken lout took up with a barmaid while we were dead in the water, waiting for a part, and I kicked his arse out of bed and told him the devil take ya', you motherless bastard. So I just sorta' jumped ship and got me a job at the hotel where I've been living happily ever after. And I pray every night that those fuckin' pirates get him at sea and cut his black heart out. No offense about 'black heart'." Luther cautiously probed her use of coke and she admitted to "sniffin a line or two when I'm feeling frivolous with my bread." Luther supplied her with several packets of coke gratis, as a missionary investment to enlist her help in developing a network at the hotel.

Cara knew all the users on the staff at the hotel and she was well connected with the yacht captains in the harbor. Luther confronted Carlos and demanded money to compensate Cara for her help. Carlos snarled that they weren't going to give him money for every bitch he scored on the island. But eventually, based on the business Luther was doing in and around the hotel, they gave him money for Cara.

Soon, Luther found himself in bed with the lanky redhead whose long legs wrapped around him with the grip of a python. And he began to have daydreams about one day taking this Irish beauty back to the states with him and making tons of money as a major cocaine player. But those were merely daydreams because Luther was still just a lackey.

In a few months, Luther, with Cara's help, had located and sold product to most of the island's users and pushers. Before the mob could move on to another island, they needed to set up an organization for handling repeat business. It was not cost effective to post Luther on the island permanently; his main value was finding and developing new customers and pushers. Luther had implicit faith in Cara and he suggested her as the agent to handle all the repeat business. She knew all of the users with whom Luther had established relationships, and she knew her way around the byways of the island so she would be a natural to handle the repeat business. When Luther suggested the Cara option to Che, his response was quick and terrifying. He produced the razor-sharp banana knife that he carried, grabbed Cara's thick red hair and pulled her violently to her knees with the menacing blade at her jugular. "You think I trust our money to your piece of ass, you *nord Americano Marica* ?" Then thrusting the twisted rictus that was his mouth so close to Cara that his spittle sprayed her angry, defiant face he screamed, "You wanna' collect our money? You wanna' hold our money for us? Huh? Maybe you think you take the money and 'run Venezuala' like the song, huh? You think I am *Marica* like your boyfriend friend?"

"Let her up, Che. Let her go. Now!" Luther was holding his little .380 pocket pistol to Che's temple. Che looked up at Luther and laughed crazily but there was a look of fear in his eyes. Che's gutter instincts told him he was about to die if he did not comply. Slowly her released Cara's hair and pulled the blade away from her throat. "Now let her up and put that pigsticker in your back pocket." As Cara rose she spat in Che's face and he giggled nervously to show his contempt for her act. Cara ran to Luther's side and stood there, glaring at the three Cubans. Jorge made a move as if to reach for something in his back pocket and Luther growled, "Don't even think about it, Jorge," and the gorilla slowly dropped his hand.

Carlos turned to Che and said, "Fuck this skinny faggot with his little pea shooter. Let's rush him, he can't get us all. Let's tear him to pieces."

Luther fired a shot at Carlos's feet and yelled, "I've got seven more shots and I swear I'll kill you all. Now, *vamoose hombres* or whatever the fuck you say in that bastard spick language."

Then the strangest thing happened; Che started laughing, almost hysterically and he threw air kisses at Cara. "That's some brave lady you got there, gringo. I know now we can trust her. And you show us you are a man, senor Luther. Let's sit down and have some drinks and work out a deal with the lady."

"You better not be out of your raving head, Che. I'm not going for any bullshit. I don't think the lady wants any part of you now."

"Let's hear what the big man's got in mind," Cara said calmly, her voice strangely flat and emotionless."

Che laughed again and said, "See? I know brave ladies when I see them. We gonna' make you a good deal. And you never gonna' steal from us, right, red lady?"

"Let's see what you call a 'good deal', and maybe we can talk some more," Cara said. Luther was speechless. He was a benighted on-looker to a facet of human behavior he had never before witnessed.

Che agreed to pay Cara five percent of every sale she made and for which she collected the proper amount. Carlos would return to the island weekly to settle with her and leave a new stash. Cara nodded her agreement. She was satisfied. Nothing more. Moments ago a madman had held a blade to her throat. She showed no emotion then and no elation now that she had a deal.

"Say something," Luther said. "For crissakes, I thought you were a dead woman. You just looked him straight in the eyes. What the hell were you thinking?"

"How long is this spik going to showboat," she said with the faintest suggestion of a grin. "I've seen the act before. Your gun just shortened the scene a little."

"Didn't seem like an act to me, and I been on the streets a long time," Luther said. "And so you think you're tough, eh, boy-o?" The brogue had thickened a bit and her eyes glinted impudently.

"You satisfied with the deal? You trust them?" Luther asked.

"We'll see. If they stiff me they won't get a penny off this rock," she said. Luther knew he could trust this woman. Thoughts of the two of them in action together in the states danced through his head. If only it had been Cara, not Lindy.

Luther and the Cubans left for St. Barths and Cara began making her rounds at midnight.

Abe yelled for Gussie one morning around five-thirty. "Gussie, there's a guy here to see you." The big guy looked vaguely familiar to Gussie, something about the shy shuffle. "You know who I am?" he said in what was almost a little boy's voice, so unexpected from this two hundred and fifty pound bulk. He wasn't a bum, Gussie quickly surmised as she looked him over. He wore clean jeans and a nice flannel shirt. Something about him. "I'm Pounder. Used to sleep across the street in that storefront."

"Oh, my God! Pounder. You look wonderful. You lost so much weight. Where have you been?" Gussie gushed as she rushed over and hugged the big guy.

"Never thanked you for fixing that cop—you know the one. I come to tell you I'm clean now, no wine, no pot, no nuthin'. The reverend and the church ladies got me into the county rehab hospital. And I go to A.A. meetings regular. I'm really okay now, clean and green."

"Pounder, how wonderful. You look so wonderful, so handsome."

"I need work, Missus Stein."

"Steinberg," Gussie corrected softly. "What do want to do, Pounder? You want to work here?"

"Gussie, we don't need no help!" Abe interjected.

"Just a minute, Abe," Gussie snapped. "You want to work here? You know how to wait on trade, Pounder?" Gussie asked, a note of dubiety in her voice.

"No ma'm. Not at first. Just want to help when they unload the trucks in the morning. You know, open boxes, put stuff away, sweep and dust and wash the windows. Everything. I'll work for very little and for food. You shouldn't be doin' all that heavy work. You and the gentleman here, why you're gettin' up there."

"Why thank you, Pounder," Gussie said, grinning at Abe. Gussie gently suggested a salary for Pounder and told him he could have all the food he needed, within reason of course. Pounder was hired and reported for work promptly at five a.m. the next morning. Reverend Graylock and the church ladies, even Vera Deering, inundated Gussie with kisses and God's blessings.

Pounder and Abe got in each other's way at the beginning, but they soon made the necessary accommodations and things started to go smoothly as the work load diminished for Gussie and Abe. Pounder proved to be a fast learner, his boyish voice and mannerisms notwithstanding. One morning, Abe awoke with a strep throat and was obviously too sick to unpack the morning deliveries. Pounder insisted that Abe go back to bed and rest. Pounder unpacked to the boxes and placed the produce attractively in the appropriate bins as Gussie watched. Gussie rewarded him with a big breakfast of ham and eggs and home fried potatoes in the upstairs apartment as Abe slept off his strep throat in the bedroom. For a guy who had lived his life in the doorways of abandoned stores, Pounder ate with surprisingly refined table manners. Where had he learned this behavior? What had his early life been like, Gussie wondered. A very unusual and lovable guy, and certainly a godsend if Abe became ill and was unable to work.

An unmarked police car stopped at the curb and an officer in a gold-braided, immaculate uniform walked into the store. "Good afternoon, Missus Steinberg, how have you been?"

Gussie recognized him immediately. "Lieutenant Carney, my God, what a surprise. Did I do something wrong?" she said with a warm smile.

"Yes, you called me lieutenant and I've been made a captain."

"Oh, congratulations. You certainly deserve the promotion. Is this a social call Captain?"

"It is, Missus Steinberg. I am so pleased that your store is no longer a source of concern since the departure of Mister Hightree. And your new employee is a walking miracle. We shine our beams into empty storefronts and no Pounder guzzling wine. Our thanks to you for keeping this store as a fine place for people in this neighborhood to shop. Just wanted to stop in and wish you continued success. Call me if I can be of any assistance to you," Carney said, shaking Gussie's hand.

"This is so nice of you, Captain. So very nice. Thank you. Thank you so very much." Gussie was moved by Carney's words. A far cry from a few years ago.

Late one afternoon, Willa Simon motioned to Gussie, wanting to talk privately. "What's up, girlfriend?" Gussie said. Her attempt at black slang amused Willa. "Ain't bein' nosey, but—is something wrong with your other half?"

"What do you mean, 'is something wrong?' Did you notice something?"

"I ain't no doctor, but he ain't the same man. He seems a little befuddled at times."

"How do mean, 'befuddled?' Give me an example," Gussie asked, getting concerned.

"Like he finds me collards a zillion times before. Today I ask him to pick me out some nice fresh collards and he looks at me kinda' blank for a long time. And I think I done something wrong; so I ask him if I done something wrong. And he finally says, 'show me what you're asking for.' It's like he completely forgot what collards is."

"What did you do, then? Did you show him where the collards were?"

"I did. And he acted like they was somethin' brand new to him."

"Did he say anything?" Gussie asked.

"Nope. Just took 'em out of the bin and shuffled over to the counter. And I mean, shuffled. He's walking kinda' funny, lately. You check him out. I could be way wrong. You see what you think, okay?"

Gussie mumbled "Okay." Her mind was elsewhere. She was concerned. Was this a symptom of old age? Abe is a strong young guy, she thought. Shuffled? What the hell is she talking about? But Gussie would watch. Carefully.

Months went by and Abe was Abe; nothing untoward about his behavior. What the hell was Willa talking about? Sometimes she could be a *yenta;* but she's a good friend. Nothing malicious about her. Still...she thought she saw something unusual about Abe. Gussie's mind ricocheted from concern to scoffing.

"Out of the clear blue sky you decide we should get married? What brought this on all of a sudden, Abe?" Gussie asked. Abe said nothing, he reached into his pocket and pulled out a small velvet box and handed it to Gussie. "Go on, open it," Abe said, strutting back and forth nervously.

"Oh, my God, Abe. It's gorgeous. The velvet box had contained a two carat diamond ring in a beautiful setting.

"Okay. So now we're engaged. Let's run down to city hall and get a license and a blood test and get married by a judge. I want to be married to you, babe. When I kick off, I want there to be a Missus Abraham Zellman to shed a tear of two for me. What do you say, kid?"

"What do I say? I say let's do it. I'm honored to be missus Abraham Zellman." And so they got married by Judge Kathleen Moriority in a simple ceremony at city hall. The ring was the most precious thing Gussie had ever owned and she couldn't stop extending her hand so she could appreciate the beauty of the large diamond.

Abe wanted to have sex more frequently now. Was he trying to prove something? Did he sense that the end was near? At any rate Gussie finally told him that people of their age should go easy... wait until the mood hits both of them. Abe agreed.

"Let's get dressed up and go somewhere fancy! What do you say, kid? How about that French joint? Or, are you in the mood for some good *schvartze* ribs?" Abe was rambling and Gussie had to slow him down.

"What, have you got *schpilkas* or something? You can't sit still and take it easy after a busy week?" Gussie said. Abe was wounded by Gussie's reply. His face dropped; he was a disappointed little boy at that moment. Didn't he realize that Gussie was only kidding?

"Okay, sport, if you've got the money, I've got the time," she warbled, trying to lift his spirits. "Let's do the ribs."

They had a good time at the rib joint where they were always treated like royalty. When they left, Abe tried to remember where he had parked in the crowded lot, and, as they stood there, their waiter came running out holding Abe's wallet, which he had left on the table. No big deal, Gussie thought. People start to forget things as they get older. But a wallet?

Morrie Rappaport's eyes filled with tears and Gussie regretted bringing up the subject of Sylvia's death. Yes, Sylvia was diagnosed with dementia. And that's what killed her. Morrie said the last years were agony. For both of them. She didn't know who he was at the end. She might as well have been dead, Morrie said. It had started out like it was no big deal. She started forgetting things; the names of people we knew. But then she couldn't remember the name of ordinary things; the refrigerator, the elevator. Things like that. "Is Abe starting to forget things?" he asked. Gussie didn't want to start rumors about Abe so she said that both she and Abe would forget the names of certain movie actors when they watched old movies on TV. Nothing really worrisome.

"So why are you here? Why are you asking questions about Sylvia?" Morrie asked. Gussie was embarrassed and she apologized to Morrie. She just wanted to be ready when their time came, she said, not knowing how to excuse herself and end the conversation.

But Gussie was getting worried. It was more than just forgetting the names of old movie actors; Abe was in the middle of ringing out a customer when he forgot how to work the register. He just stood there, frozen. Not knowing what to do. Pounder and the customer exchanged looks, knowing that something was terribly wrong. Pounder called Gussie who ran to the register and straightened out the mess. The customer was annoyed and walked away, shaking her head, a silent message to Gussie that she had better find out what was wrong with the man.

It was time for some straight talk with Abe. They both agreed it was more than just the normal forgetfulness of the senior years. Abe started to cry, after telling Gussie that he didn't want to be a burden to her. Gussie told him he would never be a burden, that he had made her life a joy and that she would never abandon him. They would fight this fucking thing out together. Gussie said he was still able to work in the store and if he got stuck, he just needed to hold his arm up to signal her that he needed help. The store would go on as it always did.

Gussie called Morrie Rappaport and finally admitted that things had progressed to the point where she felt she needed the guidance of a doctor. Morrie was kind; no "I told you so" stuff. He told her that he had taken Sylvia to see Doctor Morgenstern, the top neurologist at the Mount Sinai Hospital Clinic; a young guy who really understood dementia and would level with her after he examined Abe.

"It ain't cheap, babe," Morrie warned. His nursing care will cost a fortune and when it gets near the end you've got to face the fact that you can't take care of him yourself. You'll need to put him in a nursing home.

"Bullshit!" Gussie shouted through her tears, "I'm not sticking Abe in some goddam home. He stays with me. I'll take care of him to the end."

"And you'll get yourself sick, Gussie," Morrie shouted back at her. "And you'll go broke unless you've got some fancy insurance to pay for people to come to your apartment and help you. You ain't going to be able to do it yourself, trust me, Gussie. And you want to run the store yet! Lots of luck, Gussie."

Doctor Morgenstern was indeed a young guy, as Morrie Rappaport had said. In her inimitable style, Gussie told the doctor that he looked awfully young. Morgenstern smiled and asked Gussie if she would like to see an older neurologist.

"No," Gussie said, "as long as a you can assure me that you really know your stuff about this dementia thing." He took Gussie's hand and promised he would give her man the very best care it was possible to give. Gussie looked at him for a long time with her special Gussie look and told him that she believed him.

And so began months and months of visits and tests and examinations. And the painful minute by minute observation of Abe Zellman as he became more and more a stranger to his beloved Gussie. Had he known that Gussie had run through most of her savings caring for him, he certainly would have turned Sol's old pistol on himself.

Pounder had taken to wearing a gleaming white starched apron that Gussie bought for him. The neighborhood people had long since ceased perceiving him as the rehabilitated wino. Pounder had become a gracious, efficient master of dazzling fresh produce, meat and fish. "How's the whiting, today, Pounder?" they would ask, totally confident of his evaluation. The regulars avoided glancing at the rear of the store where sat a ghost that had once been Abe Zellman, bursting with his zest for life.

When Gussie was flush with cash from Luther's operation, she could afford to sell the premium grade foods almost at cost. She could not bear the thought of raising prices or of cutting back on quality. Her life was the respect she had earned in the community. She would never give that up. So she juggled and struggled to pay her suppliers.

But it was now at the point where they had begun to give her gentle, respectful reminders that they might have to cut her off.

She was physically exhausted; caring for Abe and fighting to keep the store afloat had aged her. When Kitty made a surprise visit she was shocked when she saw Gussie.

"My God, what's happened to you, Mom?" Kitty said. Then she saw Abe sitting at the rear of the store, a skeleton in a heavy sweater, staring at her blankly. Kitty, in many ways, was a younger version of Gussie and she was similarly given to blunt questions requiring straight answers. Abe was in the final stages of dementia and she was going broke, Gussie admitted. Kitty wasted no time. She called for an ambulance and had Abe taken to Mt. Sinai. He was dying and Kitty knew it. They put Abe in a bed and told Gussie it was a matter of days, perhaps even hours. Gussie rushed back to the store and told Pounder to stay in the store and tell the customers that they were closed due to a death in the family. He was to pack up the perishables and take them to the homeless shelter, and to tell the delivery guys that she would settle up with them when she got back. She wept all the way back to the hospital and told the charge nurse that she would be sleeping in Abe's room. Kitty called Maxie and told him she would be staying over with Gussie. She expected him to come and make funeral arrangements when Abe passed. And somehow, they had to convince Gussie that it was time to either sell the store, or simply close it up.

"Things are terrible here, honey; you won't believe how your mother has aged," Kitty said.

Maxie arrived the next morning and rushed to the hospital room at Mount Sinai. The situation, from his purview, was an utter disaster; it left him no room to commiserate, only annoyance. Who, after all, was this guy Abe? And that goddam store continued to be the *bet noir* of his existence. Somehow this melodrama that had been his mother's life had to reach a resolution so he could live his life in peace, at long last. These were Maxie's thoughts as he stood in the doorway of the darkened hospital room perfumed with the odors of death. His mother, lying on the rumpled cot on which she had spent the night, was drawn and red-eyed. She mustered only a look of apprehension when she saw him in the doorway. Kitty looked exhausted, seated in a chair, wrapped in a blanket. And Abe Zellman rasping his last breaths, was the only sound in the room. Finally, Kitty rose and embraced him.

"He's very sick, honey," were her first words, and Maxie's face registered nothing. He walked to his mother and said, "Are you okay, Mom? What's going on?"

"Her husband is dying, that's what's going on, Maxwell." Maxwell? She hadn't used that name in years. Why the hell is she angry at me? Maxie thought.

"Okay. So what can I do to help?" he said.

"I'm so happy you came, son" Gussie said. That was it.

"Mom," Kitty whispered, "I'm going down to the cafeteria for some coffee. Do you want anything?"

"No, sweetheart. I'm fine. Take Maxie and tell him 'what's going on'" Gussie said, mimicking Maxie's words as he stood in the doorway. The irony was not lost on Kitty who pulled Maxie out of the room before he could respond. Kitty had long felt that Maxie's self-concern had reached the level of abject selfishness. Could he ever change, she wondered? Yes, he loved her and he was devoted to her father. But this love, in the final analysis, was self-love, was it not? Could he ever feel compassion for the suffering of people who were not 'self'? What did he feel for his mother as her husband, a stranger to Maxie, lay dying? Gussie was facing two terrible losses—her husband and the store that had been so much a part of her life.

"Honey, your mom is going broke. The medical bills have been murder. She can't pay her suppliers and they're getting ready to cut her off. She needs to sell the store or close it up."

"Fat chance. The store's an obsession that I don't begin to understand," Maxie said.

"You don't understand it, Maxie? You still don't understand your mother. That store's her life—a source of pride. Why can't you understand that?" Kitty said. "The problem now is that she's run out of options. Can the store be sold? Would someone buy it?"

"You think she'd let it be sold even if I could somehow find a buyer?"

"This is when you have to become a human being, Maxie."

"What's that supposed to mean, Kitty?"

"The life that your mother is clinging to is over, Maxie. She's tired. She's lost your father. And now she's losing Abe and her store. The store is somehow tied up with her life with your father--her youth. All her dreams."

"It's also tied up with her dreams for Luther. Something I'll never understand."

"Luther's gone, Maxie. I want her to come live with us and be a grandmother when we have kids. We have to give her a life after the store."

"You think she's ready for that, Kitty?"

"With love, we can make her ready, sweetheart. You have to come back home, Maxie, You have to be the son that didn't change his name and run away."

"Jesus Christ, Kitty. I didn't realize I was such a disappointment to you."

"You're not, sweetheart. You're the 'poor Maxie' I fell in love with at the ZBT keg party."

"There's a Korean guy a few blocks away. A competitor. I'll talk to him. Mom doesn't need to know about it, yet."

Chulsoon was nobody's patsy. He already knew that Steinberg's was temporarily closed. "Somebody die?" he asked.

"No. Nobody die," Maxie said, unable to resist the temptation to mock the Korean's sing-song delivery.

"Then why store closed?" Chulsoon probed.

"Painting, Redecorating. Store open soon. My mother wants to retire. Go live in Florida. You interested? Store is for sale. Lots of buyers already calling."

"Why you come see me? Talk to buyers."

"You are number one competitor. Steinberg's takes many customers from you. People tell us. I figure you are the best one to buy us out." Chulsoon's enigmatic posturing continued in silence for a long minute and then he began to bargain, his execrable English tumbling out, barely comprehensible. The bottom line: he would come and examine the store and the look at the books. He wanted sales figures and expenses. Then he would make an offer.

Abe Zellman died in his sleep as Maxie was negotiating.

Abe was not a religious Jew and he had told Gussie that he wanted a quiet burial in the section of the cemetery where Sol had been buried. The rabbi could say a few quick prayers and that would be it. No sitting *shivah,* just remember to light a *Yahrzeit* candle for him every year. There were no known relatives and most of the people attending the gravesite ceremony were black customers of the store who remembered Abe. Maxie ordered a deli tray and Morrie Rappaport and few of the old-timers showed up at the apartment after the cemetery service. Even Aunt Lillian schlepped from the suburbs to offer succor to Gussie.

Abe had a paid-up whole life insurance policy with a face value of ten thousand dollars that he had forgotten about. It was the deus ex machina that would keep Gussie afloat for a short time. Gussie knew nothing of the policy until the insurance agent finally tracked her down. As Abe's legal spouse, she would automatically be the beneficiary.

She would reopen the store in a few days after she settled up with her vendors and restocked the store. Pounder had taken care of things just as Gussie had ordered and he would stay on, be her good right hand and it would be business as usual at Steinberg's Discovery Foods.

Maxie and Kitty knew nothing of the insurance policy. They had returned to the  store after speaking with Morrie Rappaport and several other real estate firms about listing the store for sale. All of the real estate people said they would need sales figures and inventory to suggest a selling price.

Gussie looked much better after having rested for a few days after the funeral. To Maxie's surprise, Gussie had reopened the store. He knew better than to question his mother about her finances; he merely exchanged looks with Kitty and shrugged his shoulders in resignation.  Kitty was puzzled and terribly worried; how would Gussie manage; she owed her vendors and she was broke. Yet there she was, the old Gussie; full of energy and running poor Pounder ragged restocking the store.  Maxie and Kitty froze in horror as Chulsoon, unannounced, came padding into the store.  Gussie and Pounder recognized him immediately and stopped what they were doing to confront the poor benighted Korean. "You want sell store?" he said.

"No, I don't want sell store." Gussie snarled.

"Yes. You want sell store. Husband die.You want sell store, I know."

"Pounder, get this fuckin' gook out of here before I blow his head off." Pounder gently moved Chulsoon toward the door. "

The lady said the fuckin' gook has to leave now," Pounder said, grinning devilishly.

"Holy shit," Kitty said to no one in particular. "Gussie, you are a piece of work, you know that?" Kitty took Gussie's arm and led her to a chair at the rear of the store.  "Maxie, come over here. We've got something to discuss with your crazy mama." Maxie joined the group, bug-eyed and pale. Both women obviously were deranged.

"What's going on?" he said. His usual, banal opening statement.

"Your mother just used a threatening epithet on a well-meaning competitor. She's a new widow, practically broke and too old and tired for this kind of bullshit." Gussie giggled her approval of her daughter-in-law's hectoring language. "What's going on?' Maxie mumbled his bewildered mantra.

"What's going on is that we are insisting that your mother apologize to that poor "gook" and listen to his offer. She is going to sell this store and come and live with us as she awaits her new role as a sane, sedate grandmother. We are going to have kids, aren't we?"

"Kids? Kids? Sure. Of course we're going to have kids. What the hell is going on?" Gussie was laughing. Borderline hysterical.

"Here's what's going on," Gussie said, choking on her laughter. "Nothing. Kitty, I love you like the daughter I wish I had, but I just ain't ready for the rocking chair. Eventually I want to be the loving grandma to your kids. But not yet. Please, kids. Not yet! Go home and enjoy your life and make babies and let me and Pounder run our business. Maxie! Go home and be a *mensch*. I appreciate everything you've done for me. Now go home."

"Gussie, you're broke. How are you going to keep the store open?" Kitty pleaded.

"I married a man with money. I'll be okay," Gussie said.

The ten thousand dollars didn't go very far; she paid the suppliers and brought her account up to date. The store had to be restocked and it would be several days before the neighborhood trade returned after the closure. Gussie was reduced to counting pennies; if she stayed with the tight markups and kept buying premium merchandise and there were no unexpected expenses, she could grind out a living. But inflation had set in and her cost of goods went up. Gussie was reluctant to raise her prices at first, and this cost her. She gradually raised her prices, but she was too timid with her increases and she continued to lose money. She tried to figure how long she could hold out;  the outlook was bleak. Her days were numbered.  In desperation she dropped to her knees in her darkened bedroom and spoke to Abe. "Abe, sweetheart, I'm going to do something and I hope you understand; I'm desperate, Abe. I need money to keep going. I know you would want me to keep the store open so I am going to pawn the beautiful ring you gave me. I swear, Abe, as soon as I get caught up I will reclaim the ring. I know the kind of guy you are. You understand, don't you sweetheart?  I love you, Abe."

Luther and the Cubans had worked St. Barths and Antigua as Cara was handling the business on St. Kitts. Luther had moved a large volume of cocaine and the repeat business had to be handled. Che was anxious to return to St. Maartin where the big bucks awaited. It was decided that Carlos would remain behind and work the repeat business on St. Barths and Antigua while Cara continued to handle the customers on St. Kitts. Luther was tired and he did not want to work St. Maartin. During their meeting on St. Barths, he told Che he would work with Cara and service the three islands with her. Same deal as Cara had, five percent. He said he planned to live on the islands permanently. But before anything else, he wanted to settle up right there on St. Barths and collect what was coming to him from the very beginning, when he made his initial contacts and sales on St. Kitts. Luther figured there was to be a big payday; close to a half million. Che listened, his dull-eyed stare revealed nothing. Luther suddenly felt the big barrel of Carlos'.40 caliber cannon at the back of his neck. "You wanna' know what I owe you? How 'bout what you owe me? You owe me your shitty brains all over the floor, pretty boy faggot. That's what you owe me. You shot at me to protect that cunt of yours. You thought you were a big man, eh, hero? I let you live then. But not now. Nobody shoots at Che and lives.

"If I don't check in with Cara tonight she will blow the whistle on you, Che. And the island constabulary will have your ass," Luther said. It was his last hope.

"Let me blow his fucking head off, boss," Carlos said.

"Better idea," Che said. "Take him to St. Maartin and put him on a plane for the States. If he even blinks, kill him right on the spot."

"I'm broke. Give me something. I made a lot of money for you, Che. Please. Give me something and I'm out of here clean. No trouble, ever. You're the king, Che. I'm pleading for a break. Be the big man I always heard you were. I'm begging you." Luther was at his best. Che peeled off five grand and threw it at Luther's feet. As Luther knelt to pick up the money, Che pushed his boot into Luther's face and demanded that he kiss the boot. Luther complied and Che kicked him in the face. Luther lay bleeding and Che and Jorge departed for St. Kitts and their meeting with Cara. Carlos would take Luther to St. Maartin and put him on a plane for the states.

When they met on St. Kitts, Che pointed a gun at Cara and threatened to blow her face off is she ever mentioned Luther's name to anyone. "He's gone. You're the boss on St. Kitts. Do your work and we pay you good."

"Did you pay Luther 'good'?" Cara confronted the choleric Cuban, coldly. Not a trace of fear on her voice.

"Not your fucking business, bitch," Jorge said.

"I want to know if you paid him for all the work he did for you."

" He's on his way to the States. He never even kiss you goodbye. That's 'cause he a pretty-boy faggot," Che taunted.

"He's more of man than you'll ever be. You're jealous of him, aren't you? You've had the hots for me for a long time haven't you, estupido?" Jorge slapped her and she licked the blood off her lips without flinching or crying out.

"Watch your mouth, bitch," Jorge said.

"If I find out that you stiffed him, our deal is off," Cara said.

"Our deal is off when I say it's off. We pay you like we say, right? You do your work and don't give us no shit about that punk boyfriend. We paid him off. Fair and square. Forget his name and nothing bad will happen. We got a deal, Red?" Che said.

"Get the fuck out of here. Make sure my money is here every week. And nothing bad will happen, " Cara said as she turned and walked away.

Luther staggered off the plane in Ft. Lauderdale, bruised and humiliated. His glib tongue had saved his life but now his main concern was Cara; would they stiff her also? Would the animal, Che, hurt her? Her defiant mouth was sure to inflame the un-

215

stable Cuban. Luther checked into a cheap hotel where his lack of luggage was not a problem. He paid in advance in cash and rushed up to his room and tried to get a call through to Cara on St. Kitts. There was a slight delay and Luther paced the room, reliving the months he had spent groveling, toadying up to the Cubans and finally acting the simpering, abject coward to save his life. Would there ever be a payback? He would need money. Money gets you power. He had to get back in action. He had to pull his guts back into his belly again. And he desperately wanted to be with Cara again. How he loved the brazen Irish heller. Finally the phone rang. It was Cara on St. Kitts.

"Cara! Are you alright? Can you talk?"

"I'm alone. The spiks had a bit of a paddy with you, eh, boy-o? Where are you, darlin'? Florida?"

"Yes, a flea bag near Lauderdale. They stiffed me, babe. Carlos wanted to kill me. Had to plead for my fucking life. Very degrading, dear girl, They threw five grand at me and put me on a plane in St. Maarten. What about you? Did they pay you? Did they hurt you?"

"Those ruddy rascals know better than to paddy me up. I'm connected on the island, darlin'. You'd perish to know who my customers are, starting with the chief magistrate. My money comes in like clockwork and it's adding up, me lad. And there you sit beat up and broke."

"I need to see you, sweetheart. Forget the money. I need to smell you when you're aroused and wet. I love you, Cara."

"I love you too, darlin'. But you best not come to the islands. Che hates you 'cause he's jealous of you. He's got a thing for me, poor idiot. I can't stand the sight of him. But they'll hurt you, Luther, if you come back to the islands. "

"Then you come to me, Cara."

"Whoa, keep your britches hitched, darlin'. What would I be comin' to? Working the streets with you peddling coke? Luther, you helped to set me up with a sweet deal here and I'm making big money for the first time in my life. I'm established down here. I love these islands, next to Ireland, of course."

"You can't keep operating forever. Sooner or later, you'll get busted."

"Sweet lad, I don't intend to push coke forever. As soon as I build up my boodle to where I want it, I'm done. Right now, I'm safe. I've got friends in high places."

"Cara, I'll get in action up here and build up a bankroll. When you're ready, cut out of there and came up here. We'll have a good life, Cara. We'll be happy." There was a long silence and Luther's heart sank. "Not going to happen, is it babe?"

"No, sweet boy, it's not going to happen. I love these warm, sunny islands and I've made a life down here. I'm too old to be startin' all over in a strange place. And if the truth be known, my dream is to return to Ireland as a rich woman and get the respect my family never had." Another long silence. "When you get to your permanent location, call me with the name of a bank. I want to send a bank draft. Maybe fifty large. I owe you, dear boy. And I love you dearly. Take good care. Goodbye, sweetheart." The phone went dead and Luther's heart broke. He had let himself be vulnerable for the first time in his life, and he was to pay for it with a sadness he could never have imagined. He sat alone in the flea bag hotel room not knowing whom to call or where to go. He had no fresh clothes, no razor, no appetite. He felt that he might as well be dead.

Luther slept fitfully for two days, on and off, and awoke with a thick tongue and an itchy, mean beard. He threw on his soiled clothes and found a diner. He was ravenous. The waitresses kept glancing at him as he wolfed down his food, his face cut and bruised, his clothes wrinkled and stained. Some kind of a desperate dude; maybe a guy on the lam, they assumed. As he finished eating, he remembered that all he had was five, one thousand dollar bills in his pocket. He called for the owner and showed him the bills. Could he make change for the one grand note? The Greek owner examined the bill, turning it over several times and holding it up to the light. "Margie, run over to the bank and tell them to give you ten, c-notes for this. Tell them it's for me." Then turning a suspicious eye on Luther he said, "You sit tight for a minute, right buddy?" When Luther got his change, he left a five dollar tip and walked out, squinted in the bright morning sunlight as he headed for the drug store where he loaded up on toiletries which he jammed into a cheap shaving kit.

He shaved and showered until the hot water ran out . He splashed the high priced aftershave cologne on his face and sprayed his body with deodorant. He wanted to look reasonably presentable when he went to the J.C. Penney store to assemble a basic wardrobe. He had spotted an upscale haberdashery and he was tempted, but he had to stretch the five grand. The last item was a carry-on bag and he splurged a bit on this item. It would get him respect as he traveled, destination unknown at this point.

"How the hell did you get this number?" Ann Rudmann hissed in anger. "What do you want? Where the hell are you?" Luther let her spew her lawyerly invective for a few seconds before he turned on the charm. "Ann, your number is in the phone book. I told you that the last time I called you. Are you through being an offended barrister? I'm in Florida and I'm coming back in town and I merely wanted to let you know that I will once again be the discreet purveyor of top quality merchandise." This calmed her down.

"Same location?" she asked.

"My old partner got remarried so I don't think that's a possibility."

"Our old friend Captain Carney said the new husband died. You better check it out. Gotta' go. Stay in touch." Click. She was gone. But she opened a door for Luther.

"Gussie, I just got word you lost your husband and I wanted to extend my sympathies and see if there is anything I can do for you."

"Luther! Are you here? Oh, it's so wonderful to hear your voice. Are you alright? You always seem to call when things aren't going so good for me."

"Gussie, I'm fine. I'm fine. I'm in Florida but I'm coming back into town. What's the matter, Mom? You got problems?"

"It's nothing you need to worry about, sweetheart. Tell me about yourself. Where have you been? What have you been doing?" Gussie jabbered on. Luther cut her off.

"Something's wrong, Gus. I can tell. Is everything all right with the store? Is business okay? Who do you have helping you?"

"I'll tell you what—when you get back in town we'll talk. Do you want to stay in the apartment? No, you probably want some fancy hotel."

"I don't need a fancy hotel. It'll be just like old times to stay in the apartment. I didn't bring a lot of stuff up with me, so I won't crowd you."

"You won't crowd me, I've got plenty of room now."

"I'll call you when I get in town." Bingo.

Luther 's facile mind had worked out the basics of the putative operation. He would eschew the fancy steaks and scampies that he had formerly employed as a ploy to justify white customers arriving at all hours. The concept of Discovery Foods as a destination store for people purportedly seeking food bargains proved to be a weak story over the long haul. This time there would be no nocturnal activity nor constant automobile traffic converging on the store. Everything depended on Gussie and his old confederate, the estimable Blue.

Gussie embraced Luther when he arrived and as usual, she wept with joy. As they stood in middle of the quiet store, Gussie studied Luther. He was thinner and he had aged a bit. The quality of the clothes he was wearing told her that things had not gone well financially for Luther. Gussie was a percipient observer with a finely attuned prescience, especially when it came to Luther. So she blurted it out. "You need money, sweetheart. It breaks my heart to have to tell you that I can't help you. I have nothing left. All the money you made for me is gone; Abe's medical bills ate everything up."

"I don't know how you do it, Gus, but you got it right. I'm hurting. Maybe we can help each other the way we did before."

"Luther, I'm afraid of the funny business. We were on the verge of getting caught. I thank God that we stopped just in time."

"Gus, when people say, 'trust me,' I get nervous. But trust me. I have a plan for doing business where there won't be people coming here day and night to buy the stuff. It will be quiet, peaceful and, I swear to God, it's absolutely foolproof."

"Now I'm really scared. 'foolproof' is a kid's word. A kid that thinks he can outsmart the whole world. You think you can outsmart the whole world, Luther?"

"Trust me, Gussie. I can beat the game this time. And none of your customers will know that anything is going on. I'll be the regular wine and beer expert in your beautiful, high quality store."

"Again, he gives me the 'trust me, Gussie' bullshit and of course I'm going to go for it."

"Trust me, Gussie" Luther says with his boyish, irresistible grin, "this ain't no bullshit... it's the real thing that's going to get us both well again."

"Do I remove the pork chops and chicken to make room for your fancy steaks again?"

"No way. No steaks, no scampies, no nuthin'. I just expand the beer and wine section a little bit. Nothing changes. Everything stays quiet and cool."

"Now you're starting to scare the shit out of me. Sounds too good to be true. And you know the old saying that when something sounds too good to be true, it ain't true."

"Yah, yah, yah. We got a deal, Gus?"

"Just tell me when it starts, okay?"

"You still use that bank down on Central?"

"I don't have much in it, sonny boy."

"I'm expecting a money draft from St. Kitts. Fifty grand. Start up money for my exclusive wine and beer operation, right here in your store."

"Luther, can I make you something to eat? You're starting to make me crazy."

Luther and Blue met at the quiet Italian joint that nobody seemed to go to and they talked into the back bar mirror, barely moving their lips. "A delivery service? You want me to deliver shit to your store? Every fuckin' morning at five? That's gotta' cost you, bro'. I mean you making me kind of a partner, the way you're talking."

"Pay attention, Blue man. My customers, the white folks from the country clubs—lawyers, prosecutors, doctors, bartenders who do a little pushing, all my regulars from the last time we worked together—they call me and place an order for a case of my top shelf wine, six bottles in a case. I get three, maybe four orders a day.

Some may want a case of my imported beer, twelve bottles. Every case will have twenty packets at a hundred per. Two grand, right?"

"I can count, crazy man," Blue said, now very, very interested. "And the packets are under the false bottom of the case, right?"

"I count on your genius for that part, Blue. You get a van and paint a sign on the side: 'International Wines and Beer' and that's your delivery truck. Every morning, when the delivery guys arrive, you're right there, in the middle, delivering my three or four cases. My customers pick up their order during the day and the drive away. Nothing to attract attention from the fuzz. No slipping packets in steaks being wrapped or shit like that. And very little unusual traffic coming to the store. Periodically I retrieve the cases and give them back to you."

"How do the country clubbers know to order?"

"I will talk to them out at the club and explain the gig. I deal with people who don't run their mouths because they got as much to lose as I do. And two g's is nothing for them when they're using."

"Sounds smooth, rolling off your silver tongue. One problem, slick."

"Tell me about it, Blue."

"I'm buildin' cases, I'm up half the night getting' ready, packin' cases and driving with a heavy load of shit in my van. Like I said, sounds like I gotta' be a partner, not just a supplier."

"How's 70-30?"

"Just listen to that jive ass nigger."

"60-40?"

"And I keep the stash you gave me to hold when you blew town."

"Not a problem, partner." Blue kisses him on the cheek.

Luther was greeted enthusiastically by his grateful friend, Pounder, who was nonetheless fearful that Luther might once again bring the peaceful store under the heel of the police surveillance. Pounder never wanted to relive those bitter days. The neighborhood ladies slowly became aware of Luther's presence as he tried assiduously to maintain a low profile, working quietly arranging his wine and beer displays. He rarely used the cash register, and seemed to have very little interaction with the food operation.

That was Pounder's bailiwick. Some, as was the case with the ubiquitous Vera Deering, felt alarm, even anger and started the gossip roiling through the community and the church. There was an unnerving disquietude surrounding Luther's activities.

After two weeks, Blue was ready and Luther vanished for several days as he reestablished his contacts at the country clubs. In casual cocktail gatherings he explained the new format: phone me when you want to place an order; the basic order is twenty pieces; Pounder would carry the case of six wine bottles containing the product beneath a false bottom, to your cars; pickup was to be during daylight hours; Luther would retrieve the cases periodically. No strain, no pain; easy does it. The two bartenders who had their own operations, could order three cases at a time in order to service their trade. Everyone liked the simplicity of the new system, Beth and Evan were planning a big party to celebrate Beth's promotion to associate chief prosecutor, and they wanted to be the first to place an order. Dino, the bartender at Riverdwood, put in for three cases. Of course there would be an extra charge for the wine; it was very much top shelf. One could order either Pinot Noir, Burgundy, or Chardonnay, discounted twenty-five percent off the citywide, market price. Everyone liked the deal. Now is was up to Blue to get the orders straight and to make formation at five a.m.

Luther had moved into Gussie's apartment where he spent a sleepless night in anticipation of the first morning's transaction: a case of Chardonnay for Beth and Evan and three cases of Pinot Noir for Dino the bartender at Riverwood.

Blue's van, smartly painted "International Wines and Beer," arrived with the truck from Dupree of the Sea promptly at five a.m. and the Blue, whistling as he worked, carried in the four cases of wine and, very businesslike, left an invoice for the transaction. Evan sauntered in and picked up his order at three p.m. and Dino shortly after, came for his four cases. Ten thousand dollars plus the cost of the wine slipped unobtrusively into the blasé hands of Luther Hightree—like shit through a tin horn. Life was going to be good at Steinberg's on Central Avenue in the ghetto.

"Lillian," shrieked Maxie, "your phone calls are like the voice of doom!"

"You want I should not call anymore?" Lillian asked, her feelings hurt.

"Lillian, I love you. You have been like a mother to me," Maxie said, now down an octave and apologetic.

"So don't *schrei* at me. I'm giving you news you should know about."

"Of course, of course, Lillian. So tell me again, is that trouble-maker back? Is he working in the store?"

"All I know is what Morrie Rappaport told me. He saw him in the bank and he was doing some kind of a big transaction. A money draft or something came in for him. He's living in the apartment with Gussie."

Mac Edmunson said the firm could spare Maxie for a few days but something in his manner gave Maxie pause. "Something bothering you, boss?" Maxie said. "Am I taking too much time off?"

"Come on, kid, we're not on a time clock here. And you've piled up enough hours here to tour the world."

"You looked at me funny,"

"What is this 'you looked at me funny' Am I a school teacher or something? What the hell is a funny look.?"

" Like you want to tell me something."

"Jesus, Max—you're like my wife. She could always tell when something was bugging me."

"So what's bugging you?"

"It's not me. It's Harold."

"Our Harold? Harold Kahn?"

"Yep. The president of your fan club. He thinks your reputation is in jeopardy."

"What's with Harold all of a sudden? Is he turning into a little old lady?"

"Turning? He's been a little old lady worrywart all his life. Part of his charm. And, his hidden strength."

"What's going on, boss?"

"He knows about your mother and her store. And the black guy she raised who turned into a wise guy. And the police surveillance. Don't ask me how he knows these things, but he does. And whenever you go back there Harold is afraid you'll be pulled into a situation where you have to defend your mother. And he's afraid that it could become public knowledge which, of course, would shake up our esteemed, lily-white clients. He's worried that they would no longer want you to be privy to what goes on in their board rooms.

"Mac, I'd cut my balls off before I'd do anything to embarrass this firm,"

"I know it, kid. Can you keep your nose out of your mother's business? I know both you and Kitty are trying to keep her from getting involved with that guy."

"His name is Luther. Luther Hightree."

"Fancy name."

"He's a punk, Mac. And I'm convinced he's using my mother. Using her as his rabbi to cover whatever hustle he's into. I thought he was gone forever after my mother remarried. But her husband passed away and this creep pops out of the ground like a poison mushroom."

"Is that why you're going back there?"

"Yes."

"What are going to do?"

"Damned if I know. I've just got to confront that guy and find out why he's back in my mother's life. I've got to do something, boss."

"Don't do anything crazy, son, Don't get your name in the paper. Harold's right. You've got a brilliant future. Your mother has no right to let her personal life ruin yours. I was going to suggest that you take Kitty with you, but she's as emotional as you are."

Maxwell confronted a startled Luther in the store and asked him go down the block to a black beer and wine joint so they could talk freely. Maxie demanded to know why Luther had returned and what was he doing in the store. Certainly, Maxie contended, it is not to become a grocery clerk…after a lifetime of hustling drugs. Maxie warned Luther that he would do everything in his power as a lawyer, and a friend to the police to prevent Luther from involving Gussie in a drug operation, and that included putting him in jail. Maxie wanted Luther out of his mother's life forever.

Luther said nothing as Maxwell ranted; his face reflected his sang-froid and contempt. Finally he began to speak, slowly and softly at first. He asked Maxie what he really knew about his mother; after all, it was he who ran away as a ten year old to live in a fancy part of town, and it was he who tried to change his identity. How the hell did he come off as a protector of his mother? Luther said he was closer to Gussie; cared more for her than Maxie ever did, his anger rising. Why did he come back? What was he doing in the store? The store was Gussie's link with her life with Sol; it was a source of pride now that she was able to deal fairly and generously with the poor people of the neighborhood, with whom she had formerly been forced to deal harshly. He, Luther, had helped build a new store of which Gussie was proud. She loved the neighborhood; the respect and love she received from the community enriched her life. A son who had changed his name and run away had left a hole in Gussie's life. So get the fuck out of here, Luther told Maxie. We're very happy without you. I'm Gussie's true son.

Maxie blew; "True son? Look in the mirror, boy. You're nothing but a lying, drug pusher taking advantage of a lonely old lady. And this fancy store was built with drug money. Gussie and Sol weren't druggies. You came from a wino mother who used her food stamps for wine instead of feeding you. You're shit, Luther. And I'm going to make you smother in your own shit. I swear to God," he shouted as he raised his arm magisterially. One of the drinkers at the bar muttered: "That honkie got hisself a mouth. Somebody oughta' close it up." That made Luther grin and he turned to the boozer and ordered him a drink as Maxie stomped out.

Maxie's conversation with Gussie went nowhere; Gussie continued to insist that nothing illegal had ever gone on in the store. Maxie protested that if she and Luther were busted, as surely they would be, his career would be ruined if he had to return to defend her. Gussie smiled knowingly. " Do me a favor and don't ruin your precious career protecting me. I have always been able to take care of myself. Take care of your lovely wife and bring me some grandchildren while I can still appreciate them." She hugged and kissed Maxie and told him to put his mind at ease. "Go and be healthy and happy. I love you."

A saturnine melancholy consumed Maxie on the plane ride back to Boston. He had heard of prosecutor Martin O'Donnell's runaway ambition to run for governor. God forbid, if he got the case when Gussie and Luther got busted, he would be merciless. Could he be talked to? Would the endorsement of a major law firm get his ear? Maybe it would never happen. He had to put his inflamed mind at rest. Maybe, just maybe, Luther was telling the truth. Please God, let Luther and Gussie be telling the truth.

"Goddamit! If that smart sonofabitch  starts his bullshit in that fuckin' store, I'm gonna' get a search warrant and tear that place apart, even it I have to lie to the honorable pain-in-the-ass Judge Morton Kaufman." Captain Matt Carney was not pleased to be informed that Luther Hightree was back in action at the Steinberg grocery store. He was going to pay Missus Steinberg a visit once again.  Only this time it was not to extend his best wishes for success.

"Missus Steinberg," Captain Carney said, his voice struggling for control. "Is it true that Luther Hightree is operating once again in your store?  I thought that was over once and for all.  Why in God's name is he back? What's the deal, Missus Steinberg?" He was now red in the face and the purple booze capillaries were starting to spread on his nose. "The last time I saw you we had a pleasant meeting.  And now we're back at square one again.  What is the hold that this man has on you?  I must tell you that I am very disappointed and angry to see Mr. Hightree operating again in my district."

"Captain, do you drink beer?  We have beer from all over the world and it would be my pleasure if you would help yourself to any brand you would like to try. This is our business, Captain. Imported beers and wines at discounted prices. We offer big discounts because customers order by the case.  Nothing else is going on. Luther is simply trying to make an honest living. You have my word on that. And please, do take whatever you would like with my compliments for the courtesy you have always shown me," Gussie sang.

"Have a good day, Missus Steinberg," the captain said as he turned abruptly and marched out.

Despite Captain Carney's anger, there was no police surveillance nor any problems whatsoever. Everyday at least one case was ordered and picked up by the buyer during the daylight hours. The neighborhood regulars eventually came to accept Luther's presence; he was the quiet, pleasant oenologist, making a modest living. He drove an ordinary looking Pontiac; no flashy cars as he formerly did. Eventually, the word circulated throughout the neighborhood that one could get real bargains buying beer or wine by the case at Steinbergs,, and the black trade increased, albeit of course, without being privy to the cocaine deal.

Blue continued to fulfill his role as the supplier or beer and wine with the punctiliousness of a conscientious merchant while Luther continued his role as the very avatar of respectability. Pounder and Gussie happily discharged their quotidian duties and life continued smoothly at Steinberg's Discovery Grocery on Central Avenue in the ghetto.

The routine was interrupted by another of Kitty's surprise visits; this time to announce that she was once again pregnant and was sure that this one would take. Her main focus, however, was Luther. Kitty felt she could see through any of Luther's subterfuges and she wanted to see, first hand, what his latest escapade was. She was, however, completely disarmed by Luther's masterful, faux naïf posturing as he explained his business model. Beer and wine by the case, ordered by phone and picked up during the daylight hours by the buyer—seemed logical to Kitty and blessedly legitimate. Kitty was vastly relieved, though she continued to perceive Luther as an essentially lubricious character.

As Gussie and Kitty huddled in girlish excitement selecting names for Kitty's baby, Luther lapsed into a lugubrious introspective mood; he had cleverly deceived Kitty and all the neighborhood customers. Was there content in his makeup other than mendacity? What else had he done in life other than deceive? He imagined a life with Cara, both of them working at something honest and productive. Would he ever be a father? Was duplicity in his genes? Was he nothing more than Anna Mae's unwanted bastard?

He thought about Gussie.  Was this new operation going to be perdurable?  Deep in his heart he knew that it eventually would crap out.  All grifts eventually did.  What would happen, then, to Gussie? He loved Gussie; she was, in his heart, his mother.  Why then, has he put her at risk?  Or, did Gussie secretly love the excitement that Luther brought to her otherwise empty life?  Luther wanted to snap out of his mood.  Maybe a line of coke would do the job; he always carried a few packets of the magical powder on his person.  He went upstairs to the apartment to try to forget who he was for a few minutes.

Officer Siwinski, now Corporal Siwinski,  continued his nightly patrol of the of the lower Central Avenue section of the ghetto. He routinely shined his spotlight on empty store fronts and deserted alleys.  At a morning muster, he asked a question that disabused the Irish cops of their perception of Siwinski as the district's dumb Polack.

"Who the hell is International Wines and Beer?"  he asked.  An annoyed look on Carney's face was presage of a condescending, singsong retort:  "Why do you ask, Corporal?"

"Because I seen that van at five a.m. when the delivery trucks hit the Steinberg store.  And I never heard of a beer distributor with that name. So I looked them up in the phone book and they ain't there."  The other cops guffawed, shouting that maybe their phone got disconnected!  Carney didn't find it humorous and his gaze demanded silence. He sent a sergeant to check the various bureaus where businesses are registered with the city and county  to see if there was a listing for International Wines and Beers. They did not exist.  Carney thanked Siwinski for his alertness to the dismay of the Irish cops who had lost their patsy.

At five the next morning, Carney and Siwinski, in plain clothes and driving an unmarked cruiser, parked unobtrusively down the block from the Steinberg store. The first arrival was the Dupree of the Sea truck, followed by the van of International Wines and Beer.  As Blue was routinely removing three cases from the van, Captain Carney appeared out of the darkness. "Hold it there, sir," Carney barked. Blue froze, a bowel movement imminent.

"Let me see some ID" Carney demanded. Blue quickly produced a chauffeur's license and his social security card. "Where is your place of business located?"

Blue was ready. "6900 Grand Avenue." Smartly. Businessman-like.

"Why aren't you in the phone book?"

"Getting ready to do it. Only been in business for three months." Blue answered, a paragon of cool. Carney turned and disappeared into the darkness. Blue sighed and continued with his delivery and the paper work inside the store. Luther ambled over to him and whispered, "What the hell was that?"

"Copper playin' Dick Tracy. Don't mean shit. Gave him everything he asked for," Blue answered proudly.

"That cop ain't Dick Tracy. He's a captain. Boss of this district. This is bad shit, Blue. They're on our ass."

" How you mean, 'on our ass?' They ain't got nothing.'"

"What are you going to do if they grab one of your cases and start to break it apart?"

"They better have one of them search papers."

"Ever hear of probable cause?"

"Cop's is real careful with that searching shit. They ain't about to grab my cases. Stay cool, man," Blue said.

"Since when are you a lawyer?" Luther asked.

"Been on the street a long time, bro. When I think the fuzz is ready to move on us, I just stop delivering. I be long gone."

"What does that do to me, Blue? You suddenly disappearing."

"The bum went broke and blew town. You're looking for another wine and beer supplier. Simple story. They won't have nothing but a fairy tale. Trust me, bro. We're turning heavy sugar here. I ain't ready to fold and run after all the work we put into this operation. I want to milk this gig for all it's worth," Blue said, full of conviction.

"Let the good times roll," Luther said without very much enthusiasm. And he laid down a line of coke and snorted it in.

"What you doing that shit for, bro? Ain't gonna' change nothing," Blue said, big brotherly.

" Takes the place of a round ass chick, Blue."

"Chicks? Name your tit size and I'll deliver," Blue joshed.

"Ain't like that, Blue. I'm missing someone special."

"Oh, like that, huh? Can't help you there, friend. Don't burn your nose out brooding. Keep working. Let the cash take the place of that pussy."

"Give me a goddam definition of probable cause, Marty," Carney importuned the long-suffering prosecutor.

"It's when you've got physical, tangible evidence that a crime has been committed or is about to be committed," Martin O'Donnell replied, not unsympathetically. He knew that Captain Carney had the proverbial bit in his mouth. He simply could not help his old friend out in obtaining a search warrant from the immutable Judge Kaufman.

"Can we go to another judge?" Carney asked, almost pleadingly.

"No way. Kaufman's your man, old buddy. And he ain't budging unless you've got some real strong evidence going for you."

"Wait 'til that Jew bastard asks the FOP for a contribution next election cycle." Carney was uncharacteristically out of control.

"Control that mick fuse of yours, Matt. Kuafman has been a good friend of the deparment's.

In desperation, Carney ordered Siwinski to park in the alley across Central Avenue from the store, several times during his all-night patrol.

Several months rolled by without any trouble. Luther was moody and his coke use had increased. Gussie knew he was lonely and that he was doing too much thinking about his mother and other heavy-duty subjects. Finally she told him to be careful walking around town with packets of cocaine on his person. "Give them to me to hold in my apron and I'll give you one if you need it. I just hope you won't need this stuff." Good old Gussie; nobody was going to search her. Always thinking about what was best for Luther.

And, actually Luther's use diminished. He had met a decent looking girl in the local bar and he started spending time with her.

He rarely asked Gussie for a packet anymore. Still, she carried a three packet supply out of habit.

Luther's new companion's name was Missi—that was the spelling she preferred; she had come up from Mississippi not long ago and she had many Southern mannerisms that amused Luther. He had asked Gussie if it was alright to let Missi spend the night in his room. Of course it was okay with Gussie. She was delighted that Luther had lightened up a bit.

One of the heaviest users was a customer name Bradley Caxton IV, a very old name in town. Caxton was a big stockbroker working on his third marriage. From their brief conversations, Luther got the impression that marriage number three was in trouble and wifey was threatening divorce. This time there were kids involved, apparently, and mama was threatening to go for full custody of the kids, contending that Bradley was an unfit father because of his drug addictions. This had Bradley very agitated and he had hired the top divorce lawyer in town to fight for parental rights.

What worried Luther was Bradley's drinking; the last time he had come to pick up his case of wine, he was half in the bag and his driving was erratic. That scared Luther. If Bradley got stopped and searched, the cops might just find the coke hidden under the false bottom of the case. When Bradley called to place an order two weeks later, Luther informed him that he was cut off temporarily because of his drinking. Bradley begged to be allowed to place an order. Luther contended it was too risky at that point in time. He suggested that he should see Dino at the bar for his needs for time being. When he was able to assure Luther that he would not show up drunk, they could resume their relationship. Bradley agreed reluctantly,

Gussie heard Luther and Missi laughing and slurring their words as they stumbled up the stairs to Luther's bedroom. They had been partying heavily, drinking and snorting coke. They literally passed out in their clothes when they hit the bed. Gussie was pleased that Luther had brightened up and was having some fun.

Brad Caxton IV, on the other hand. was overcome with sadness and seething with anger. He was loaded with cocaine and booze as he drove wildly through the night, weeping and screaming threats to his estranged wife. She had been awarded custody of their children in court, that afternoon. Bradley had used the last of his cocaine and he wanted more. He knew where to go. His car had jumped the curb and hit the lamppost, as he lurched to a stop at the Steinberg store. He staggered from the car, leaving the doors open and the headlights blazing. He tried the locked store door and began pounding on the door, screaming…begging for someone to get him some coke. Gussie shouted for Luther but got no response—he was in a drugged sleep so she threw on a coat, turned on the lights and ran down the stairs to the store. Siwinski had just turned the corner onto Central Avenue when he saw Bradley's car. He killed his lights and glided to a stop in the street in front of the store. Siwinski watched as Bradley pounded on the door, screaming and crying. Gussie had to do something; someone was screaming for help. So she unlocked the door. Bradley brushed by her and stumbled toward the cash register and began pounding on the counter pleading for someone to sell him some cocaine. The man was crying like an infant; a thick stream of saliva hanging from his mouth. "What's wrong? What do you want?" Gussie asked.

"Goddam you, sell me some coke." He threw a handful of hundred dollar bills on the counter. "Now get me some fuckin' coke! Can't you see I'm hurting!" Gussie ran to the wall hook where her apron was hanging and she fished out three packets of cocaine which she threw on the counter.

"Here! Take it and please get out. Please go away!" Bradley grabbed the packets and staggered outside. He teetered momentarily and then fell to the sidewalk where he thrashed and quivered in a convulsive heap. Gussie screamed for help. Luther came staggering into the store trying to clear his head and make sense of the nightmare that was taking place. Missi followed him into the store and Luther told her to run. Siwinski had called for EMS help which quickly arrived and began ministering to the convulsed man on the sidewalk. Siwinski then pulled his cruiser on the sidewalk, drew his weapon and entered the store, shouting in a high-pitched, near hysterical voice for Gussie and Luther to freeze and raise their hands. He fumbled awkwardly as he removed his handcuffs and commanded his prisoners to put their hands behind their backs, after which he cuffed them. "Stay where you are—don't move," Siwinski shouted, far louder than was necessary, his weapon shaking in his nervous hand.

"Point that thing away from us, we ain't going nowhere," Luther pleaded. Gussie was shaking, in shock and disbelief. Siwinski finally holstered his weapon and began frisking Luther who was still wearing his suit. The search produced three packets of cocaine that Luther had carried with him for the night of heavy partying. Siwinski grinned savagely as he pocketed the three packets of cocaine.

"Planning to do a little selling, wise guy?" Siwinski squeaked.

EMS medics came in and announced that the man had had a seizure, probably a drug overdose. He handed Siwinski the three packets of cocaine Gussie had given Bradley. We found these on him. Probably what he OD'd on," the medic said as he departed for the ambulance, which sped away with its siren wailing; a familiar sound in the night air of the ghetto.

Soon, Captain Carney arrived with several uniformed officers. Siwinski began babbling, trying to give a comprehensive report. "Take it easy, Ski," Carney said. Then he saw Gussie shaking, near collapse. "Did you cuff her behind her back, you fucking half-wit. Take those things off of her and get her a chair." Carney finally got the picture; Siwinski witnessed Gussie selling several packets of cocaine to the man ID'd as Bradley Caxton. Luther Hightree was arrested with three packets of cocaine on his person. Four, one hundred dollar bills were found on the counter as payment for the cocaine sold by Missus Gussie Steinberg. "Allow Missus Steinberg to get dressed and secure the prisoners until I return," Carney ordered the uniformed officers. "Siwinski, maintain the premises. Keep bystanders away from the store and arrange for a tow for the Caxton vehicle. I will return shortly."

Feldman Bros., the produce supplier and Blue arrived at the scene at the same time. Blue knew immediately that a bust had occurred and he wheeled his van into a u-turn and sped away, followed by the Feldman truck. Shulte Meats and Durpee of the Sea would get the word through the grapevine.

Captain Matt Carney was experiencing an exhilerating sense of vindication as he planned his visit to the residence of Judge Morton Kaufman whom he was happily planning to awaken at four a.m. Being a cop was not such a dumb- ass mick deal after all. He was once again proud to be a policeman.

Carney had radioed district headquarters and ordered the young law student on part- time duty to draft a search warrant document for the judge to sign.

Judge Kaufman answered the door after a few minutes, properly robed and shod, and greeted Captain Carney with judicial comity. "Sorry to disturb you at this hour Your Honor, but this is a matter of great urgency," Carney said,

"Please come in, Captain. How can I help you?" the judge said, thoroughly masking his anger. He knew that Carney enjoyed the little drama that was being played out. Carney had finally gotten probable cause evidence and he could now demand a search warrant from the Jewish judge who had thwarted his requests in the past, because Carney was unable to show acceptable evidence.

"Your Honor, a police officer witnessed the actual sale of cocaine and the exchange of money between the buyer, who OD'd on the sidewalk, and Missus Gussie Steinberg at the Steinberg Grocery Store on Central Avenue. A store employee, Luther Hightree, who has long been a suspected drug dealer at that location, was arrested with cocaine packets in his possession. Your Honor, this store has been a cancer for several years, as you know." Carney recited his evidence with a barely concealed tone of gloat.

"Good work, Captain. You have a properly prepared document for me to sign?"

"We do indeed, Your Honor." Carney presented the search warrant document which the judge quickly read before reaching for a pen and scribbling his signature. "What's next, Captain?" Kaufman asked.

"I am ordering the narcotics squad to the location and we will tear that store apart until we find  the stash of narcotics which we are sure is hidden on the premises."

"Good hunting," Kaufman said, to signify the end of the meeting.

The eight man narcotics squad thundered into the store, armed with pry bars and axes and attacked Gussie's beautiful store with a gleeful vengeance. Gussie screamed in anguish as the neatly stocked shelves were ripped from the walls, and the axes split the wall open for the pry bars to probe inside. The noise and the dust and the gratuitous destruction were more than Gussie could bear and she fell from her chair in a dead faint.

Luther, handcuffed, was unable to help her and he screamed for someone to assist Gussie. A sympathetic uniformed cop ran over and lifted Gussie to the chair and shook her face until she awakened, a look of horror and disbelief on her face. "Open one of those wine bottles and give her a sip of wine. She's about to have a stroke for crissakes," Luther begged. The cop complied and Gussie almost choked on the wine and began coughing violently. Luther moved next to her and leaned down to speak words of comfort to her.

"You!—move away. Now!" a narc cop shouted at Luther.

Part of the crew had found its way into the apartment upstairs and a new cacophony of horror filled the room; pots, pans, ripped drapes, and the crash of dishes. Again Gussie screamed, her eyes wild and empty of reality—"Don't break my grandmother's china! Please, please, please." And she collapsed into a wrenching, gasping weeping that moved some of the narc officers, who glanced sympathetically at the pitiful, handcuffed old lady begging for her priceless china to be spared. Nothing was spared. Clothes were strewn everywhere. Coffee, sugar, cooking spices and cans of Crisco lay in a tortured mess on the carpets. Empty boxes were used to salvage the meats. The wine bottles were carelessly pulled from the shelves and piled into empty boxes. The imported beers were happily salvaged for future distribution. The empty beer and wine

239

cases were checked carefully but nothing was found. Gussie's un-controlled, piercing weeping  unnerved Carney and he ordered the unformed cops to take Gussie and Luther to the station lockup.

"Keep a watch on the old woman, she may be suicidal," Carney said.

Carney had vented his hatred of Luther and the years of being fooled by the very store he was now raping.

When they were through, the store was a garbage dump; canned goods coated in plaster dust amidst splintered wood and broken glass. Someone had thoroughly hated this store and had wreaked a mindless revenge for every wrong the store had committed.

It was as if the store had been anthropomorphized and was now getting the shit beat of it by a guy that if had offended too many times. But the store won one last time; no stash was found.

When daylight broke a silent crowd had gathered outside the store.  They stood there, stunned, wondering what had brought this cataclysm upon their store. It was as if a beloved friend had died a horrible, painful death. There was an almost physical di-mension to the silence—it seemed to weigh heavily on every mute bystander. Finally someone shouted, "motherfuckers!" No one looked around at the shouter. He had spoken for everyone there. Soon there was the sound of muffled sobbing and weeping. Then people began to give vent to their feelings: *It was such a beautiful store, why did God take it away from us? God punished them for selling drugs. Shut your evil mouth Vera—that's not your business.  Did they kill dear Gussie? Where is she? I knew that boy would bring her to grief. Where we gonna' get that nice fresh whiting? It was just plain white man's mean-ness—meanness, Look how they broke everything to pieces. They didn't need to do that. Lousy cops, honkie devils.*

A misshapen heap weeping silently on the curb—it was Pound-er. Life had once again cheated him out of a home.

The Boston Globe carried a humorous little squib about a grocery store run by a little old lady who was also pushing cocaine along with her broccoli. Mackenzie Edmunson read the Globe assiduously every morning as he sat on his toilet throne. The little old lady's name rang a bell—Steinberg! Wasn't that Maxie's real name? Jesus Christ, I hope to hell I'm wrong. Should I mention it to the kid?

Mac motioned Maxie into his office and told him to close the door. "I'm fired, right? It always scares the crap out of me when you tell me to close the door. What's up, boss?" Maxie said, smiling and relaxed.

"Tell me I'm a befuddled old sap, but I want you to read something I saw in the Globe this morning," Mac said as he stared into Maxie's eyes. He had circled the little article with his marker pen. He handed the newspaper to Maxie who had suddenly realized that something terrible was about to happen. Maxie read the item and sat motionless staring at Mackenzie Edmunson.

"It had to happen. Goddam her to hell," Maxie said, tears flooding his eyes.

"Is it your mother?"

"In all her fucking glory."

"Don't speak of your mother that way, son. Go and help her."

"You know, of course, if I go there, my name will get spread all over the papers. My value to this firm will be zilch."

"We'll worry about that later. Go and get your mother out of this jam."

"I am going with you or I will take a plane down there myself," Kitty said, her eyes red and puffy.

"You're seven months pregnant. You want to lose the baby? God only knows what's going on there," Maxie said.

"I'm going. Help me pack some things."

They rushed into the Justice Center Holiday Inn and breathlessly registered, instructing the bewildered desk clerk to have their bags taken to their room. Then they rushed to the courthouse where Maxie identified himself as defense counsel in the matter of Gussie Steinberg. They were directed to the office of clerk of courts where Maxie presented his credentials as a partner in the law firm of Edmunson, Peterson and Kahn of Boston which produced an immediate response and a tone of awed respect from the clerk. "We're registering as defense counsel for the defendant, Missus Gussie Steinberg."

The clerk shuffled a few official documents and said, "Okay, the defendant has been remanded to the county jail awaiting bail. Are you here to post bail, sir?" the clerk asked.

"Yes, we are going to post bail. How long has she been in the county facility? When was the arrest made? What is she charged with? "

"Mister Stonehill, the charge write-up is in the prosecutor's office, in the next building. All the details you request are there. I can direct you to the bail offices if you wish."

The clerk directed them to the bail office. Kitty half ran to maintain Maxie's frantic pace. The sight of the very pregnant, tastefully dressed woman panting after an agitated lawyer raised eyebrows in the legal fraternity walking down the various corridors.

Gussie's bail had been at two-hundred thousand dollars, and, as a property owner, she was entitled to the ten percent ruling, meaning that she could post a bond of twenty-thousand dollars which would be returned to her when her matter was resolved. Kitty, pulled out her checkbook and wrote a check for twenty thousand dollars from her personal trust fund account. "I'll reimburse," Maxie said absently.

"Fine," Kitty answered, still breathing heavily from the frantic dashing.

"Go back to the motel and lay down, please baby," Maxie said, suddenly aware of Kitty's near exhaustion.

"Exercise is good for the pregnancy. Don't worry. Let's go— your mom's in the county jail which is probably a horrible place." The clerk began to blather out instructions for the release of a prisoner with a legally posted bond. Maxie nodded his head in acknowledgment of the instructions. "Where's the prosecutor's office?" Maxie asked. The clerk gave specific direction. Maxie then remembered that he did not know the prosecutor's name. The clerk told him that Martin O'Connell was the County Prosecutor.

"Where now?" Kitty asked.

"I need to read the charge write-up which is in the prosecutor's office. It's what she's actually charged with. It'll give me a head start to know that."

Then it occurred to Kitty: "Are you going to defend your mother? You realize what that means? Your entire life will be an open book. You'll be Maxie Steinberg defending his mother Gussie Steinberg, arrested on a drug charge. Your clients in Boston will love that, I'm sure."

"Already talked to your father about that. We'll just have to see how this mess plays out. Are you ready for all this, babe?"

"Poor Maxie, the ZBT, reincarnated. Sounds like fun. Are you pissed at Gussie for outing you?

"I'm beyond pissed. I'm operating on some kind of neural reflexes.

"Good! Let's go get your poor mama."

Martin O'Donnell, the County Prosecutor, was in his office as Maxie and Kitty walked in. When Maxie presented himself as the defense counsel in the Gussie Steinberg matter, Martin O'Donnell began pontificating, ex cathedra until Maxie handed him his card, identifying him as a partner in the vastly prestigious law firm of Edmunson, Peterson and Kahn. Then O'Donnell began speaking in the respectful cadence of an officer of the court doing obeisance to a powerful adversary. He presented Maxie with the charges write-up folder and offered them coffee and a comfortable sofa on which to rest, as they read the charges against Gussie. After reading that Gussie was charged with felony sale of a controlled substance, Maxie graciously thanked O'Donnell for his courtesy and asked if it would be presumptuous for an out-of-towner to invite the prosecutor to a quiet, get acquainted dinner? O'Donnell jumped at the invitation. He had never played with the big boys before and he was excited. Sure they could have dinner. O'Donnell knew the perfect spot where they would not be bothered. And could he do anything to expedite the bailout for Missus Steinberg?

Kitty and Maxie were not prepared for what they saw when the matron unlocked the door and led out this scarecrow-like creature in an orange jump suit, that was the prisoner, Gussie Steinberg.

"Orange has never been a good color for me," Gussie shrugged. It didn't help. Maxie was destroyed and he buried his face in her thin shoulder and wept.

"No contact with the prisoner," the matron barked. Kitty pulled Maxie away from Gussie.

"She's being released. Bond has been posted. Where are her clothes?" Kitty asked.

"When the paperwork comes down, we'll dress the prisoner and bring her out to you," the matron said mechanically.

"Hurry, goddamit," Maxie snapped.

" Cussin' ain't gonna' help, mister. Just sit down and wait," the matron said.

Gussie came out wearing the robe and coat she threw on the night that Bradley Caxton pounded on the door of the store. "This is all I have. My clothes are back at the apartment."

They got Gussie a two-room suite at the motel and Kitty pulled back the cover on the queen-size bed, fluffed the pillows and coaxed Gussie into the bed. Maxie sat at bedside holding Gussie's hand, not knowing where to begin. "You look tired, honey. You shouldn't put a strain on yourself. What are you, in the seventh month? Come on, lay down next to me. There'll be plenty of time to talk later."

"Maxie, call room service. Maybe Mom would like something to eat."

"Just some tea, Maxie, and those little cakes—what do you call them—?"

"Petit fours. That sounds wonderful, Mom," Kitty said as she kicked off her shoes and laid down next to Gussie. "Maxie, can you handle going back to the apartment? See what you can salvage of Mom's stuff."

"The place is probably still sequestered as a crime scene. I'll see what I can work out with the police. You guys get some rest. I'll see you later."

"Captain Carney. He's in charge. He's a decent guy," Gussie said, her voice getting thick as sleep overtook her.

Maxie got an okay to remove clothing and personal items under the supervision of two officers who checked every item that Maxie threw into one of Gussies ancient trunks that he found buried under some wallboard. Maxie choked back tears as he picked up Gussie's dresses and shoes. Her lingerie lay strewn everywhere and he felt a strange sense of intrusion as he packed Gussie's undergarments. He found a picture of himself and Sol, covered in plaster dusk, the glass shattered. Shattered pieces of Gussie's grandmother's precious china lay everywhere. Everything he touched induced a shock of memory, a phantasmagoria of life episodes best forgotten. Finally, he could bear no more, and he and the officers carried the trunk to Maxie's car. The policemen seemed to share Maxie's sadness as they helped him load the trunk into his car.

The women were sound asleep when Maxie returned to the hotel room. He sat quietly, nibbling on the leftover petit fours, thinking about all the problems that lay ahead and all the words that needed to be spoken. And he dreaded it.

Later that evening, they sorted through Gussie's clothes. Some were sent to the dry cleaners, others were suitable to wear and were stored in the closet. When the clothes came back from the dry cleaners, most of Gussie's wardrobe was neatly packed in the trunk and given to Willa for safe keeping. They had decided that the Holiday Inn at the Justice Center was the logical place for Gussie to stay until everything was resolved. Gussie was concerned about money; she did not want Maxie and Kitty to pay for everything. She wanted to know who put up the money for her bail. Kitty said not to worry, that she had taken care of it. Gussie then revealed that she had a safe-deposit box and that she had squirreled away thousands of dollars, her share of the money Luther made over the past two years. "Money Luther had made?" Maxie repeated Gussie's words. "Money he had made from drug sales?" Maxie asked.

"Yes. He gave me a percentage. I don't know much. But it was a lot," Gussie said flatly, emotionlessly.

"Is the safe-deposit box in your name, Mom?" Kitty asked.

"Yes. At the bank on Central Avenue, near the store."

"I want you to go to the bank with Kitty, and sign the box over in Kitty's name. It's possible that they might want to come after that money. Kitty won't withdraw any funds without your written permission," Maxie said.

"Written permission? Don't be such a lawyer. You take whatever you need, for heaven's sake. Kitty, you take the twenty thousand you laid out for my bail. And Maxie, you take money to pay for the hotel expenses and for lawyers for Luther and me."

"Mom, I'm going to be your lawyer. Luther can take care of himself."

"No. Absolutely not. I don't want your name smeared defending a drug mother."

"Mom, listen to me. You're charged with felony sale of a controlled substance. You could go to prison for the rest of your life. I'm the best lawyer you could find. I won't let anyone else touch this case. We've had our differences, but you've got to let me do whatever it takes to keep you out of prison."

"But what about Luther?"

"I can't represent Luther. He's got to find his own lawyer. I'm sure he's got money stashed away." The twenty thousand dollars for your bail will be returned to you when everything is resolved. Luther will have to find a bail bondsman and pay him the twenty thousand for his bail. He's a big boy and he can take care of himself."

"One of his customers is a big lawyer in town. Maybe she'll represent him. Ann Rudmann is her name. "

"I'm sure they'll connect, Mom. Worry about yourself."

"Luther means nothing to you, does he?

"No, he does not," Maxie answered with a note of finality.

"Let's go to our room and unpack, babe... Kitty and I will be staying down the hall, Mom, so if you need anything, just ring us."

"Kitty, you rest. No more running around. Maybe you should go back home so you can take care of yourself better."

" All us Steinbergs have got to stick together, Mom. I'm sticking here," Kitty said.

"Leave it to my son to marry a *michigina,. "* Gussie sighed.

Martin O'Donnell puffed up when the maitre d' at Giovanni's greeted him by name as he walked in with Maxwell Stonehill, the big hitter from a big Boston law firm. This was to be their get acquainted dinner and O'Donnell was determined not to appear impressed; but to no avail. Maxwell's thousand dollar suit and Ferragamo shoes awed the round shouldered prosecutor in his shiny-elbowed blue suit. It was the drink order that did it, however. Maxwell asked for a single malt scotch, Glenlivit or Glenfiddich, twelve years old if they had it. O'Donnell's usual Seven and Seven would be a disaster, so he mustered his pitifully limited savoir-faire and said, "That sounds like a good idea. Bring me the same, Luca." The poor devil didn't have a clue what he was about drink, and the staggering amount that would appear on the bill that Maxwell, blessedly, insisted on picking up.

Things were different when they finally got down to the deal that Maxwell was proposing. Martin O'Donnell was now the dominant actor and he had no compunction about injecting long interludes of mysterious silence as Maxwell pitched his deal. He'd put the smart shit in his place and show him who was in charge. Finally O'Donnell, his tongue loosened by the alien scotch, said: "What's all the heat you're laying on me to spring an old Jew-broad drug pusher?"

Maxwell unconsciously stiffened in his chair and stared silently at O'Donnell for several moments until the prosecutor became uneasy. Maxwell knew that what he was about to say would change his life forever. "The old Jew-broad is my mother."

O'Donnell giggled, nervously, inappropriately, as his face reddened.

"But her name is Steinberg."

"So is mine."

"Holy mother of God. I am so sorry, Maxwell. How terribly rude of me."

"You had no way of knowing. Let's continue our conversation," Maxie said. "And by the way, my friends call me Maxie."

" So what's the real deal, Maxie?"

"Okay. You're considering a run for governor, I know. A conviction of a big-time drug dealer would give your campaign a big boost."

"It's not just the governor's race. I hate that smart-ass pusher—that Hightree guy. He's been screwin' us around for years with that smug little smirk of his. I'd like nothing more than to put him away for a long, long, time."

"Gussie Steinberg can help you."

"Speak to me," O'Donnell said.

"Gussie's dream has always been to run a quality store down there in the ghetto. She feels she owes it to those folks for all the crap people have been selling them for years."

"So?"

"This Luther character has played on Gussie Steinberg's sympathies for years. His mother froze to death in the alley next to Gussie's store after they sold her a half gallon of cheap wine that she bought with her food stamps instead of buying food for little Luther.

The Steinbergs adopted him and raised him until he took off when he was around sixteen. He was gone for years, and then he came back when Gussie's husband died. He offered to help her rebuild her crummy little store into a beautiful, modern place; and he promised to show her how to sell good quality food at low price. The catch is, she has to let him peddle cocaine from the store. She doesn't know beans about coke and he convinces her it's a white man's harmless party substance. And he'll only sell to whites who can afford it—never to poor blacks. That's the honest to God truth, Martin. When they busted Gussie, she was trying to get a guy who had OD'd out of the store. He was begging for coke, so she reached under the counter where Luther stashed his packets and she threw a bunch of packets at the guy and begged him to leave. The guy threw some bills at the register and grabbed the coke. When he got outside, he collapsed and convulsed on the sidewalk. And that's what the officer saw. Gussie wasn't selling, she was trying to get a lunatic druggie out of her store. I swear to God, Martin, that's the living truth."

"Sounds believable, Maxie…so, what can I do?"

"Give Gussie probation with no restraints and she rolls over on Luther, big time. Right now you've got him for a little chicken shit three packet possession beef.

Gussie will testify that he had been selling kilos of cocaine at that location for two years."

"Maxie, they found no stash when they busted the store."

"Martin, you're a strong prosecutor. Make Gussie's story stick. She'll play great in front of a jury. Trust me, I've been in front of lots of juries in big cases. I know a winner when I see it."

O'Donnell sat silently for a long time, weighing Maxie's logic. He desperately wanted to nail Luther Hightree for something bigger than mere minor possession.

"Let me write it up. You talk it through with Missus Steinberg. If she buys it and is willing to swear to it in front of the grand jury, we've got a deal. That may be kind of scary for an older woman because she's going to be there without you, as her lawyer, present. What do you think?"

"I think we've got a deal, mister prosecutor."

"Then let's have another one of those Glen-what-the-fuck-do-you-call-'ems

"So what happened with the prosecutor?" Kitty asked as the lay in bed, exhausted, but unable to sleep.

"We made a deal. Mom walks without restraints—"

"Yes….now tell me the bad news."

"She's got to roll over on Luther and tell the grand jury that he's been selling kilos of cocaine for the last couple of years, while she was running the grocery store." Kitty said nothing, as she stared up at the ceiling.

"Well—say something," Maxie said.

"I think it's horrible. How could you put Mom in a spot like that! You want her to rat on a person that she has loved and protected all his life?" Kitty was outraged.

"Luther is a lying piece of shit who would sell Mom out in a minute if he got the chance."

"You are wrong. And you know it. Luther loves your mother and he made her happy when her life was bleak and empty…when you were long gone living your bogus life."

"Bogus life? Is that what you call our life together? Who's turning on whom?. The man turned my mother into a coke dealer, for crissakes! "

" And don't give me any of that phony crap about the cocaine. Coke is a party drug for people who can afford it. He didn't force people to buy it, did he?" Kitty pounced. "You've had a thing for Luther since you were ten years old, and you're willing to get him locked up for the rest of his life. That's kind of sick, Maxie."

"Sick, huh? I'll show you sick. I'll take you down state to the womens' federal penitentiary and let you see the animals my mother will be thrown in with because 'Luther loved her' so fucking much."

"Okay, Maxie, the silver tongued barrister. You sell it to Gussie."

"I'll do whatever it takes and I thank you for your love and understanding."

"Maxie, I do love you. I just don't always understand you."

Maxie had decided to take Gussie for a ride through a quiet park area so that they could talk uninterrupted. He slowly, passionately explained his plan for keeping her out of jail. Gussie listened without responding. Maxie's frustration boiled over. "There is no other way, do you understand?" Then, slowly, ponderously he said it again emphasizing each word by pounding on the steering wheel: "There…is…no…other…way." Gussie's face was frozen; an expressionless mask. "Do you want to go to jail?" He spoke as though addressing a child.

"No," she barely whispered.

"Then listen to me. I'll tell it to you again. Luther forced you to let him sell cocaine in the store. He threatened your life if you went to police. He ordered lots of cocaine every week. You were not involved. You were busy running your grocery store…Are you listening to me?" She remained silent.

"I ask you again, do you want to go to jail?"

"No."

"Then I beg you to make that statement in court, Momma. I am begging you!"

"If I say what you're telling me to say, I'll make it worse for Luther." They stare at each other silently for what seems an eternity. "I won't do it. Find another way to keep me out of jail."

"There is no other goddam way, you stubborn, crazy woman. How long are you going to keep torturing me? What is it you want from me? " He grasps her face in his hand and turns her head to him. "Answer me—what is it you want from me? I wanted you to love me but your life revolved around a little *schvartze* orphan. The kids at school laughed at me—I felt like a fool. I hated that dirty little store and the way you and my father cheated the poor people in the neighborhood. I had to change my life or I was going to kill myself. I had to run away. I was ashamed. Ashamed! I've loved you all my life, but I know that deep in your heart you and Dad never forgave me for running to Aunt Lil and changing my name."

"Maxie, I don't want to torture you. I know you're risking your whole career, your whole life to help me. Your father and I have always loved you. Dad was always so proud of everything you did. We love you, Maxie. Don't throw your life away to save me. I'll survive, you know that."

"No, I do not know that," Maxie said angrily. "You think I care about my lousy career? You're my mother. You're my mother for God's sake." He loses control and weeps uncontrollably, his face buried in his mother's chest. Finally Gussie pulls away and opens the car door. They were back at the hotel parking lot.

As she left, she kissed Maxie and softly said, "I love you, Maxie. Let me think about what you want me to do." And she walked slowly to the entrance. Maxie was saddened at the sight of her labored gait as she walked into the darkness.

Gussie pleaded with Kitty to take her to visit Luther at the county jail; she knew Maxie would never agree to take her there. Kitty stayed with Gussie until the guard brought Luther to the window. He picked up the phone and motioned for Gussie to pick up the visitor's phone on her side of the protective glass. He whispered so as not to be overheard by the guard. He told Gussie he needed twenty thousand in cash for his bail. His cash was in a safe-deposit box and his friend Blue had the key. You can trust him. You're the only other authorized signature at the bank. Get the key from Blue and go to the bank and get the money. You can find Blue at the Gold Dust tavern. Don't be afraid to go there. Blue knows who you are. Get in touch with Jake Jablonski, the bail bondsman and get the cash to him, so I can get out of here until I go to trial. You understand what I'm saying, Gus? When you get the key from Blue, you keep it until I get out. Am I confusing you?"

"I'm not senile yet, sonny-boy. And I know who mister Blue is. And I'll get the money to Jablonski. I'm at the Justice Center Hotel. Come there as soon as you get out."

"I love you, Gus," Luther said.

"I love you too, Luther. You'll be out soon, don't worry."

"What was that conversation all about? What did he want from you?" Kitty probed.

"He needs bail money."

"Does he want you to put up the money?" Kitty was alarmed.

"No. He's got money in a safe-deposit box and he wants me to get the money to the bondsman."

"Will the bank let you open his box?"

"I'm the only other authorized signature. They'll let me open the box."

"Don't you need a key or something?" Kitty asked, befuddled and frightened.

"I know where the key is," Gussie said, as she patted Kitty's cheek reassuringly.

"Are you going to tell Maxie what you're doing?"

"No. I can take care of this myself. Don't worry, honey. It'll be alright. I'm not doing anything illegal. Just getting bail money. Luther has a right to get out on bail. And it's his money. Not a big deal, honey."

"Mom, Maxie will kill me for letting you get involved with Luther."

"You didn't 'let' me do anything, sweetheart. I'm still my own boss."

Gussie knew exactly where the Gold Dust Tavern was located and she walked in like she was a regular at the joint. A few black eyeballs sized her up briefly as she looked around for Blue. She spotted him sitting in a booth at the back of the tavern, doing business. Blue recognized her immediately. "What's happening, Momma?" Blue said. "Sorry about what they done to your store. You seen Luther? You gonna' make bail for him?"

"Luther's fine. The store's not so fine. Blue, Luther said you've got the key," Gussie said cryptically.

Blue glanced around and removed a key ring from his trouser pocket. He removed the safe-deposit key and handed it to Gussie. "You're a fine momma. Hold on to that key. Luther's got lots of bread in that box. Tell him to see me when he makes bail."

Gussie went to the bank and after a long identification procedure, she gained access to Luther's safe-deposit box. It was loaded with hundred dollar bills. Gussie nervously counted out twenty thousand dollars after several false starts during which she became rattled  and lost count.

Jake Jablonski was a crude apple who barely looked at Gussie as he counted out the money. "When will Luther get out?" Gussie asked.

"When I tell the clerk of courts that I'm good for the two-hundred grand. You follow?  So you tell that bandit not to run somewhere, you follow?"

"Just get him out. You follow?" Gussie said, mocking the rough bondsman.

The phone in Gussie's room rang and the hotel operator asked for Missus Steinberg. Gussie identified herself and the operator said she had a call for her. It was Luther, being careful to speak only to Gussie, knowing that Maxie would not want her to have any contact with him. "I'm out. Thanks, Mom," he said in a hoarse voice.

"Thank God," Gussie said. "Will they give back the twenty thousand?" she asked.

Luther laughed bitterly. "The twenty grand belongs to Jake Jablonski. Don't worry about money. Just stay well and let Maxie take care of your trial."

"What about you? Do you have a lawyer? Who's going to take care of you?"

"Remember Ann Rudmann? She's a tough, shrewd lady. She's going to represent me. For a price, of course."

"Is she expensive?"

"Like they say, 'is the Pope Catholic'?"

"I want to see you," Gussie said.

"Can you get away by yourself?" Luther asked.

"Don't talk to me like I'm an old *schleppter*. Where should I meet you?"

"Meet me a the Gold Dust Tavern. The place where you met Blue."

"Hey, I'm like a regular at that joint. I'll meet you tomorrow around noon."

The meeting was very emotional. Even Blue was touched. Gussie had many questions and Luther tried his best to assuage her anxieties. Finally she brought up the unthinkable. She told him that Maxie had made a deal with the prosecutor; if she testified against him, she would get off with probation.

"But you've got to say I was a big pusher, right?" Luther said.

"Right," Gussie answered and she started to weep.

"Leave it to Maxie to make life difficult."

"So what will happen to us?" she said through her sobs.

"You go free. If they had convicted you of what they charged you with, 'selling a controlled substance,' you'd probably get five years. Maybe more."

"So what happens to you?"

"Right now, they've got me for procession of three packets. I could get a year. Maybe two to five if the judge really hates me."

"And if I say you were a big pusher?"

"I'm gone for a long, long time. Maybe twenty-five years."

Gussie screamed, "Oh God! No!" and everyone turned around to stare.

"Momma, stop. Please stop crying. Maxie's got us in a pickle. Do what's right for you. Rudmann will take care of me, I'm not worried. You do what's best for you. Go back to the hotel. I'll see you in court. Don't try to call me. It's better if we leave things alone." He hugged Gussie and led her to the door and waited until he could wave down a cab. "I'll always love you, Momma," he said as he closed the door of the cab.

Luther's trial date was set; it would be a two month wait. If Gussie agreed to Maxie's plan, she would be the State's star witness having testified under oath before the grand jury under the watchful eye of Martin O'Donnell. She would appear in court without a lawyer, as a witness for the prosecution.

Gussie pleaded with Kitty to return home to have the baby which was due any day now. Kitty agreed to return home but before she left, she and Gussie had a final conversation about the trial. Kitty realized that Gussie was faced with a terrible decision so she did not attempt to influence her one way or the other, but as a parting shot she simply said it would be wonderful to have Solomon Mackenzie Steinberg's grandmother present for the *bris.*

"How do you know from a a *bris?*" Gussie asked, pleasantly surprised.

"I'm taking lessons," Kitty said.

Gussie kissed her warmly and said, "You're an unusual young woman, Kitty. Maxie is a very lucky boy."

"He's not a boy anymore, Mom. I want him to start acting like a man," Kitty said as she turned to leave. "Maxie will be back before the trial. Relax and enjoy this nice hotel."

"You relax and have a beautiful, healthy baby boy. Sol would be so proud that you're going to name the baby after him. God bless you, Kitty."

The days dragged by slowly and Gussie wanted desperately to contact Luther but she did as Luther wished, and resisted her desire to call. She spent her days reading. All of her life she had wanted to read *Anna Karenina* by Leo Tolstoy. It had been required reading in her senior year, but she never got around to it because she was so preoccupied with her job at Pete Randazzo's platform at the food terminal. Now she had time so she went to the library and registered for a temporary card, and obtained a copy of the great novel. She became deeply invested in the characters and it took her mind off her terrible dilemma.

Then the news came; Solomon Mackenzie Steinberg arrived and he was a beautiful eight pound, two-ounce healthy boy. Kitty was ecstatic, out of her mind with joy. They were going to have a "regular, old-fashioned *bris* on the eighth day. I wanted an old-fashioned *mohel* but Maxie and my father insist on having an M.D. to do the circumcision. But—are you ready for this—my Dad is going to be the *Sondek*—the guy that holds the baby. He'll probably pass out! Oh, I'm so excited, Mom. And you're coming, I insist. Maxie is sending a ticket. Have you ever been to Boston? Oh, you'll love it !"

"Kitty, take a breath. I'm coming, I'm coming. More important, how did it go for you? Was it hard on you?"

"Piece of cake. Like those peasant ladies that have their babies in the field."

"You're father is okay with all the Jewish stuff?" Gussie asked.

"Mom, my Dad is out-of-his-mind happy and I've got him reading some of the stuff the rabbi gave me to read."

"What's with the rabbi giving you things to read? What for?"

"I'm planning to convert to Judaism. I love the sheer oldness of the traditions. Is oldness is a word? Anyhow, you know what I mean."

"You probably know more than I do about the traditions. You're sure you want to do this? It ain't easy being Jewish, you know."

"Absolutely, Mom. We can't have a split family. Sol-Mac is going to have a Jewish momma."

"Sol-Mac? That's what you call him?"

"He's got a million names already. You call him whatever you like, Mom."

"I can't wait to see him. Take care of yourself. Get enough rest. Don't run around like a wild woman."

Luther had several meetings with Ann Ruddman and she continued to build his confidence in the defense she had planned. She assured Luther that she would convince the jury that Gussie's testimony was "pure bullshit," a self-serving device to save her ass.

Rudmann was one tough broad and she was a source of succor for Luther, as the date of trial got closer.

The *bris* was a huge success. Mac held the baby manfully during the circumcision and Harold Kahn, Mac's longtime partner, was the *Quvater,* the guy that carries the baby to the baby holder. Maxie held up a wine glass and made a beautiful toast. Then everybody, including the M.D., got shit-faced.

The next morning, Maxie read the signal; Mac motioned him into his office and told him to close the door. Heavy duty conversation inevitably would follow.

"What's this shit?" Mac said, holding up Maxie's letter of resignation.

"I'm the son of a drug-pushing, Jewish mother and we're both going to make national news. I had to out myself to the prosecutor to work a deal to get Mom probation. I'm Maxie Steinberg, son of Gussie Steinberg former partner of one Luther Hightree, a big-time drug dealer. Our New England puritan clients should be thrilled to read about the double life of their former counsel, Maxwell Stonehill, aka, Maxie Steinberg, wheeler-dealer defense counsel," Maxie ran on and on.

"You finished?" Mackenzie Edmunson peremptorily ended his son-in-law's, mea culpa screed. "Your job is to make sure your mother walks on probation. You're the top litigator of the firm of Edmuson, Petersons and Kahn. You concentrate on that prosecutor and leave the client relations up to me. And when this is over, if your Mosaic sensitivity makes it uncomfortable for you to continue to practice in 'Brahmin' Boston, I have another opportunity pending for you."

Mac's arcane reference to an "opportunity" took Maxie by surprise. "Dare I ask what this opportunity might be?" Maxie asked, smart-alecky with the impunity to which he had become accoustomed.

"Ah! Mirabile Dictu! He emerges from his cocoon of opprobrium." There was a note of asperity in Mac's voice. He had been annoyed at what his perceived to be Maxie's pusillanimity. "We're buying Bronstein and Gangloff in Chicago and we need a managing partner there. You interested? Steinberg would be an acceptable name in Chicago and they like people with shady pasts," Mac said, grinning savagely.

"If ever there was a deus ex machina, this is it," Maxie said, speaking to the ceiling.

"What the fuck is that supposed to mean?"

"The machine from God. In Greek drama; a god lowered by stage machinery to extricate the protagonist from a dilemma."

"You know, Maxie, when Kitty brought you around I had grave doubts about you, but now I realize what a blessing you were. You and Kitty were made for each other. You're both fucking crazy."

"We'll find a little horse farm in McHenry County and Kitty will be in heaven."

"This meeting is over, Mr. Steinberg," Mac said as he started signing documents.

The day of Luther's trial had arrived. Kitty dressed Gussie in a stark, dark gray suit and combed her hair back into a bun. They spoke not at all of Luther's trial. Only Gussie knew what Gussie would say when called upon as a witness. Maxie had run to the toilet several times during the morning; he was suffering from nervous diarrhea as the time for the trial drew near. Martin ODonnell had passed him in the corridor leading to the courtroom and winked conspiratorially. Kitty insisted on sitting with Maxie at the side table near the judge's bench. Gussie, pale and stiff, sat at the table with the prosecutor prior to being called. The tension was palpable. Luther, dressed meticulously in a brown suit, sat expressionless, except for a brief smile at Gussie when he was brought into the courtroom and seated next to his counsel, Miss Ann Ruddman, smarty attired in a burgundy suit.

The bailiff's entrance added to the tension. Finally, he said "All rise," and he intoned the name of the ancient Common Pleas Judge, Calvin Sledge who would be presiding over the trial. Charges against Mister Luther Hightree were read and the judge ordered the state to present their first witness. Stoop-shouldered Martin O'Donnell slowly rose and said, "The state calls Missus Gussie Steinberg." A gray cloud of dread suffused the courtroom as Gussie sat frozen and wide-eyed. The elderly judge instructed the bailiff to escort Gussie to the witness stand. Maxie felt his chest muscles tighten and for a moment he was unable to breathe. He was sure he was having a heart attack. Kitty, wrinkled her nose, sniffing; Maxie had passed gas. Gussie walked stiff-legged to the witness stand and awkwardly mounted the steps to the witness chair, where she sat, staring wild-eyed like a frightened animal, at O'Donnell, who had pushed his face close to hers. He attempted a reassuring smile, but it emerged ghoulish. And in his nasal, Gaelic voice he began. This was it. O'Donnell would ask the question and if Gussie agreed with the statement, it would, for all practical purposes be over. *Please God—let her do what I begged her to do,* Maxie prayed.. *Let her save her life and end the torment that's tearing me apart.*

"Now, Missus Steinberg, can you point out the defendant, Mister Luther Hightree?" O'Donnell asked. Gussie seemed dumbfound. "Missus Steinberg, can you point out Mister Hightree?" he repeated. Finally she seemed to understand and pointed feebly at Luther.

"Now Missus Steinberg, is it your testimony that the defendant, Luther Hightree, over the past two years had sold many kilos of cocaine weekly in a store owned by you on the thirty-eighth block of Central Avenue, and that you allowed such transactions because the defendant, Luther Hightree, threatened your life if you refused to allow him to operate in your store?"

"Objection!" Ann Rudmann shouted.

"Overruled. Please continue, Missus Steinberg," the judge ruled.

O'Donnell continued. "Missus Steinberg, was this your sworn testimony before the grand jury?" All eyes focus on Gussie. A quick smile flickered across Luther's face as he glanced at Gussie. She remained silent. Maxie's eyes bore into her, pleading. Still she remained silent.

Judge Sledge softy said: "Missus Steinberg?" Gussie looked up at the judge, her voice barely audible.

"I'm sorry, I did not hear you," the judge said, leaning over the bench.

"No," Gussie said, somewhat louder now. Maxie wailed, "Oh, God."

The judge learned forward, straining to hear every word that was spoken. O'Donnell was actually green as he glared at Maxie.

Then the judge said, "You said 'no.' What exactly do you mean by 'no,' Missus Steinberg?" Maxie's face was buried in his hands and Gussie looked at him with a terrible sadness as she turned to face the judge. Then Gussie said, "No. That was not my testimony."

"But we have a record of your testimony before the grand jury and—"

"I lied," Gussie shouted. "I lied to save myself." The courtroom exploded and the judge gaveled it to silence.

"Were you instructed to lie to the grand jury by anyone in this courtroom?" the judge demanded.

"No, Your Honor. I was the one who sold the drugs to the man who collapsed. Luther only had the three packets they found in his pocket." The court roared again as Rudmann screamed for a mistrial.

"There will be no mistrial. The state will proceed with its case against Mr. Hightree for possession and the witness is charged with contempt of court and lying to the grand jury. She is hereby remanded to the County Jail where she will be held without bail until a date can be set for her trail on the charge of felony sale of a controlled substance. There will be a brief recess and then we shall proceed with the trial of Mister Hightree for possession in bulk, of a controlled substance."

Rudmann was hugging and kissing Luther, and Maxie and Kitty wept bitterly in each other's arms. They jumped up and kissed Gussie as the matron led her away, handcuffed, to the county jail. O'Donnell stopped at Maxie's table and snarled: "You lied to me! Your little scheme backfired, on you didn't it! Your own mother fucked you up. Well I'm going back to the grand jury to charge her with felony sales. Get her a good lawyer, 'cause I'm going to send her away for long time, brother Steinberg."

"Don't try to run for governor you Irish prick," Maxie said as he jumped up and ran to the bench. "Your Honor, Your Honor—a word with you, please!"

"Are you of counsel in this matter?" the judge asked.

"I am an attorney, Your Honor, but not of counsel in this matter. I am the son of the witness and I respectfully ask to court to authorize bail for the witness in view of her age."

"Your request is an inappropriate disturbance and I must ask you to return to your seat or I will have the bailiff remove you from the courtroom." Maxie glared at the judge and then turned and returned to his seat muttering "lousy old bastard." At that moment, Ann Rudmann disentangled herself from Luther and introduced herself to Maxie and Kitty. At first, Maxie prepared himself for an adversarial confrontation but relaxed when Ann Rudmann extended her hand and said that she was well acquainted with Missus Steinberg and that her associate might be of assistance in having bail set for her. "Did I hear you say you were her son?" Rudmann asked. Maxie introduced himself and they exchanged cards. Kitty, tears streaming down her cheeks introduced herself. Rudmann signaled Luther to relax, that she would soon return. "My boss's name is Dave Moskowitz and this judge knows better than to tangle with Dave. O'Donnell is steaming because your mother wouldn't come down against Luther. I can't blame you for trying to set up a deal, but I'm happy for my client that it didn't work out. I happen to know that your mother and Luther are very close. Who's going to represent your mother?"

"I don't know, yet. I didn't think she would be going to trial."

"Count on it. O'Donnell and that cop, Matt Carney want to nail her and Luther. If I lose my case, Luther will probably get two or three years for possession. But your mother is a whole different ball game. It they can convict her of felony selling, she could be looking at the full five years. Maybe more. They've got their witness, the cop Siwinski, all primed to swear he saw her selling and taking money for the sale. You're going to need to play hardball. I'm not hustling business for my law firm, but I would talk to Dave Moskowitz. He'll tear that punk cop to shreds on the stand."

"I'll call Moskowitz. Many thanks for your help. I only wish I could represent her myself in this state."

"Don't even think about it. It could be a disaster. Call Moskowitz and good luck." She threw a quick smile at Kitty and returned to Luther at the defendant's table. Rudmann put up a ferocious defense for Luther, arguing that the three packets the prosecution said were found on Luther's person were the result of a faulty search conducted under chaotic conditions. The jury was split and stayed in session for two full days before delivering a guilt verdict.

The judge, sensing that the prosecution's case had not been convincing, sentenced Luther to the minimum, two to five years.

Maxie met Dave Moskowitz at the Barrister's club. "I can't get her sprung on any amount of bail. That senile old bastard is being pressured by some people not to set bail." Moskowitz's gravel voice barely audible with his mouth full of pastrami. I think I know who's behind it but there's not much I can do. All I can do is move the trial date up. I can bring her to trial in a month. I hate to have her languishing in that shit hole of county jail for a month, but that bastard judge wanted to set a trial date six months hence. I went through hell getting it moved up, believe me. Get some rest. You both look like hell. I'll take care of things from this point on. Don't worry kid, I won't let them bury your mother."

Maxie and Kitty visited Gussie at the county jail, expecting to see her utterly depressed and frightened. They were surprised by Gussie's panache. She appeared to be a seasoned jailbird, confident, almost cocky as she learned to navigate her way through the grimy, putrid cellblocks and corridors. Kitty was prepared to bring her any food for which she might have a craving. Gussie asked only for *halvah*, the Turkish confection made of ground nuts. Kitty looked perplexed but Maxie nodded his recognition and promised to bring some on their next visit. Gussie took the news of the one month wait for her trial with equanimity and seemed pleased that Dave Moskowitz would be defending her.

Finally Gussie took Maxie's hand and the strength seemed to drain from her and her eyes filled with tears. "You worked so hard, Maxie, and I caused you grief. I couldn't turn on Luther—I just couldn't, don't you understand? It's not that I love him more, Maxie. You know how much I love you—you're my son, Maxie, you're my son. But Luther is close to me in a different way. I couldn't send him to prison."

"But you'll go to prison yourself to save him. There's something you feel for that man that I will never understand," Maxie said.

"Please don't feel bad that I'm in jail. I'm not afraid. Whatever happens, will happen."

Maxie exploded. "Don't feel bad? Don't feel bad? How do you want me to live while you're in the women's reformatory for five years? Should I just forget about it? —pretend that everything's fine? Tell me how you expect me to feel. I really need some help here—I need to understand how that mind of yours works. Let me inside of your secret brain so I know how to live. I've been confused for a long time, Momma."

"That's enough, Maxie," Kitty said. "Can't you see she's going through hell?

...Mom, did you finish Anna Karenina?"

"Not yet. It's such a big beautiful story. I left the book at the hotel."

"I'll bring you another copy and some of that *halvah* stuff. Don't think about Luther and Maxie will be fine. I think he understands why you refused to turn on Luther. He's just having one of those Maxie tantrums. He'll get over it. We love you, Momma."

Kitty stayed in town for two weeks and both Maxie and Gussie insisted that she return to Boston and get some rest. Maxie stayed on, planning strategy with Moskowitz and visiting Gussie at the county jail. The cuisine did not agree with Gussie and she lost weight and began to look somewhat haggard which bothered Maxie terribly.

The days dragged by slowly but finally the trial date arrived. Kitty flew in and sat at Maxie's side at the defendant's table. It was impossible to have a conversation with Dave Moskowitz; he was completely in his own head determined to break down the testimony of the state's prime witness, Corporal Emil Siwinski.

The trial began and the state called Emil Siwinski, who reiterated in careful detail what he observed at 4:15 on the morning in question as he patrolled the thirty-eight hundred block of Central Avenue. He had total recall of the position of Brad Caxton's metallic brown Lexus coupe with two wheels on the sidewalk and the hood smashed against the light pole in front of the Steinberg grocery store. He even described the plaid lining of Caxton's open raincoat and his position as he leaned forward pounding on the counter, apparently screaming at Missus Steinberg who seemed to be trying to placate him. He described how Missus Steinberg reached beneath the counter under the cash register and produced five packets of a white powder which she tossed at Mister Caxton who in return placed five one hundred dollar bills on the counter and then lurched unsteadily through the door and collapsed on the sidewalk in a convulsion, at which time Siwinski used his radio to call EMS, which arrived on the scene within approximately five minutes.

Moskowitz practically ran to the witness stand when it was time to cross examine. He had recreated the actual scene, photographed at 4:15 a.m. from the perspective of a police car, with actors taking the positions of Caxton and Gussie Steinberg in the store.

A car from a wrecker yard was positioned where the Caxton vehicle had crashed into the light pole. Audio/visual people brought in a large screen and a slide made from the photograph of the scene was projected. Then Moskowitz, practically salivating with anticipation, proceeded to tear Siwinski's carefully rehearsed testimony to shreds. He particularly relished the chance to prove how utterly ludicrous Siwinski's claim was to have actually observed the lining of Caxton's open raincoat.

"Ladies and gentlemen of the jury, let's get real here," Moskowitz pleaded with arms spread wide, "you're hearing the testimony of a wind-up toy mouthing the words that have been forced fed him by the overly zealous prosecution." Of course, O'Donnell croaked out his outraged objection which the judge allowed.

The only thing that Siwinski could have seen, Moskowitz crowed, were two blurry figures as he looked through his windshield and the dirt streaked window of the store.

It was a powerful and beautifully crafted cross-examination and Moskowitz slumped into his seat exhausted. Maxie kissed him on the cheek in a burst of gratitude and professional admiration. But to no avail. On re-cross by the prosecution, Siwinski gave a snarling, convincing reiteration in detail of his previous testimony insisting with the full might of his stolid Polish rectitude that he saw what said he saw. And the jury believed him.

Moskowitz agonized over whether or not to put Gussie on the stand. He knew that under cross examination the prosecution would hammer her on the issue of why she reflexively reached under the counter, knowing that the cocaine was stored there, even though she claimed she was merely trying to placate a violent addict in order to get him to leave the store. The state would vehemently insist that was not the case. Gussie was spared the agony of cross examination.

The jury came back with a guilty verdict and judge Sledge, solemnly, his extreme satisfaction barely contained, sentenced Gussie to the maximum of two to five years in the women's reformatory in Martinsville, Illinois. Kitty and Maxie were stunned and horrified; Martin O'Donnell was ebullient. He might yet make it to the governor's mansion.

Kitty and Maxie found their little horse farm in McHenry county, a long but pleasant commute to the law offices of Bronstein and Gangloff on Michigan Avenue in downtown Chicago, where Maxie assumed his duties as managing partner. Their son was growing into a strapping, beautiful young boy and Maxie liked his new position well enough.   Kitty made the two hour drive to visit Gussie at the women's reformatory in Martinsville once a month. Gussie assured Kitty repeatedly that she would survive and live to be an over-indulgent grandma for little Sol-Mac, who kept asking to see his grandmother. But always the thought of Gussie confined to a cell  blighted their otherwise happy lives.

But they needn't have tormented themselves; Gussie would find a way to beat the game. Her survival instinct manifested itself when she was assigned to clean warden Mason Phelps' living quarters. Late one afternoon as she was finishing her work she smelled the cooking odors emanating from the kitchen.  As the warden passed by, Gussie drew upon her *chutzpah* to engage the warden in conversation. She blithely asked what was  being  cooked for dinner. The bemused warden answered that he never really  knew what would be presented to him for dinner. Gussie boldly told him that whatever was being prepared  smelled rather bland and that it was probably tasteless. Gussie said that if the current cook would not be offended, she could probably improve on whatever it was that was being cooked.  Go to it, the warden said; he was open to anything that would improve the quality of what he was regularly served.  The cook was attempting to make Hungarian goulash and it was dismal failure. Gussie brought her inherited Czech-Hungarian culinary instincts to bear.  She rooted through the cupboards for paprika and other spices and asked if there was any red wine available. She totally seduced the bewildered warden with her version of a proper goulash.

As a consequence, she spent the next three years as the warden's personal cook. Kitty was thrilled to see the color return to Gussie's cheeks and a sparkle to her eyes. Gussie now had the time and solitude to devour all the classics that she had finessed when she was in high school. The warden was duly impressed that her taste in literature transcended the comic books and beef-cake magazines that were the common currency among the inmates.

The congregation at the Resurrection Baptist Church had not forgotten Gussie. They were freighted with anger at the needless destruction of their beloved grocery store. The store had been so clean and appetizing and the destruction was foudroyant and overwhelming. Reverend Amos Graylock asked the congregants if there were members who knew how to drywall and plaster. There were several and they wondered what was on their preacher's mind. He asked if there were any carpenters and painters. There were. Did anyone know where they might borrow a rug shampooer.? Of course, Willa knew where they could borrow one for a few days. It soon became apparent what the soft-spoken preacher had in mind—resurrection! "Let us resurrect, in the name of this merciful congregation a store owned by a loyal friend that was wantonly destroyed by angry men seeking vengeance in the name of the law which is so often careless in its targets."

Pounder emerged as the straw boss as the small army of dedicated tradesmen plunged into the skeleton of Gussie Steinberg's store and began their mission of resurrection. It took them several months to complete their work; many of the workers arriving at the store exhausted after a hard day's work at regular jobs. But eventually the structure and the upstairs living quarters were ready to receive the dewy fresh produce and gleaming fish. And they prayed with their collective hearts for the return of Gussie Steinberg to bring the store back to life. God willing, she will have the strength and desire to do it.

The warden shouted to Gussie, as she worked in the kitchen, to come into his study. There was a huge stack of letters piled on his desk. "Gussie, I'm getting inundated with letters from people in a church in the neighborhood where I believe you had your business."

"What to they want?" Gussie asked.

" Essentially, they want me to release you. They say you're a saintly person. You're a damned fine cook and housekeeper, but I don't think that qualifies you for sainthood. They said you financed a recreation center for the poor kids in the neighborhood. Did you really do that?"

"I gave them some money."

"Well, they really love you. What else did you do in that store beside pushing cocaine?"

"Well, it was a good store. Clean. Nice. Fresh produce and fish. And good meat. They liked to shop with me. There aren't any nice stores down in that neighborhood."

"Too bad you had to sell other products," the warden said.

"Yes," Gussie answered quietly.

The warden called Gussie into a meeting room where several men and women sat around a table shuffling through important looking papers. The warden spoke. "Missus Gussie Steinberg, you're the best cook I've ever had during these past three years but unfortunately these fine people have determined that, having completed the minimum of your two to five sentence with a perfect record, you are eligible for parole.

"This lady," he said pointing to Mona Hoffman, "is with the APA, that's the Adult Parole Authority. She will meet with you over the next few weeks to discuss the terms of your parole and to work out a plan for your life outside these walls. So I will now turn you over to Miss Hoffman. Everyone present congratulates you and wishes you only the best in your new life as a free woman." Everyone stood and applauded as Mona Hoffman led Gussie to a private room where they proceeded to discuss the terms and obligations of her parole.

Gussie was coming to grips with the realization that she was a convicted felon and that she was accountable to the state and her new parole officer. She and Mona Hoffman however, hit it off instantly and they established a pleasant rapport. In talking through the "plan" for Gussie's life after prison, they determined that Gussie did not wish to live with Maxie and Kitty, much as she wanted to be near her grandson. A mother-in-law should visit and then get the hell out after three days, because, as the old saying goes, "after three days, like fish, things begin to smell." Mona suggested that Gussie not attempt to find a job because of the difficulty felons encounter when seeking employment. Rest up, take nice walks through the park, feed the birds, go to the movies, and continue reading all those classics you've been reading, Enjoy your leisure; you've earned it, Mona counseled.

Gussie had money in the safe-deposit box that was now in Kitty's name. Mona felt that the box could now be transferred back to Gussie. Mona computed the Social Security benefit to which Gussie would be entitled. All in all, Gussie would have the wherewithal to live a moderately comfortable life.

Gussie's clothing was stored in a trunk that Willa Simon had kept in her apartment. Stay away from the store, Mona said, even though it was cleaned up and refurbished by the church members; too many traumatic memories. Gussie asked permission to maintain ownership of the property, agreeing to continue paying taxes. It was decided that inasmuch as Gussie would be living in her hometown, that someone from the town should pick her up when she was released and drive her home. How about your friend, Willa Simon? Does she have a car? Mona would call her to make arrangements and provide a small stipend for gas.

Where was home to be? That was the next issue to be decided. Because she had eschewed living in a mother-in-law suite with her children, the next logical option would seem to be a small apartment in a retirement facility where medical assistance and meals would be available. They decided on the Rolling Hills retirement Community. Gussie could stay with Willa for few days until the apartment was readied at Rolling Hills.

Mona said she would waive the monthly visits to the parole office; every three months would do fine and eventually the visits could be eliminated, assuming of course, that Gussie didn't decide to do anything crazy. Much laughter. Gussie's cocaine days were a thing of the distant past.

When the departure day arrived, Mona hugged Gussie and walked her to the gate. They shook hands, sort of business-like to mask their sadness, and took leave of each other. Gussie was a lonely figure as she slowly walked, dwarfed by the immensity of the barren, empty, gravel-covered field that led to the windswept dirt road. Waiting there, was the ever-reliable Willa Simon in her ancient Oldsmobile, ready to take Gussie home again.

Well, there were only so many walks in the park and so many card parties and bingo games. After six months at Rolling Hills, Gussie was bored shitless. What finally got to her was the broken-down, ex-borscht belt comic. "Take my wife—no you take me wife"—ha, ha, ha. Gussie walked outside to escape. She found a nice bench under a big Linden tree where she sat thinking about the food terminal and Pete Randazzo and the rest of the old gang.

Unbeknownst to Gussie, Luther had walked up the driveway and stood silently behind her. He was thinner and grayer and the trousers of his cheap, prison issue suit were too short. Gussie sensed the presence of someone behind her and she turned to look. Now they played their little game. She pretended not the be shocked by his sudden arrival. He grinned his little boy grin and said nothing. The only sound was the faint voice of the pathetic comic in the dining room.

"This your idea of fancy living?" Luther finally said.

"That your idea of a fancy suit?" Gussie riposted, dead-panned. "Take a load off," she said. And Luther sat down next to her on the bench. A passel of clucking old *yentas* walked by, all heads focused on the handsome black man sitting with the "gangster woman."

"When did you get out?" she asked.

"Got a break. Good behavior."

"How'd you find me?"

"Parole office. Nice lady. Ain't supposed to be hanging out with a felon, but she said it was okay 'cause I'm a relative. Kind of a son."

"Mona. She knows all about you. She's my officer."

"How's Maxie?" Gussie fumbled through her purse and produced pictures of Solomon Mackenzie Steinberg, his mother Kitty, and of course the great barrister, Maxie Steinberg.

"Nice family," Luther sniffed. "You hear from them?"

"All the time. They come to see me and Maxie sends me money."

"Ain't you got anything stashed away?" Luther asked, somewhat shocked.

"Yes. So?"

"Just askin'."

"Don't start up with any of your shit, sonny boy," she warned.

"Hey, I got to be a solid citizen or I'm gone, Gus." He lights a cigarette from a crumpled pack. "What's with the old store?"

"I still own the property. It's not worth anything, except maybe to me for the memories. I still pay the taxes. Why, I don't know."

"Let's take a ride down there—look things over. Who knows? Folks down there really did dig you, Gus."

"Okay. You got one of your fancy cars, mister big shot?"

"Hell, let's take a bus. Won't kill us." They got up and together, they slowly walked to the bus stop.